I0784771

RECONCILE RUN

Brock C. Edwards

Copyright 2022 by Brock C. Edwards

All rights reserved. No part of this book may be reproduced in any form or by any electronic or mechanical means, including information storage and retrieval systems, without permission in writing from the publisher, except by a reviewer who may quote brief passages in a review.

First Edition

The characters and events in this book are fictitious. Any similarity to real persons, living or dead, is coincidental and not intended by the author.

Published by:
Rustic Roads Publishing
www.BrockCEdwards.com
brock@brockcedwards.com

Artwork by Cassidy Fink.
Interior layout by TWA Solutions.

ISBN: 9798986068107 (paperback)
ISBN: 9798986068114 (ebook)

Printed in the United States

Follow Rustic Roads Publishing on Social Media.

"Everything about me is a contradiction, and so is everything about everybody else. We are made out of oppositions; we live between two poles. There's a philistine and an aesthete in all of us, and a murderer and a saint. You don't reconcile the poles. You just recognize them."

—Orson Welles

"This world is full of conflicts and full of things that cannot be reconciled. But there are moments when we can… reconcile and embrace the whole mess, and that's what I mean by 'Hallelujah.'"

—Leonard Cohen

CHAPTER 1

Counting Green Cars

"Are you serious!" The six-foot-two-inch professional wrestler wore grim black attire. The muscular entertainer paced because of excessive anxiety from his current cell phone conversation. His steady march, similar to that of a ferocious caged lion, was taking place in front of a backstage monitor, televising his best friend's wrestling match. With half-heartedness, he watched the fast-paced bout while he plugged his left index finger into his ear with ample force, hoping to drown out the overwhelming noise from the excited fans in the sold-out Tallahassee arena. "You can't marry that jackass and take Josie from me! I still love you and I know, deep down, you still love me, too! We can make this work, love bug!" he declared with an impelling assertion in his voice, as a silver cross emphatically dangled from his neck. The two combatants on the monitor were more than persistent in wowing the crowd as the discussion on the mobile device continued to intensify.

The delicate but frustrated voice on the other side of the line responded with considerable exasperation. "Please, don't call me that anymore, Richie! We've been over this a million times before. I simply can't be with you anymore! Watching you get beat up over and over, not really knowing if you got hurt or if you're just selling to the audience. All the injuries you have suffered, the broken bones, the torn muscles, the stitches, and the concussions. I hope you know that I felt every single one of those injuries, too." She vehemently disclosed her perspective on the situation as her head abruptly flipped back. "I know you and your brother lived for this stuff and I'm so sorry he passed away, but I can't support you in this profession like he could. I can no longer be a part of this."

"John only supported me in this because he didn't want me to get killed in a racecar like he almost did. After he lost his leg in the Atlanta crash was when he really started pushing me in this direction. He didn't want the same thing to happen to me." The slender Black competitor, his longtime pal, wearing bright orange trunks, performed a perfect monkey flip to his stocky White opponent in the neon green singlet, to the onlooker's delight. This caused a surge of noise, which made Richie pause for a moment as he was pleading his case to her. "Just hold out for a little bit, Mary. I'm getting ready for a title run, which will bring in some serious cash. After that, maybe I can take some time off and we can get back on track."

"This isn't about money, Richie. Even if you weren't always getting hurt, this relationship still wouldn't work because you're never home. Our own three-year-old daughter doesn't even really know who you are!" Mary spoke with harshness as she brushed her curly auburn hair out of her light peach-colored face.

"Come on, that's simply not true and you know it! I know I'm not Father of the Year mat—" Richie tried to reply to the rueful comment, but Mary promptly interrupted him.

"I'm sorry, but it is. She looks at pictures of my parents and my sister and she tries to say their names. If I show her a picture of you, she just stares for a moment, then runs off to play. You're not a bad father, Richie. I know you love Josie, but she needs stability in her life; a constant routine with her paternal figures. Nate can offer her that." Mary's voice held dissatisfaction that matched the sadness in her round hazel eyes. She took no joy whatsoever in stating that to him, but felt that it needed to be said.

The match on the monitor had now reached a fever pitch, and so had Richie's blood. The thought of another man raising his daughter left him beyond furious. She was his greatest achievement. His one and only baby girl. No one was going to take her from him. With immeasurable irritation, he pulled his finger out of his ear and ran his hand through his short-styled, dyed, jet-black hair. During which his face turned from a pale shade of white to an intense crimson red. Then he took a long deep breath. Without warning, the wrestler in the orange tights performed a sunset flip off the top rope, rolling up his opponent into a pinning predicament. Just as Richie was going to respond to Mary, the match instantly ended and the already loud racket from the people in attendance exploded into a deafening roar. There was no possible way she could hear him now, so he regrettably pressed the end call button on his phone and made a beeline to the staging area.

"You're up next, Richie. You ready?" A rather large and older backstage attendant walked beside him.

Trying to compose himself after the upsetting conversation, Richie briskly spoke back, "You know it, Gino! Where's the key fob?" The two men approached a stunningly deep and shiny black muscle car sporting subtle red stripes on the sides.

Gino pulled the key fob out of his pants pocket and with cautious repose, he moved his hand closer to Richie. "Just like we practiced, nice and easy."

"Oh please, Gino. I think I can drive a car to the ring." Richie imperiously smirked and snatched the key fob from the well-experienced staff member and former wrestler.

Gino's forehead wrinkled up, appearing as if it was a beige-colored raisin under his well-receded and scarred hairline. "I'm sure you can, but it ain't every day you get to drive a car like this. Vaughn put me in charge of it, so it's my hide on the line if something were to happen."

Richie stared intensely at the conspicuous coupe. "Sorry, Gino, just got a lot on my mind." The competitor in the orange trunks appeared through the entrance to the ring and approached them. Richie beamed. "Sherrod!" The two friends greeted each other, performing an overzealous fist bump. "Great showing out there, man!"

"Yeah? Did you get to see it?" Sherrod wiped the sweat off of his head and swept his tightly woven dreadlocks back out of his face, using a small white towel.

"Most of it." Richie daintily opened the door to the car and took great care, sliding down into the amazing ride. "I was a little distracted on the phone with Mary."

"You two finally talked? It's about time!" Thrilled for his constant confidant, Sherrod bent down to look in the car as Richie settled into place. "Damn, this thing is nice!"

"Yes, it is. Very nice. The most amazing car I've ever been in and you know I've been in a lot of cars."

The new car smell strongly filled the car as the two took in the majestic sight of the flawless interior.

"It's a real shame that it's not green. That's about the only thing that could make this ride any better."

Richie was quick to disagree. "No way, man. Green cars are cursed."

"Cursed? Nah, I ain't buying that bull, Rich."

"Hey, think about it for a minute. How many green cars do you see on the road? And I don't mean aqua, teal, turquoise, or anything like that. I mean something like forest green, grass green, or hunter green. Colors along those lines…they are far and few between."

Sherrod was quiet as he thought about Richie's statement. "I guess I'll pay a little more attention when I'm driving to see if you're right."

"I'm telling ya, man. I don't know why, but there seems to be something to it. Plus, the founder of Chevrolet's little brother was killed in a green racecar. They say that's where the curse started. I heard about it when I was a kid, but I didn't believe it either 'til I saw the great Cotton McCready himself have the worst crash of his entire career in a green car. It was a special onetime paint scheme for one of his sponsors and he almost got killed."

Not sure how to respond, Sherrod half-shrugged. "So, how did your conversation with Mary go?"

"Not good." Richie was dejected as he disclosed the new information. "She's getting married in Mt. Hood, Oregon, this Saturday to that blood-sucking politician I told you about. He's giving her the perfect textbook fairy tale spring wedding." Then he snarled in disgust.

"That's enough for now, you two! Richie, your music will be starting any minute!" Gino clamored out in a stern voice.

Sherrod patted Richie's shoulder a couple of times. "We'll talk after your match." Then he promptly closed the door to the Camaro.

"Here, hold this!" Richie tossed Sherrod his phone through the rolled-down car window. After which he suavely slipped on his small, round, dark glasses, and his left foot pushed down the clutch pedal. Right before he pressed the start engine button, a strange sensation overcame him. It was like déjà vu, but it lacked the mysteriousness that usually follows that feeling. It was more of a sense that it was closer to belonging. He sat still for a few seconds and basked in the odd atmosphere before finally starting the car. The automobile thundered to life like a Greek mythical beast, producing an eerie and deep rumbling sound. Gripping the steering wheel tightly, Richie slowly released the clutch as he slightly pressed on the gas with his right foot. The vehicle menacingly lurked forward.

CHAPTER 2

An Unforgettable Entrance

A shroud of silence blanketed the fan-filled arena after it went pitch-dark. Sporadic flashes from countless cameras and cell phone lights seemed to only escalate the anticipation of the next wrestler's arrival. Thereupon Richie's intimidating entrance, the eerie whine of the guitar fiercely brought the spectators to life, resulting in thunderous cheers. Without warning, the sleek machine made its brazen appearance. The lights slowly came back on, reflecting off of the car's flawless paint, making it appear as if it were black glass.

"Oh, my goodness, here comes the Priest!" an older, play-by-play commentator belted out, pushing his thick-framed glasses back into place.

The former wrestler turned commentator nodded, as guitars thrashed out threatening sounds. "That's right, Jack, it's The Minister of the Sinister, and he's coming out to the squared circle in a 2018 Hennessey Exorcist Chevrolet Camaro ZL1!"

"Did you say, 'Exorcist,' Steve?"

"Yes, sir." Steve nodded, making his straight bleach-blond hair lightly sweep back and forth over his wide muscular shoulders.

"Well that sure is appropriate, The Priest arriving in an Exorcist."

The imposing voice of the lead singer blasted throughout the building. "Don't look for me in the darkness, or out in the deep. Just call my name and you'll see me!"

Steve shook his head and chuckled. "Driving to the ring in an Exorcist Camaro while Metal Fate plays "The Lost Hours," it doesn't get any more badass than that. I couldn't think of a better way to make an appearance at I.W.L.'s biggest event, Ruckus Among Us."

Richie was having a hard time enjoying such a memorable entrance. It was, by far, the most amazing one of his career, but his phone call with Mary had his emotions rattled and his focus greatly skewed. Without a doubt, this match was going to be one of his biggest ever, but he couldn't get the thoughts of losing Mary for good out of his mind. Trying his best to concentrate on his job of entertaining the fans, he revved the powerful engine, which made the exhaust bellow out as the car approached the heavily lighted wrestling ring. Meanwhile, the car's supercharger produced a ghastly whine that caused some kids by the ringside to smile in astonishment, and it made others grab onto their parents in fear.

"That car is absolutely stunning!"

"It sure is, Jack. The Exorcist was designed to defeat the evil hellions from the other car manufacturers out there."

"It sure appears that it could certainly do that!"

"You can get you one. It will only cost you in the neighborhood of one hundred and twenty thousand bucks."

"Oh, my goodness, Steve!" Jack gasped dramatically, then grabbed his chest, pretending to have a heart attack.

The iconic band, Metal Fate, continued playing. "You cannot stop me. You can only stare. I am the tension in the air."

"With a top speed of two hundred and seventeen miles per hour, which makes it the world's fastest sixth-generation

Camaro, it's worth every single penny, Jack. It is equipped with the ZL1 package and that alone makes it one of the most powerful Camaros Chevrolet has ever produced. Hennessey Performance Engineering took it even further by adding a bigger supercharger, upgraded intercooler, ported heads, long tube headers, an improved intake system, an aggressive camshaft, and a returned ECU. All of which allows that car to produce over one thousand horsepower! Nine hundred and fifty-nine of those horses make it to the rear wheels. That is almost unheard of for a street-legal car! This thing is absolutely incredible!"

"I have no idea what you just said. I take the bus most of the time, Steve. I might be able to find the steering wheel on that thing." Jack astutely covered his microphone to prevent the viewers watching the pay-per-view at home from hearing what he was about to ask Steve as he leaned over. "Did you write all that down or have you been kicked in the head by a mule?"

Steve chuckled as he shook his head. "The boss handed me that info before the show started and told me to say it. I think he just worked out this deal for Richie to drive this car to the ring so that he could get a cheaper price on it for himself by advertising for the two companies."

Jack nodded his head, signifying that Steve's long-winded comment now made sense to him.

With slow and deliberate purpose, Richie exited the car and walked over to some onlookers leaning against the railing surrounding the ring. He handed out rosary beads to the younger kids and then he pulled out a small white plastic bottle with a golden cross on it. Next, he poured supposed "holy water" onto his hands and touched it to the energetic fans' foreheads. "Bless you, my child." Eventually, he made his way to the steps that led into the ring.

Richie methodically stepped through the ropes as the spine-chilling Metal Fate song still produced its creepy vibe. "Do not talk to demons, they just don't care. Don't step into the devil's lair."

Jack spotted a massive Black man speeding on foot past the Camaro. Then he quickly rolled under the bottom rope, entering the ring. What's this? Look out, Priest!"

"Mean Milo Jones got tired of waiting for this match to begin. He wanted to get an early jump on The Priest."

Milo sprang to his feet with amazing swiftness, especially for a man of such outstanding size, and clubbed Richie from behind, knocking him to the mat violently. Richie's entrance music came to a screeching halt and the crowd's excitement immediately turned to vociferous boos. The referee was in a frantic state as he tried to get the match officially started by signaling to the timekeeper with his flailing arms to ring the bell, while the ring announcer scrambled out of the ring to avoid being caught in the sudden melee.

Jack raised his arms in exasperation. "Our ring announcer didn't even get to do his job this time!"

"He jumped out of the ring like someone had rung a dinner bell. It doesn't matter anyways. Everyone knows who these two are. They have feuded off and on for years."

"Yes, they sure have, Steve, but this time there is a lot more on the line. This is a number one contender's match. The winner gets a shot at the I.W.L. Heavyweight title!" Jack made that fact clear to all the fans listening to their commentary.

Richie finally got his jacket and collar off between punches and kicks, leaving him in his usual wrestling outfit of a tight sleeveless top and long pants covering shiny laced up wrestling boots, all of which were black. The barrel-chested college football lineman, now a professional wrestling strong man, easily picked Richie up into a body-crushing bear hug.

His athletic body lay limp against the starred and striped American flag tank top and tight shorts of Milo's.

"Mean Milo has the Priest right where he wants him, Jack!"

Richie's supporters were fervent with their chants, encouraging The Priest to break out of the powerful man's arms. He gradually showed signs of life. Feeding off of the crowd's immense energy, Richie threw occasional punches at his competitor's big bald head and black-bearded face.

"The Priest is coming back to life! After repeated punches to Mean Milo and now elbow shots to his head, he has managed to break himself free from that devastating bear hug, Steve."

Richie ran into the ropes to gain momentum and narrowly dodged a clothesline attempt from Milo. Next, he bounced off the ropes with immense fury from the other side and drop-kicked Milo squarely in his face, sending his mighty foe flying out between the ropes and crashing to the ringside area. Once again, Richie ran directly into the ropes, gaining speed.

"Here he goes, Jack! The Minister of the Sinister has engaged his angel wings!"

Richie ran fast and hard toward Milo, springing off the top rope, flying squarely onto the huge man, and they both fell hard to the concrete floor. Moments later, the competitors slowly made their way back to their feet as the referee performed a ten-count protocol. Right before the official reached the match-ending number ten, both men crawled back into the ring just in the nick of time. They continued their vicious battle back and forth for fifteen minutes to the satisfaction of ravenous wrestling fans.

Milo discreetly asked Richie, "You ready for the turnbuckle spot?"

"Yeah, let's do it," he murmured between heavy breaths.

To perform the last set of moves before bringing the highly competitive match to an end, Milo grabbed Richie's arm and flung him toward the turnbuckle. Richie raced like a greyhound toward the intersection of the white ropes that were covered in black pads and labeled with the conspicuous I.W.L. logo. He took great care as he leaped onto the second turnbuckle, jumping back toward Milo with great force while spinning sharply around in the air, attempting to connect with a flying lariat. Milo easily caught the agile performer and slammed him violently to the mat with a large portion of his body weight landing, by accident, solidly on Richie.

CHAPTER 3

Badger Day, Again

"Absolutely unreal," Gino mumbled, as Richie drove out of the dimly lit backstage area to start his match.

"What's that?" Sherrod curiously asked.

"The way you kids get to make an entrance these days. Hell, we didn't even always have music to come out to when I first started. Now, there are all kinds of fireworks, songs, flashing lights, and even lasers. Don't get me wrong, we eventually got most of that stuff, too, but not to the extent of what it is now."

"Is that a bad thing, Gino?"

"Nah, it just blows my mind how much has changed." He smiled for a second, but then it transformed into a wry look, turning his gray mustache sideways. "Well, on second thought, maybe nothing really has."

"Whaddya mean?"

"Best I can tell, it's like this. We can take this show, event, circus, sport, whatever it is or whatever you want to call it." He paused, gazing toward the ring. "We can take this thing and repackage, repaint it, rebrand it, do whatever to it, but at its core it is always the same thing. Good versus evil, heroes fighting villains, my favorite competitor against yours. This thing speaks to us. It speaks to us on some primal level. Kinda like cowboys and Indians or cops and robbers."

"Yeah, you're right, it does." Sherrod nodded in agreement. "I know one thing. It sure is a crazy way to make a living."

"This is more than a job, son. This is like that damn zombie show you guys are always talking about. This business gets in your blood and it consumes you. Hell, it becomes you."

"I never thought of it like that before, but you're spot on with that thought, Gino."

"Some people out there in the world just don't get it. They say crap like, 'Oh, that's so fake' and 'You don't believe that's real, do you?' Those snobs hate it, but people like us, those of us that actually get what this is and what it's about, are hooked. We are truly hooked on this thing for life. Even if some of us go through periods where we don't watch or those of us that have been in the ring may give it up for a while, but we always come crawling back like damned junkies to a dealer."

"For real, you've been in this stuff for a long time now, ain't ya?"

"Feels like forever. Three ex-wives, two estranged kids. Lord knows how many more illegitimate ones out there." He chuckled. "And I'm still here. I can't break free, Sherrod. I have finally just accepted that this is my life. I can't go perform in the ring anymore, but at least I'm still involved. Vaughn is a pompous ass, that's for sure, but I can't hate him. He lets me stick around, so here I am."

"I'm real sorry to hear that about your kids, Gino." Sherrod said with a downcast gaze.

"Nah, don't worry about it. It is what it is. Here's the thing though, I tried, and I mean really tried hard, to be a good father and a good husband. I even had what they call a real job at one time. I drove a forklift at a factory. But the whole domestic bliss thing just didn't work out for me. I had been gone far too long already. I'm sure I got on their nerves, always talking about wrestling and telling the same ol' stories over and over. I lived in the past and they needed me in the present. I guess what it all really boiled down to was that we tended to rub each other the wrong way when I was there all the time. I really hate that it didn't work, but I sincerely tried to fix it. For the most part, I don't really have any regrets, though. I regret, of course, that we're not closer than we are, but how can a salmon regret going back upstream? It's just doing what it's supposed to." Gino shrugged, then his demeanor grew somber. "I'll be here working behind the scenes for as long as I can or as long as they will let me stay. Then I guess it's off to the nursing home to die. This business probably took thirty years off my life and destroyed any hope of a real relationship with my family, but at the same time, it gave me an amazing ride. I got to see the world, meet so many amazing people and got paid a lot of dough to do it."

"I guess it's like that old saying. No free lunches, huh?"

"Yep, no free lunches, kid. I just overheard Richie on the phone with his old lady and it brought back a lot familiar memories. I'm here to tell ya; he can quit this business and go and try to be a perfect dad, but it will eventually start to eat at him. And over time, it will eat his insides up, always being stuck at home. I hope I'm wrong, but that's exactly how it was for me."

Sherrod slowly nodded in agreement. "Yeah, it's a tough situation." Hoping to lighten the mood a little, he changed the topic. "You're going on the European tour with us, right?"

"Yeah, definitely. I love it over there. I can't believe Vaughn actually chartered an entire plane for us all, though. That's a first. It's even going to have an open bar!" Gino stretched out his arms in exclamation. "Can you believe that?"

"Oh, God, no! An open bar with some of these guys? What was he thinking?"

"I don't know. It's probably going to be like that *Con Air* movie." They both shared a nervous laugh. "Hey, let's sit together so we can watch each other's backs."

"Hey, that's a good idea! I'll catch you later, Gino." Sherrod looked down at Richie's phone as he headed back to the locker room area. As he turned a corner, he saw a very familiar brown-haired man enter one of the backstage offices. "It can't be!" he whispered. He crept up to the room, using a fair amount of caution, and peeked through a partially open door. This enabled him to get a better look at the chalky complexion that was on the arrogant face of the now recognizable man. *What the heck? Why is that sorry piece of crap here?* he thought. Wanting to be careful, he looked around and, since he didn't see anyone coming his way, he eased his way ever closer to the door to eavesdrop.

A short cocky man in an exuberant light pink shirt held a fat cigar in his thick, gold ring covered fingers. "Considering you left a very successful and dominating career to try and become a professional hockey player, the fans aren't going to be very accepting of you. Especially after that amazing insult you gave them on your way out. What was it you told them? Oh yeah, 'Every single one of you fat-ass, backwoods inbred, welfare drawing, waste of human lives can go eat dog turds with toothpicks.' Then you said, 'I completely regret ever spending a single second entertaining you drooling dingleberries.'" Awkward silence filled the room for a moment. "As a heel, that comment will definitely draw you some serious heat."

"Yeah, well, I don't give a rat's ass what those stupid marks think. I'm here for one thing, the paycheck." The very cocky competitor folded his arms formidably. "Besides, my name carries a lot of weight in the sports world and it can make huge loads of money for us both, Mr. Vaughn."

"Yes, a very true statement indeed. That's why you're here and also the main reason we're going to put the title on you straight away." Vaughn rubbed his well-groomed, salt-and-pepper-colored beard that led up to his horseshoe hairline. "Bad Badger Timberland will dominate the wrestling world once again, which will allow me to put over any ham and egger out there that might have the smallest glimmer of a chance of beating you. All the while saving this company tons of cash in the long run by not having to pay out to bigger named performers."

"That sounds like a good plan." Badger's eyebrows rose inquiringly. "So, when do I beat Overkill?"

"Oh no, he carries way too much prestige to suddenly lose the title out of the blue. We're going to have him lose to The Priest due to an existing injury from a previous bout. Then at the next television taping after that happens, you are going over The Priest in a record setting title match."

Badger looked confused. "Record setting?"

"Nine seconds. You're going to catch him off guard with a devastating blow before the bell even has a chance to ring. Next you will set him up for your patented Avalanche Slam, thus defeating him in the fastest heavyweight title match in the entire history of the I.W.L.!" Vaughn smiled with great delight.

"Nice!" Badger cracked a haughty smile, which was a rarity for him, followed by a nod of approval. "So is Priest getting the axe or what? Not that I care. It's just that most transitional champions are usually on their way out the door."

Vaughn cleared his throat, then a cold and lackluster stare covered his face. "He will have the option to become a trainer or he can hit the road. It doesn't make a difference to me either way. It's becoming apparent that he's gone about as far as he's going to here in the I.W.L. Besides, the Vatican has been on my back since day one after the debut of his character. They've contacted me several times over the years, urging me to get rid of the whole sinister priest gimmick. They don't like the negative way it portrays Catholicism. It was edgy at first and got a lot of attention, but now it seems to have finished running its course."

Oh, man, Richie's going to be super pissed about this. Sherrod stealthily scampered back to the locker room.

CHAPTER 4

Two Birthdays, One Contender

Richie had been super excited as he lit the number two birthday candle on Josie's beautiful pink cake. The love for his daughter was easily detected in his voice as he and Mary sang to her. After the song finished, the happy couple helped her blow out the candle, but she seemed mildly interested at best.

Mary looked at Richie with a long face. *"I'm sorry she's not into it this time."*

"It's okay. I imagine that your second, second birthday can be a little boring. I'm just glad to be here with my two most favorite ladies." He hugged Mary and gently kiss her forehead.

"You know I love it when you kiss me there. I'll show you the rest of the video from her first, second birthday from last week in a little bit." She sighed while enveloped in his arms. *"Josie was so excited with all the presents and kids running around."*

"I'm really sorry I missed it." Richie's voice held deep regret. *"The schedule just didn't allow for me to have time off then. I barely got here this time."*

Mary broke their embrace, stepped back, folded her arms over her chest, and pursed her lips. *"I know. I hope all this time you are missing with us is worth it. I hope you get whatever it is you are after."*

Richie became somewhat defensive. *"I'm after supplying you two a good life. I want you to be able to have everything you need and want."*

"I need and want you here with us, Richie! Instead of talking to you on a five-inch screen sporadically. I make good money. You don't have to live on the road all the time to provide for us."

"I know, love bug, it's tough right now, but it will be worth it." Richie had tried to convince her, as well as himself. Then the cute couple embraced in a genuine, warm hug. *"I love you, Mary."*

"I love you—"

∞

"Two!" the referee shouted out. Thereupon, Richie barely kicked out of the pinning predicament as he desperately gasped for air.

"Looks like that slam took the wind right out of The Priest." Jack's voice reeked of concern.

Steve nodded. "Sure did. He's having a hard time getting to his feet. We may have a serious injury on our hands."

The referee used his authority to back Milo into a corner to give Richie some time to recuperate, since he could tell he was really hurting. He walked over to him as he awkwardly climbed back to his feet. "You okay, Rich? That was a nasty bump you just took." Richie reluctantly nodded while he tried to get air back into his lungs. "Good, let's take it home."

Milo looked out at the crowd and gave them two big thumbs down.

"Uh oh, Jack, he's giving the signal for his The Star Spangled Splatter! That's one of the most dangerous and feared moves in this entire profession!"

Then Milo threw his longtime colleague into the ropes.

Richie bounced off them and to everyone's surprise, he landed a big blunt kick directly to the gut. As the humongous man held his midsection and grimaced in pain, Richie made the sign of the cross. The noise from the crowd seemed like it could literally blow the roof off of the entire stadium.

Now consumed with excitement, Jack yelled out, "It's his call sign for his finishing maneuver, The Last Rites!"

Richie grabbed the strongman's head and firmly pressed Milo's face against the top of his head and, without warning, dropped to his knees, appearing to crush Milo's mug, sending him flying backwards before he landed hard onto the mat. Richie stayed on his knees for a moment and clasped his hands, appearing to pray. Then he forcefully grabbed his opponent's tree trunk of a leg and pulled it toward his upper body while covering Milo's head and shoulders with his own back.

The referee shouted out in a loud and clear voice as his arm slammed the gray sweat-ridden canvas. "One, two, three!"

The audience erupted with deafening cheers.

Richie got to his knees, and the referee raised his arm to verify him as the winner of the match. Then his entrance music played, which also signified his historic victory. Next, he gingerly exited the ring by rolling under the bottom rope.

"I think The Priest is still hurting from that big slam off of the middle turnbuckle," Steve speculated.

"He very well could be; he usually hams it up with his fans more than that, his congregation as he calls them, even more so after a big win like this one. I'm going to go see if I can get a few words from him." Jack stood up from the announcer's table and walked toward The Priest.

As Richie tried to shake off his pain from the heated battle, he noticed that the beautiful, black machine was gone. Gino had already taken it backstage. *Man, wish I could have driven it at least one more time*, he thought.

Jack caught up to Richie and after congratulating him on his big win, he punctually inquired, "Priest, I gotta know. How does it feel to be the number one contender for the Heavyweight Championship here in the Infinity Wrestling League?"

Richie grabbed the cordless microphone from Jack, and after somewhat catching his breath, he spoke in character. "A lot of people have tried to stop me on my mission to win the heavyweight title here and they have failed miserably time after time. They didn't realize my mission has been ordained from a Higher Power. These sinners were only mere speed bumps on my glorious highway to Heaven. Forgive them not, Father, for they knew exactly what they were doing." Richie shoved the microphone into Jack's chest and intensely stared into the camera with his cold, grayish-blue eyes.

"Wait, Priest, before you leave. Do you have any words for the current I.W.L. Heavyweight Champion, Overkill?" Jack cowardly stood down beside Richie, making sure to stay out of his way while holding the microphone close to his mouth for it to pick up his response.

Richie used great intensity in proclaiming, "Don't expect mercy, don't expect forgiveness, and don't expect to win. Overkill will be roadkill." Richie made the sign of the cross and delivered his famous catchphrase. "Ashes to ashes and dust to dust."

The spectators quoted his famous tagline along with him and cheered as he walked to the backstage area while holding his side.

CHAPTER 5

Cooler Heads Peculate

"Ow, I think my rib is cracked," Richie groaned while easing down onto a worn-out wooden bench in front of a row of gray, dilapidated metal lockers.

"Probably happened from that big-ass slam off the middle turnbuckle. I heard the whole locker room groan out loud when it happened." Sherrod finished changing into his street clothes. He was now dressed in shiny black track pants that laid over white sneakers and a bright orange shirt that carried his persona's logo.

Richie held his left side. "Oh yeah, it did. So you saw my match then?"

"No, but I saw that slam." Sherrod quickly changed the subject. "Hey, I've got some bad news, bro."

"What, did you shart yourself again?" Richie chortled with a mischievous smile, then grabbed his sides even tighter. "Oh crap, it hurts to laugh."

"As a matter of fact, I did, smartass, and I'm wearing your underwear," Sherrod snapped back with a smile of his own. "Speaking of which, where is your stuff? I was going to put your phone in your bag, but I didn't see it."

"By the door; I was late getting here."

"Oh yeah, well, someone else was, too." Sherrod's face held a grim look.

"Who?" Richie perked up to listen closely to his old pal.

"Badger Timberland."

"That's a total load of bull, Sherrod. Don't you know liars go to hell?"

"Oh well, I'll be in line right behind you then, I guess."

"Come on, man, Bad Badger Timberland did not show up here. He basically dropped his pants and took a huge metaphorical dump right on this company, the fans, and the industry as a whole before he ran off to go be a big hockey star. That had to be about four years ago, I think."

"Yeah, he did, and how did that work out for him? I think he played two seasons for a farm team before being cut or something like that. Anyways, who cares? But Timberland showing back up here isn't all of it." Sherrod dreadfully explained the rest of the bad news after rubbing his forehead. "I saw him talking to Vaughn, so I listened in on their conversation."

"You did what? Damn, Sherrod, I never figured you for a Nosy Nelly." Richie chuckled.

"Shut up, dumbass, you make it sound like I'm a creepy peeping Tom or something. For real though, man, you need to hear this! Vaughn is putting him over on you and quick, too! After our tour in Europe, he's putting the strap on him and it's at your expense."

"Sherrod, come on, man, you can't be serious." Richie refuted his friend's statement in disbelief. "I've worked years for this opportunity. Vaughn is a low-down snake, but surely he wouldn't do something like that."

"Hey, guys, come check this out. You ain't going to believe this!" Milo yelled out to Sherrod and Richie from another row of lockers. They wasted no time and ran over to a monitor that was steaming the action from the ring so they could see what the fuss was about.

Sherrod stood beside his friend, standing akimbo. "I told ya, Richie,"

Badger Timberland was swaggering toward the ring to announce his return to the I.W.L. His familiar-sounding entrance music was playing, which completely shocked the attending audience, who thought they would never see him in a professional wrestling ring ever again.

"What the hell is he doing here?" Milo barked in anger.

"I don't know, but I'm going to find out." Richie headed out of the locker room at a fervent pace to track down Vaughn. After a quick search, he located his current objective, his employer, setting in an elaborate office with his complete attention focused on a television monitor. He seemed to be very excited as he gawked at the live feed of the event. Richie's adrenaline was running dangerously high, so he took several deep breaths, hoping to calm himself down before he entered.

"Hey, boss, gotta second?" Richie fought off the ever-growing feelings of anxiousness.

"Can it wait? I'm trying to watch this," Vaughn, with his back to Richie, uttered back with an all too familiar arrogant attitude and, to make it worse, he didn't even bother taking his eyes off the monitor.

"Well, not really. I need to talk to you about some time off. I just need a week or so. It's really important or I wouldn't be bugging you about it right now."

"Come on in then. Let's watch this while we talk." Vaughn's eyes were still glued to the monitor. "Are you seeing this? I can't believe we actually managed to get Badger Timberland back into the company. He's been plastered all over the national sports channels as well as the mainstream satellite radio stations and social media outlets in the recent past. His decision to come back here will bring in tons of free exposure for the I.W.L."

"I wish I could share in your enthusiasm for this, sir, but I just can't stomach his total lack of respect for this business and all of the legends that paved the way for guys like us." Richie had blurted that out before he even realized what he was saying.

The heartfelt comment went against Vaughn's excitement and finally got his eyes off the monitor for a moment. He glared at Richie. "Well, I'm sorry you feel that way but you might as well get used to Timberland being here. You are going to be working with him real soon, by the way."

Gino walked in. "Excuse me, Mr. Vaughn, here is the key fob for your new car." then he laid it on the desk.

"Oh, thanks, Gino. You know, I had completely forgotten about it." Vaughn snickered smugly. "When you have as many cars as I do, it's hard to keep up with them all. How did you like driving my car, Richie?" Before he could even answer, Vaughn blurted, "I bet you've never been in anything that nice, have ya? I got a killer deal on it since we're advertising for Chevrolet and Hemingway at the event tonight."

"Hennessey. It's Hennessey." Richie pointed out while thinking, *What an idiot. He doesn't even deserve that car.*

"Yeah, whatever. It will set next to my Vette collection." Vaughn smirked. Being corrected by an employee seemed to have aggravated him. "Gino, make sure the ring crew carefully packs up the Camaro. We leave for Europe after the show. I won't get to drive it 'til we get back."

With moderate hesitation and dread building in the pit of his mid-section, Richie butted in on the current conversation. "That's what I wanted to talk to you about, sir. I know it's a bad time to ask, but I must insist on a week off. I have some personal issues I need to deal with, and I was hoping I could catch up to the tour in Germany before I win the title."

Vaughn sat up in his chair and actually gave Richie some of his attention. "Oh, I see. Regrettably, the answer is no. I'm sorry, but that just can't happen." Shaking his head, the tone of his voice was cold and hollow. "We appreciate all you've done for the company, but we are going to need you to take on another role here. This is going to be your last big run before shifting gears, so to say." He didn't want to reveal this information to Richie until after the tour of Europe, but this conversation had forced his hand on the matter.

Richie could feel his heart beating in his throat as his blood pressure spiked. His fears of what Sherrod told him were coming to fruition. "What do you mean, exactly?"

"We want you to be in more of a trainer type position. You'll be helping the new guys finish honing their skills, what little they have these days, as well as helping them choreograph their matches. You have a knack for coming up with exciting spots. I think it would be a perfect job for you." Vaughn wasn't very convincing.

Richie stuttered, "Okay," with overwhelming uncertainty growing in his voice. He felt like his mind was going a thousand miles per hour and his stomach was now tied up in knots. Questions poured out of his mouth without any control. "Would I still be active on the roster? What would my schedule be like? How much would my pay be?" He couldn't believe this was actually happening. He had sacrificed so much of his time, his body, and his whole adult life for this job, and Vaughn was taking it all away from him in a single instant.

Vaughn's main focus was no longer on the monitor at all, as he could feel the tension in the room reaching a higher level. He was prompt in replying to the many questions, hoping to sugarcoat them without distorting the facts too much. "Well, your pay, sorry to say, will be decreased somewhat. Our trainer's salaries currently top out around just north of thirty thousand; still a decent amount of money. Enough to lead a modest little life with, but I'll talk to my accounting crew and see if I can get you a touch more than that. Your schedule would basically be the same as it is now and no, regrettably, you wouldn't be on the active roster at all anymore. Hey, on the bright side, you wouldn't be prone to any more serious injuries either."

Richie sat in silence with a blank stare on his face.

"I hope you can understand our point of view on this. We really need your help with Badger Timberland's return. We need you to help put him over as fast as possible, so—"

"So you're telling me that Badger is basically going to bury my career!" Richie could no longer keep his composure. The news of Mary getting married already had him upset, but now finding out he was losing his job, how and who to, was more than he could handle.

"Hey, I understand that this information is unsettling, but let's calm down here." Vaughn held his hands out, making a pressing down motion. It was clear to see how angry Richie had become. "This doesn't have to get ugly. I totally get that you're upset, that's expected, but we can make the best of this situation. It's nothing personal."

Gino watched with growing concern. His secondary job was to protect Vaughn.

"Oh yeah, let's calm down!" Richie shouted with blatant sarcasm, sticking out his chest and swaying his head back and forth, seeming to mock Vaughn. "Let's stay calm because I'm not about to lose my relationship! Let's stay calm because I'm not about to lose my daughter! Let's stay calm because I'm not about to lose my career! Let's stay calm because I don't have to job out to the biggest douche that ever worked in this industry!"

Vaughn's face became beet red. A man of his stature didn't take well to being talked back to, and especially in that manner. "Don't you take that tone with me, you ignorant piece of trash.

If you were any good, this wouldn't be happening right now. It's not my fault that you're a middle card performer, at best."

"I've done damn good considering this stupid gimmick you put on me! There are very few other guys in this business these days that could have portrayed this character as well as I have! I got over with the fans and I still manage to get a good pop from them to this day!"

Vaughn sneered. "Those ignorant wretches don't know what they want. They have to be told what to like and what not to. It's up to me to do the thinking for them." He adjusted his flashy necktie with an exaggerated motion.

"And we're all just your puppets to be used at your disposal to make it all happen! Well, not me, not anymore!"

Gino feared things were about to get out of control, so he moved closer to the desk.

Vaughn stood up, pointing his finger in Richie's face. "Let me tell you something, you piece of crap, you'll show up for all your scheduled matches and be a transitional champion for Timberland or you won't get a cent of the money left on your contract!"

Richie's eyes widened then sharply squinted, giving Vaughn a haunting death stare.

That reaction made Vaughn realize that he now had Richie right where he wanted him. A domineering smile came across his face. "That's right, and the last time I checked, it was just a little bit over a hundred thousand. You can kiss every last single cent of it goodbye."

Richie pointed his finger at Vaughn. "I worked damn hard for that money and I earned every single last penny. I wrestled matches filling in for other guys, I made appearances I wasn't required to, and I even used my own money at times when it could have been an expense for the company!"

Sherrod and Milo heard Richie yelling, so they made their way over to the office and stood just outside of it.

"I don't give a sewer rat's ass about what you have done. You will show up, and you will do what you are told!" Vaughn stood erect, with overwhelming confidence in his now coarse voice. "You're bought and paid for. Your sorry stinking carcass belongs to me, and if you don't show up, you'll pay the price. Let's see, for starters, I can have some of my friends at the TSA put you on the 'No-fly list'. How's that for a parting gift? It'll be hard fixing your personal situation if you can't even get there, won't it? You don't cross Terence Vaughn and get away with it! No one does!"

Richie realized this predicament with Vaughn had become hopeless. He hung his head in defeat, but at that very moment, the Camaro key fob laying on the desk caught his eye. It was as if it were a lighthouse sending out a bright beacon of hope. *This is my only chance!* he thought, taking a deep breath. *Here goes nothing.* "I tell you what, Vaughn. You can keep the damn money and you can destroy my career. But there's one thing that you will never be able to do."

"Oh really, hot shot, and what might that be?"

Richie got up into Vaughn's face. "Look at yourself in the mirror and say, 'I am a real man.' Everything you've got and everything you've done has been because of someone else. You brag about being in charge of a multi-million dollar company, but you didn't do a single thing on your own to get here. I'd bet that you can't even wipe your own ass!"

Vaughn grabbed Richie by his shirt and got in his face with immense anger. "I oughta bust you up, you damn hillbilly!"

Richie shoved the egomaniac off, sending Vaughn back into his chair and it toppled over onto the floor with him in it. Gino went running over to check on his boss. Richie grabbed the key fob while they were distracted and kept it hidden in his left hand. *Yes! It worked! That idiot fell for it!* Richie thought, pleased that his impromptu plan was an immediate success.

Vaughn regained his footing and tried to attack Richie, but Gino was holding him back, momentarily at least.

"Damn it, Richie, you've gone too far! Get the hell out of here now!" Gino barked as Sherrod and Milo rushed into the office to help him gain control of the explosive situation.

Sherrod grabbed Richie by the left arm and Milo grabbed his right, pulling him toward the door. "Let's go, man, come on."

"You're through, you piece of crap!" Vaughn shouted. "Nobody talks to me like that!"

Yeah, well, I'm not a nobody, Richie thought, as the three men made their way back to the locker room area.

CHAPTER 6

Capes or Cabs

Sherrod looked at Richie in disbelief. "You done lost yo damn mind!"

"Shhh! Keep it down. I probably have." Richie nodded in agreement "But please tell me, what else am I supposed to do? That thieving bastard took my career, my money, and possibly will have me put on the no-fly list as a parting gift. How am I supposed to fix my relationship with Mary if I can't even get there?"

"Can he really put you on the no-fly list?"

"It's Terence Vaughn."

"Yeah, you gotta point there. I still don't know about this, Richie. Taking his car is insane!" Sherrod moved in closer, speaking quietly to keep from drawing attention from the other wrestlers in the locker room. "Where did you say Mary was at?"

"Oregon. She's getting married in Mt. Hood Saturday."

Sherrod's jaw dropped, and he gave Richie a blank stare.

"Come on, man, stop fooling around."

"Oh, I ain't fooling around. I'm just trying to get this craziness straight in my mind. You're going to take Terence Vaughn's brand new stolen car and drive clear across the country—from Tallahassee, Florida, to Mt. Hood, Oregon? Especially after insulting the man and getting him good and pissed off? You even shoved his old ass onto the floor!"

"Do I have another option? Either way, my career at I.W.L. is over. If I can get to Mt. Hood, then I can convince Mary to give me a second chance."

"Bro, can't you do that over the phone?"

"She won't take the time to really hear me out on the phone. If I can talk to her in person, I know I can fix this mess. And now since all this has happened with Vaughn, I will be able to explain how I gave up my only chance of being the Heavyweight Champion to be with her, then I'll definitely be back in her good graces. She knows how bad I wanted that title. She'll have no choice but to send that damn communist wannabe, Nate Rainer, packing."

Sherrod carefully listened to Richie's reason for wanting to go to Oregon. "Okay then, let's stop this crazy talk about stealing a car and get you a bus ticket to Mt. Hood."

"And let that slimy subhuman Vaughn get away with stealing over a hundred G's from me? That's why I was planning on taking his car. Lowlifes like him need to be taught a lesson."

Looking confused, Sherrod held his arms out. "How's that going to teach him a lesson?" With blatant sarcasm, he then asked, "You want me to go get you a cape and a mask?"

Richie now had a confused look as well as he questioned his agitated ally. "Why would I need that?"

"Well, if you're going to go all vigilante, you might as well look the part." Sherrod rubbed his forehead. "Look, he'll just go buy another one and then you'll be stuck with a car you can't drive or sell, for fear of being caught with it!"

Richie's demeanor changed. He stopped talking back and stared down at the floor. "Yeah, you're right, man. It's just that I can't beat him in court, so taking that car was the only way I could come out of this debacle somewhat even."

"It's never even with Vaughn."

"Yeah, ain't that the truth." Richie nodded.

Sherrod's eyebrows rose out of curiosity. "Wait, I know it's your money, your business, but how's he stealing a hundred G's from you anyways?"

"I made the mistake of setting up my contract for the minimal monthly allowance then the large payout at the end of it."

"Not trying to beat you up even more than you already are, Rich, but that was a huge mistake."

Somberly, Richie exhaled and looked at his friend. "I know. I got greedy. I chose that setup 'cause the more money you leave in it, the greater the interest it draws, but now all I got is the shaft."

The two friends sat quietly for a bit.

"I remember this one time when I was a teenager, John told me this outrageous story about cars."

Sherrod smiled. "I thought that's all he ever did?"

"Yeah, but this one was different, way different. I don't know if he had smelled too many exhaust fumes that day or what, but he only told me this story once. That wasn't like him; he usually made you listen to his tall tales over and over but not this particular one."

Sherrod turned to his left and sat up to get a better view of Richie telling the story. "Well, let's hear it."

"He said to me, 'Whenever you go to buy a car, never be in a hurry. Sit in it with the engine off for a minute or so before you start it and listen.'"

"Listen to it with the engine off?"

"That's what I asked him and he said, 'Yes. Leave the engine off and listen.'"

"What are you supposed to hear?"

"That's what I said, too. What am I listening for? Wind noise, loose interior panels, bees in the trunk?"

"Wait, why would there be bees in the trunk?"

"Out in the country, if a car sits in the summertime, even for just a little bit, bees, well actually wasps or yellow jackets, will sometimes try to build a nest in the cracks, especially in the trunk jamb."

"Oh, that's just like them lil' bastards. Hide in the trunk and 'bam!' Ambush you at the grocery store."

Richie chuckled lowly, not quite enough to hurt his ribs this time, before continuing to tell his story. "Anyways, he said, 'You're listening for the car to speak to you.'"

"So like Knight Rider then?"

"That's exactly what I asked him. He said, 'No, dumbass, you're listening for the car to speak to your soul.' Then I said, 'What? Have you been drinking?' He said, 'Yeah, but that's beside the point.' Then he got real close and spoke just a notch above a whisper while saying, 'Only trust a car that speaks to your soul. A car that does that will never let you down.'"

Sherrod turned his head and cut his eyes at Richie. "That's crazy. Just how much had he been drinking that day?"

"That was the very next thing I asked him. He got a little aggravated at that comment and said, 'I'm serious, dammit! Now listen close to what I say. Check the car for rust, engine knocks, and everything else, but no matter how good of shape it's in, don't buy it if it doesn't speak to you 'cause it will only give you trouble. I'm tellin' ya right now. If a car speaks to your soul, it will never let you down, especially when you need it most. Don't pick the car, let the car pick you.' I told him that I kinda understood what he was saying, but it was kinda crazy, too. He said the Indians did the same thing when they picked a horse. Why should it be any different for a car? So, I don't know if he had been watching too many westerns that week or what, but to this day, I never forgot that story. And of all days, the day I lose my job, lose my money, and possibly lose my family, I actually had a car speak to me." Richie looked straight into Sherrod's eyes. "Vaughn's car spoke to me."

"No way. You're fooling with me. First, you're talking about cursed green cars and now it's talking cars. Next, you're going to tell me something about flying cars. What's the matter with you, man?"

"That car spoke to me, Sherrod, just like John said. I'm dead serious. I know it sounds crazy, but I could feel exactly what he was talking about when I was in it." Richie gave Sherrod the most serious and unwavering look that he'd ever seen him make.

Sherrod gazed back at him as if he was in a trance. Hearing him talk about John reminded him of how badly Richie was hurt when he died. Now, if he lost Mary and Josie too, he would end up worse off than Gino. At least Gino still had a job here. If Mary turned him down, he wouldn't have anyone or anything left. *I can't let that happen,* he thought. *If something about this car gives a part of John back to Richie, then, well, he at least deserves that.*

"I'll get changed and catch a cab to the nearest bus station." Richie hung his head low. All hope seemed to be vanquished from him as he realized how desperate and insane his plan sounded.

"Wait! Oh snap, man, this is deep." Sherrod rubbed his forehead as he looked down. Without warning, he looked up with an anxious expression and grabbed Richie by his shoulders. Then he got close to his face as if he was having a regrettable 'aha' moment. "If you're going to do this, you gotta go now. You need to be long gone from here before the main event ends."

CHAPTER 7

Go West, Young Masked Man

"What? Now you think taking Vaughn's car is a good idea?" Richie looked at Sherrod with a wrinkled-up face of pure confusion.

"Hell no! It's a terrible idea, and to be honest, it's probably the worst idea you ever had!" Sherrod held his arms out to the sides of his torso. "But you're definitely right on the matter of saving your relationship with your family. Also, you're right about Vaughn. He shouldn't get off that easy for screwing you over. At the very least, we're going to make his sorry ass buy another new car." Sherrod pointed his finger at Richie, then shot him a cunning smile.

"Wait! Am I really going to do this?" Richie's heart beat fast as the realization that this was actually happening was setting in.

"Let's see." With his hand on his forehead, as the daft plan's details processed in Sherrod's excited mind. "Vaughn shouldn't see the car again 'til sometime after the European tour. All we need to do is keep him from knowing it's gone 'til then."

"That's right! He told Gino to make sure the ring crew packed it up. He won't have any idea it's gone! That's Brilliant!" Richie pumped his clenched right fist in excitement.

"Then I will make sure he thinks they did. I'll keep Gino distracted by getting him to tell me some more of his stories from his good ol' days."

"K, good." Richie nodded with satisfaction at that idea. "What about cameras? Are there any back there?"

"I don't know for sure but I've got an idea. I can't believe I'm doing this. Get your street clothes on, I'll be back."

"Where you going?"

"To get you a cape and a mask!" Sherrod took off in a flash while Richie changed into his black sneakers, blue jeans, and a black ZZ Top tee shirt. Moments later, Sherrod was back with Milo's American flag-striped ring coat and a black mask. With urgency, he motioned for Richie to come with him, and the two fled the locker room and went into a dark hallway.

"What are you doing with those?"

"Trying to cover your ass! If there are cameras back there, hopefully they won't know it's you. Quick, put them on! I told Perplexitor he was my nephew's favorite wrestler, and he gave me his backup mask to give to him."

"You wasn't kidding about getting a mask, huh? Gah, this thing stinks! What about Milo's coat?"

"I just took it."

"Oh, geez! Man, he's going to be so pissed." Richie chuckled.

"I hope so. That's a part of the plan. You can send it back to him later. Give me your cell phone." Sherrod outstretched his hand.

Richie's eyebrows rose. "Why do you want it?"

"Just in case Vaughn suspects you took the car, he won't be able to track you. You better not use your credit cards and stay away from any cameras. If they pick up your face with the car nearby, you're busted for sure. Same with cops, too. Most have body cameras. If they try to pull you over, you're done."

"Yeah, I know. I guess I'll just have to outrun them."

Sherrod leaned in closer to Richie. "Listen, first chance you get, you better get the GPS, OnStar, and any other thing that could track down that car disabled. The second he reports it stolen, that's the first thing the cops will do."

"Oh, yeah, that had completely slipped my mind. Get Mary's number off my phone and find out the address of where she will be in Mt. Hood. My passcode is 244866. I will call you from landlines or borrowed phones, so be sure to answer any unknown numbers."

"Will she give me the address?"

"Call her from your phone and tell her that even though you think she should give me another chance, you want to send a wedding present." Richie put on Milo's coat. "She always liked you, so I think she will go for that. I don't have any cash on me. Do you have any I could borrow?"

Sherrod reached into his pants pocket and pulled out a small wad of bills and quickly counted them. "Fifty-three bucks. That's all I got." He slapped the worn and wrinkled-up cash into Richie's hand. "That's not going to get you very far."

"Thanks, man. At least it is something to start out with. You know I will pay you back. If I don't get busted, that is."

"You better not get busted! I might need a tag team partner one day."

"It would be beyond awesome if we could finally tag up like we're always saying. We won't be able to do it here, though."

"You never know. Vaughn is all the time bringing back guys that we thought we would never see here again, like Badger Timberland, for example."

"Good point. What are we calling ourselves? Heaven and Hell?"

"Sinners and Saints."

"Ha, I love it! We can call our finisher the 'Purgatory Plunge' and come out to a badass version of 'When the Saints Go Marching In.'"

"That'd be so perfect. I really hope it can happen one day." He gave Richie a quick bro-style hug. "Get outta here, man. Call me when you can."

Richie slipped out a door and headed for the back lot like a bat out of hell. He was in a frantic state as he approached the car and scanned the area for any movement, checking to see if anyone was nearby. The coast seemed to be clear, so he hopped into the Camaro and threw his bag in the back seat. He groaned as he felt a sharp stabbing pain in his back. "I definitely have a cracked rib." At that exact moment, a couple of guys walked out from behind the building. Richie tried to duck down, but the pain wouldn't allow him to do it. They walked straight toward the car. Richie's heart was now pounding like a furious war drum. *I'm not even out of the parking lot and I'm busted*, he thought.

A back door to the building flung open and someone yelled out, "Hey, guys, get your asses in here! You gotta see this. Milo is tearing the locker room apart!" The two sprinted by and didn't seem to notice Richie.

"Halleluiah! Sherrod's plan worked!"

He watched the two guys enter the door, then he started the car. The black beauty roared to life, and Richie wasted no time exiting the arena lot and onto the road. Soon thereafter, he pulled off Perplexitor's mask. Satisfied the arena was far enough away, he turned into a dimly lit strip mall parking lot to figure out which way he should go and to further familiarize himself with the car's features. Satisfied with his route, he set up his portable music player. *I sure am glad I kept this thing around. Who's laughing now, Sherrod?* he thought as his close friend had jokingly poked fun at him for holding onto the dated electronic device. Next, he used the utmost discretion, pulling back out onto the road.

The lead singer for one of his favorite eighties bands sang out loud through the premium nine-speaker sound system, "Head west, young man, before this life is over."

Must be a sign, Richie thought as he pressed down on the accelerator and drove west into the night.

CHAPTER 8

An Unexpected Angel

About two hours had passed, as Richie drove with great caution. He was trying his best to avoid people and the police in hopes of not getting caught in a stolen car, so he stuck to back roads when possible. It was 11:42 p.m., and he seemed to be somewhere around River Falls, Alabama, on this soon-to-be Monday morning. Fortunately for him, he gained an hour when he crossed the Apalachicola River in Florida, putting him in the Central Time Zone.

"Finally, a gas station that's open!"

The low fuel light had been on for quite some time. Richie turned right into the station and pulled up to a pump. The area grew somewhat eerie and quiet after he turned off the thundering engine. He reached into the back seat to get into his bag and before he could get what he wanted from it, there was a sudden and unexpected knocking sound on his window.

"What the heck!" he uttered as he turned around too fast, causing his rib to hurt.

Someone was now standing beside the car and staring straight into it. "Hi there. Does Lord Vader know you have his car?" A young woman stood beside the vehicle. Her black feathered coat gently ruffled around in the cool night air. Then she noticed he was hurting. "Are you okay?" The smell of her perfume rolled through the partially lowered car window. It had an aroma similar to fresh cotton candy.

"Yeah, I just got some rib issues. What do you want?"

"Well, I could use a ride." She inched closer to the window. Her eyes were thorough in checking out the car's interior while peeking inside it. "Wouldn't you like some company tonight?" She shot him a surreptitious smile.

Surprised, Richie looked into her black, olive-like eyes. They seemed like two astonishing black holes that continually sucked in his attention without ceasing. He also noticed a subtle hint of a Spanish accent. As he was about to ask her to leave, he realized she could be very useful.

"I would normally say no, but I could use some help."

"Oh, okay." She appeared somewhat confused.

"I need you to pump my gas and go inside to pay for me."

"Well, that's not very gentleman-like. I've had guys ask me to do a lot of things, but this is a first." Her half-smile was insincere.

"Yeah, well, I'm not trying to be rude bu—"

"No, it's okay, I don't mind. You'll have to give me a card, though. They're closed."

"Really? All the lights are on." He looked with a focused gaze at the building.

"Yeah, they do that here. It fools a lot of people."

"Dang it! I'm on fumes and all I have is cash."

"Wait, I think I got one we can use." With some hesitation, she pulled a small stack of credit cards out of her light-colored, fashionably torn jeans. Richie noticed her very dark hair had black cherry-colored tips as they slightly blew into the opening of the window.

"That would be great. I can pay you back."

"Okay." She nodded.

As she walked around to the pump, he rolled down the window more. "Put ninety-three in, please."

A classic rock song about a young woman, surprisingly similar to the one Richie just met outside his window, now played on the radio as he watched her pump the gas.

I don't want to bring someone along into my mess, but she sure could be a help, Richie thought. *She seems to have a way to pay for gas, food, and rooms. I can pay her back later. It sure would cut down on the chances of my face being picked up on camera by having her do all of those things for me.*

The radio continued to play. *"She was too old to cry for being all alone, so she dialed her last number and screamed into the phone."*

She walked up to the passenger window and knocked. Richie just barely rolled the window down. "Okay, it's full. I'm Lucia, by the way."

"Are you a cop?" He didn't think she was. He just wanted to see how she would react to the question.

"No, that's so funny!" Lucia laughed. "So what's your name?"

"You can call me Richie."

"So, now what, Richie?"

"I've got to get to Mt. Hood, Oregon, by Saturday afternoon. I'm kinda in a crazy predicament and I really need help staying off the radar. Would you be interested in accompanying me? No funny business, strictly professional. I'm being completely honest."

A Chevy Tahoe turned into the gas station and pulled up behind them.

"*Estupendo!* Not again!" Lucia rolled her head back, then smacked the top of the door.

Richie was furious at her actions. "Hey! Watch it, lady! Don't smack the car li—"

"So you're the cop and this is a sting, right?" Her Spanish accent grew a slight bit stronger as she now yelled at Richie.

"What is it? What are you tal—?" Richie was very confused until he looked into the rear-view mirror and before he could finish his sentence, he saw the sheriff's vehicle behind him. In that very instant, he felt as if his heart had stopped, and he panicked.

∞

Richie had sat in the back seat of the bright yellow service vehicle that was rushing to the hospital. *"What floor are you on, babe? My cab is almost there."*

"What did you take, the Cash Cab? This is ridiculous, Richie! You should have been here hours ago!" Mary's sister scornfully spoke into her phone.

"Is this Dottie?"

"Yes, they took Mary back already. If you're not going to be here, I'm going back there with her." Her declaration was hateful.

"I'm almost there! My stupid flight was delayed at the last second." Richie was anxious as the cab sat at a red light with its turning signal agonizingly ticking away as it waited to turn into the hospital.

"We're on the third floor." Dottie pressed the end-call button.

After getting through the crowded lobby and a very slow elevator ride that felt like two eternities, Richie came rushing into the waiting area.

"She's in room three. Hurry up!" Dottie shouted.

Richie ran down the hall like a madman and right before attempting to enter the room, a serious, petite nurse stopped him.

"Hold it right there." She held out her hand with great confidence, merely touching Richie's chest and staring up at him from her short stature.

"It's okay, he's the father." Mary beamed, followed by a painful wince.

Richie ran over, grabbed her hand, and stroked her forehead. *"I'm so sorry I was late."*

Mary clenched her teeth. *"It's okay. I'm just glad you're here now."*

After a few short but intense painful moments for Mary and Richie getting through being queasy and nearly passing out, he was now well beyond astonished at the amazing sight of Mary holding their newborn baby on her chest. It was as if it was a magic trick. All those months in the womb, making this special little person and presto, in an instant, she arrived into this world.

Richie cuddled up to Mary. *"I can't believe she's actually here now. Look at how beautiful she is."* He gently stroked Josie's cheek.

"I know. She's so amazing. Oh my goodness, she looks just like you."

Richie smiled. *"She's got your nose, though."* He shot Mary a smile and followed it up with a kiss on the cheek. The happy new parents soaked in the amazing moment of their daughter's birth.

The next morning, Richie regretfully looked at the clock and dropped his head. *"I've got to catch my flight soon. I really, really don't want to go. It's absolute torture, leaving you two."*

"I don't want you to either, but I'm so glad you got here before she was born."

"Two weeks, then I'll be back for a month. I'll be counting the seconds 'til then."

Mary had responded with a loving smile. *"We'll be here waiting for you to—"*

∞

"Get in!" Richie banged on the steering wheel. He was totally frustrated that the police were already a problem for him this early in his journey. "I'm not a cop!"

Lucia stared at him with uncertainty for a split second.

He started the car. "If you're going with me, then get in right now! Otherwise, get out of my way!"

His new friend wasted no more time and jumped into the passenger seat after grabbing her pink suitcase.

Meanwhile, the deputy exited his vehicle with no delay and headed toward the driver's door, with his right hand on his weapon, ready to pull.

CHAPTER 9

We Can Drive 55

"Turn off the car and come out with your hands up!" the deputy demanded with a nervous but still very threatening tone of voice.

"Buckle up!" Richie instructed.

Now in a hurried rush, Lucia threw her stylish but worn suitcase into the back seat and pulled the red seatbelt across herself, and snapped it in.

As the approaching deputy closed in on the door, Richie hit the gas hard and rocketed toward the gas station's exit. He slid out onto the road, narrowly missing the ditch by the entrance, and turned toward the opposite direction from which he had driven in.

Richie's brows rose in amazement. "Holy crap! The power of this thing is insane!"

Even though he had been driving it for hours, that was the first time he had really driven it hard. He shifted through gears with great precision and gained incredible speed, zooming down the road out of sight before the deputy could even get back into his Tahoe.

With a look of concern, Lucia looked at him. "I knew it! You stole this thing, didn't you?" The powerful car had her pinned back in her seat as she waited for an answer.

An awkward moment of silence forced Richie to answer her. "It's a long story. Do you want out?"

"No! Up here on the left, after this sharp curve, there's a dirt road you can take."

Richie downshifted and made a hard left turn onto the dirt and slammed on the brakes. He put the car in reverse, backed out onto the road, and started driving back toward the gas station.

"What are you doing? You're driving right to him!"

"Just watch. I hope this works." Richie was clearly nervous as he turned on the high beams before turning around the sharp curve again. Back on the straightway, the deputy was coming with his lights flashing. Richie slowed down to the speed limit and let off the accelerator and coasted, hoping to disguise the sound of the powerful car.

"Turn your brights off, asshole!" the deputy shouted out his window in anger as he passed the Camaro.

"Did it work?" Richie looked in the rearview mirror.

Lucia was looking back over her left shoulder, watching. "Seems like it. Did you learn that trick from the *Dukes of Hazzard* or something?" Before he could answer, she said, "Wait, I think he hit his brakes. I can't be sure, he's outta sight now," as the car turned downward and to the left on the narrow and curvy back road.

"We're going to keep it that way." Richie downshifted to gain speed and stormed down the dark two-lane road. Both of them were quiet for some time while Richie worked the gears as if he were in a timed road course race. Lucia watched in amazement as her hands clung tightly to her seatbelt. "Are you familiar with this area?"

"Yes, somewhat. This is Highway 84."

"The El Camino east-west corridor. I think I saw a documentary about this road."

"Yes, I've heard it called that before. Most of it is two lanes of road that has plenty of wrecks and traffic jams, depending on the areas and times."

"Well, it's been pretty good for nighttime driving, 'til now anyways. I've been able to avoid a lot of people, but we need to get off of it right away. The heat is probably on us."

"I think Highway 55 is coming up on the right. We could go that way for now." Lucia looked back to see if the deputy was in sight.

"Was that a friend of yours?"

She snarked, folding her arms in disgust. "Not that stupid pig!"

"Hey, you watch your mouth! That's a thankless job. You need to appreciate the fact someone is willing to do it. That man is sacrificing time with his family to do a job that doesn't pay well, all while risking his life."

"If he had harassed you the way he has me, you would feel completely different, so I'm sorry that I'm not that appreciative of him." A look of disgust was plastered on her face.

"Maybe you shouldn't break the law for a living."

"Says the man who's driving a stolen car! I knew it was stolen when I saw that it was missing a license plate."

"Look, it's a long story. I know that's an old and worn-out cliché, but it's the truth."

"I'm sure it is, but Oregon is days away, so I think you've got plenty of time to tell it."

Richie glimpsed at her, then he stared out the windshield. His favorite mix of songs continued to play on his music device as he contemplated what to do.

"A man took something from me, so in retaliation, I took this car from him."

Lucia took a few seconds to process his answer. "Okay, that makes sense. So, why are you going to Mt. Hood? Is that where you live?"

"No, I'm trying to save my relationship."

"Couldn't you just have left the car somewhere safe and caught a flight out there?"

"That's another long story."

"So, what is the plan? What do you want with me?"

"I need someone to pump gas, get food and hopefully pay for rooms. I can't use my credit cards and I can't let my face be recorded. I need you to help me with those things and I will compensate for expenses and pay you for your time."

Confused by the request, an uneasy look appeared on Lucia's face. "Are you in the mob or something? Why are you worried about your face being recorded on cameras?"

"I'm not in the mob, but the man I stole this car from has connections similar to them. I have to be super careful."

"Listen, I need to get out of Alabama. I have worn out my welcome here. I would love to go across the country in this Batmobile you have, but you're going to have to tell me everything. Who you are, why you stole this car, and who you stole it from? If you can't do that, then I'm not sure that I can be of any help to you."

Richie thought about his options and decided he didn't really have a choice. Before he gave her answers to all her questions, though, he needed to know one thing. "How do I know I can trust you? How do I know you won't sell me out for a quick buck?"

"Just because I work outside the law doesn't mean that I can't be trusted. I have to stay low-key, so why would I bring any unnecessary attention to myself?"

"Okay, I guess that's a fair statement. But if I tell you everything, you have to keep it confidential. You can't tell anyone anything. Not a single word, is that clear?"

"That's no problem. I completely understand. Fifty-five is up here on the right." She sat with a slightly self-assured grin on her face.

Richie turned onto the alternate road and thoroughly told her his story as they roared down the black narrow road.

CHAPTER 10

European Wedding Gift

The minor glow coming from a cell phone belting out the musical sounds of a synthesizer faintly lit the darkened room. It was playing the first few lines from the classic seventies song, "City of Funk," as it lay on the nightstand.

"Who in the world?" Mary fought off excessive grogginess while sitting up in her warm and cozy bed, rubbing her eyes and face. Without any aim, she reached for the phone and knocked it to the wooden floor, lighted side down. "Really!" She threw her hands up and slouched. As she stumbled out of bed to pick it up, she accidentally kicked it under the bed with her foot. Consumed with total frustration, she yelled, "Aw, come on!" Wanting to avoid the overhead light from blinding her, she turned on the television instead for some aided light in finding her phone. She finally located the mobile device and answered in a blunt and direct tone. "Hello!"

"Mary? Is this Mary?" The voice from the other end spoke with shyness and uncertainty.

"Yes, sorry, I dropped my phone. Who is this?"

"It's Sherrod, Richie's friend. I hope I'm not calling too late."

"Oh! Sherrod! I knew I recognized your voice. It's actually not that late. I had just gone to bed a little early tonight, but anyways, is Richie okay? Are you? What's wrong?" Concern grew within Mary. It wasn't normal for Richie's friends or coworkers to be calling her.

"No, sorry, didn't mean to worry you. Nothing's wrong." Sherrod thought of Richie zooming down the road in a stolen car. "I'm getting ready to board a plane to Europe and I don't know how good my phone will work from over there, so I figured I would call you before I left the States. I was hoping to get the address for your wedding reception so that I can send a gift."

Flattered at Sherrod's thoughtfulness, Mary gasped. "Oh, Sherrod, you don't have to do that."

"No, I insist. Look, I'm not happy about you moving on. Richie's going to be an absolute wreck because of it, but you are my friend, too. Also, Uncle Sherrod has to spoil little Josie!"

"Well, I appreciate that, Sherrod. You mean a lot to us. Give me a minute so I can find the venue's address." Mary left the room to find the information for him. The television was playing the nightly news.

The neatly dressed woman news anchor looked into the camera, reading from the prompter. "The F.B.I. has been notified that an escaped male convict that has been on the run since the nineteen-eighties has been spotted back in America. Peter Mitchell Simms, a then notorious drug runner, now drug lord kingpin, was serving a life sentence in a California prison for multiple murder convictions and countless drug law violations. Simms promptly escaped from San Quentin State Prison in California after only severing six months. Authorities say he is to be considered armed and very dangerous. He has been spotted throughout Mexico and Cuba over the years and most recently in Miami. Officials have reason to believe that he could be anywhere in the southeast or possibly southwe—"

"'Kay, I'm back. Are you there, Sherrod?"

"Yeah, I'm here."

"Listen, I don't doubt at all that you care about us, but I smell a rat. What are you two up to?"

Shocked that she caught on to him so fast, he sounded confused, hoping to throw her off the trail. "What are you talking about, Mary? I just want to send you a wedding gift."

"So, let me get this straight. You're getting ready to board a plane to Europe right after the biggest wrestling event of the year and amongst all that chaos you want to send your best friend's ex a wedding gift right after he found out she was getting married?"

After a long pause, Sherrod came clean. "Fine, you got me, Mary." He hung his head in defeat, knowing his charade was over. "Look, Richie just wanted to talk to you before the wedding."

"We already talked."

"In person, though. He thought you wouldn't give him the address, so he put me up to getting it for him."

Mary let out a deep sigh. "Let me talk to him. Put him on the phone, please."

Sherrod's heart sank. "He's, uh…he's not here."

"Can you tell him to call me then?"

"Um, He can't."

"Why not?"

"I, uh, I have his phone."

"What? This doesn't make sense. You have his phone and he's not there. What is going on?"

"Look, he's on his way to see you before you get married. He, um, he kinda quit."

"Quit? What are you talking about, Sherrod?"

Sherrod was uncertain if he should tell her the story, but then he figured it couldn't really make things any worse at this point. "Well, you see, Richie found out Vaughn was going to have him drop the title to Bad Badger Timberland. After doing that, he was going to be busted down to a trainer position, all without being consulted about it beforehand."

"Wait, what? Let me get this straight. Badger Timberland is back in the company and Richie is being demoted? He told me he was going to finally have the strap put on him." Mary was very confused by all this new information.

"Yeah, that's right, but only as a temporary transitional champion. Richie had originally went back to talk to Vaughn about getting some time off so he could work on things with you, but after that heartbreaking bit of information from the boss, he pretty much felt like he had the rug pulled out from under him. So he became even more hell-bent on fixing things with you and threw away his only chance of finally being the champion, after telling Vaughn off, of course. You know how he is."

Marry was quiet as she processed that Richie had finally quit his job to be with his family. Then she giggled to herself at the thought of him putting Vaughn in his place. "Okay, so where is he now? Why do you have his phone?"

Sherrod rubbed his head in distress, as he didn't want to tell her all the details. "Look, all I know for sure is that he is on his way to Oregon and nothing is going to stop him. I know none of this is my business, but can you please just give him five minutes? Besides, if he's single for too long, my sister Angela will be all over him. He's a big enough pain in the ass as my best friend. I couldn't imagine having him as my brother-in-law, too."

Mary chuckled. "Yeah, I guess I owe him five minutes. I'll text you the address." Her face turned serious. "Sherrod."

"Yes, Mary?"

"Tell Richie he'd better not get his hopes up."

CHAPTER 11

Millennial Transmission

"Wow! This is just so unbelievable." Lucia was having a hard time comprehending Richie's outlandish story. The whole situation genuinely shocked her.

"Look, if you're not up for all this, I'll let you out somewhere safe. I'd totally understand."

"No, I still want to go. Just isn't every day you end up in a celebrity's car."

Richie blushed. "I don't really consider myself a celebrity."

"I actually meant Terence Vaughn." She held back a grin. "I wonder if he would give me a reward for returning this thing."

"Oh, yes, of course, he would." Richie rolled his eyes to the left. "I'm starting to regret telling you this information."

Lucia's face lit up. She laughed out loud. "Sorry, I'm only messing around. This is just so exciting! Plus, it's nice being in the presence of someone famous for once instead of all the usual cheating assholes and scum-of-the-Earth types."

Richie's face turned serious. He looked Lucia over, thinking *She is way too pretty and seems too smart for this kind of life.* "So, it looks like we're outside of Beatrice." He noted the sign they passed, showing the town was thirty miles away. The radio still played continuously as the car rolled down the road.

"Yeah, the Mississippi state line should be about two hours away."

"So, how do you know this area so well?"

She was hesitant to respond at first, but then she finally answered in a monotone voice. "I've pretty much been all over the southern United States. I'll grow tired of one place, or it will get tired of me, so then I move on. I'll catch a ride with traveling salesmen types, lonely businessmen on trips, and sometimes truckers. I just keep moving. I don't like to go too far north, though."

"How come?"

"I don't like the cold and snow. Besides, there's too many people the further up you go."

"No, I mean, how come you do this? You're so young and seem really smart. Why do you live like this?"

Offended by Richie's question, Lucia became defensive. "Look, I do what I have to! I survive so please don't worry about it! We can't all be famous wrestlers."

Embarrassed and not knowing how to reply, Richie readjusted himself in the seat.

"Speaking of which, how much does this job pay?"

"Well, what sounds like a fair price to you?

"I'd say five grand should do it."

Richie coughed from the shock of the amount. "Five grand! How about twenty-five hundred?"

"Four."

"Thirty-two and you cover all the expenses."

"I can try, but my cards don't always work."

Richie became concerned. "Why?"

"'Cause they're stolen!" She threw up her hands. "My accounts at 'Hooker One' and 'First National Prostitute' are all maxed out at the moment."

"You have a smartphone in your lap, so I figured you also had some legitimate credit cards to pay for the monthly service on it."

"It's a prepaid phone and I lift cards off my customers from time to time. Lucky for us, that one at the gas station hadn't been canceled yet. Why does it matter anyways? You said you have cash on you, right?"

Richie took a deep breath. "Well, that's just great. I had you use stolen resources to pay for my gas." He shook his head in disappointment.

"Why does that matter? Did I mess up your karma or something? It's the credit cards of unfaithful idiots who are cheating on their wives, so don't feel too bad."

"Well, when you put it that way." He shrugged. "Fifty-three dollars. I got fifty-three dollars from my best friend before I left Tallahassee. I don't feel that it is safe to use my credit cards because it would most likely get me caught."

Lucia palmed the top of her head. "You stole Terence freaking Vaughn's car and planned to take it across the country with no license plate and fifty-three dollars! I think you have took one too many chair shots to the head there, Champ!"

"Look, I knew it would be a problem, but I was hoping I would come up with some way to make it work."

"How?"

"You, for one! I saw your stack of credit cards, and then you used one to get gas. That's why I told you to get in when that cop pulled up!"

"So you're telling me that you would have left me there if I hadn't bought you gas?"

Hesitant to answer, Richie sat quietly for a few seconds. "Most likely."

Lucia's jaw dropped and her mouth hung open as she gave him a look of shock.

"Whoa, take it easy." Richie held out his right hand, showing her his palm. "It wasn't anything against you. It wasn't a personal issue at all. I wasn't looking for a good time. I was looking for gas. You seemed to have a way to pay, so that's why I hired you. Look, this simply boils down to me needing your help to get to Oregon."

An awkward silence filled the car. After processing that comment, she thought, *I can't really argue that logic. I do hire myself out for a living.* "Sorry for the confusion. I have forty dollars on me. Maybe we will catch a break and these cards will keep working."

"Yeah, that'd be nice. Oh, I just remembered, I always keep a few restaurant gift cards in my bag."

"That's good news. Any particular reason you do that?"

"When I see someone in need, I give them one. I don't like giving out cash, but I really don't like not helping when someone truly needs it. Maybe now someone will help me for once."

"So you do believe in karma?"

"I believe that what goes around comes around."

Lucia chuckled. "I'm pretty sure that's what karma is. I didn't think Catholics could believe in it, though."

"I'm not a Catholic. I just play one on TV." Richie grinned.

Lucia gave him a false smile since she didn't get his joke. "We can use those gift cards for some food, at least."

"The stack is getting low, but it beats nothing." Richie groaned and repositioned. "My back is killing me. Can you drive a straight drive?"

Lucia smirked. "Of course, I can drive straight."

"No, I mean, can you drive a car with a manual transmission? Drive stick, pressing in the clutch pedal to change the gears."

"Oh." Her face lit up, finally realizing what he meant. "No, I can't. Sorry."

"I guess that meme I saw a while back is true then. Manual transmissions really are 'millennial anti-theft devices'."

Lucia shot him a smirk in response to his snide comment. "Why is your back hurting?"

"'Cause I got slammed by a four-hundred-pound powerlifter and he fell on me while doing it."

"I thought pro wrestling was fake? You did just say you weren't actually a Catholic." Lucia chuckled as she looked at him, waiting for a reply.

That statement more than aggravated Richie. Within a split second, his face wrinkled up and transformed to a dark shade of red, as he gripped the steering wheel. "I wish I had a godd—"

"Chill, chill, chill! I'm sorry! I know it's choreographed, not fake, right?" Lucia backpedaled on her joke in haste with her hands held up once she saw how bad it had upset Richie. "I knew a former Luchador one time when I was a child and he was always talking about injuries he'd suffered from when things didn't go as planned. He was old and senile. Nobody knew when he was telling the truth or not. Regardless, he always thought he was."

He gave her a cold stare, then focused on the road. He was tired, hurting, hungry, and had to use the restroom. "I gotta get out of this car for a while." He groaned.

Lucia was checking the map on her phone. "Seems like we're pretty much in the middle of nowhere. Beatrice doesn't look too promising either." She looked up from her phone. "Watch out!"

CHAPTER 12

Padiddle

Startled by Lucia's warning, Richie swerved the car far to the left and slammed hard on the brakes. A loud and disturbing thud came from the right front side of the vehicle before it finally came to a stop. Lucia gasped and grabbed her face.

"No! Damn it, no!" Richie placed the gear shifter into neutral and pressed the parking brake button. The car idled as he quickly got out to assess the unwanted and potentially disastrous situation.

Lucia rolled her window down. "Is it still there or did it run off? How bad is the damage to the car?"

"Ugh!" Richie groaned and grabbed his head. "I can't really tell, but it definitely broke the headlight. Bring me your phone light, please."

Lucia was quick to do what he asked, and the two of them were very thorough in inspecting the car.

"I ain't believing this! Look, the only damage seems to be the headlight. There is some scuff marks on the bumper below it, but I thought we had destroyed the whole front end and right fender."

"Me too, especially considering how loud it was. Did it run off?" Lucia searched along the roadside. About ten feet back from the car lay the unfortunate creature. "Aww, poor thing." She yelled over her shoulder, "I found it!"

Richie came running. "Be careful. Wounded animals can be very dangerous." He took the light from her. "Stay here. I'll check it out." He was very cautious as he inspected the wounded buck. "Looks like he didn't make it."

Lucia came up behind Richie as he was bent over, examining the animal. "This is so horrible."

"It's not like I meant to do it."

"I know, just makes me sad. I've never seen one up close before. What's wrong with his horns? Why do they look furry?"

"They're antlers and they're in what's called the velvet stage. He's still growing 'em in. Well, was. See how it's like a solid mass right there? That had to be what hit the headlight. Must have pushed him away from the car and broke his neck." They stood there for a few seconds, looking at the carcass. "Okay, we better get going."

"What? We can't just leave it here, can we?"

Richie shot her a confused look. "What do you think we should do with a dead deer?"

"Put it in the car and take it to a vet?"

Richie looked at her sarcastically. "Yeah, we'll do that right after I put on a little coat."

Lucia now had a very confused look. "What do you mean?"

"It's from a movie, never mind. Just get in the car."

Seconds later, they were back in the now slightly damaged vehicle and headed on their way.

Richie sighed. "It was bad enough not having a license plate. Now that we have a headlight out, we'll be an even bigger cop magnet."

"It's definitely harder to see. Being down a light makes a bigger difference than I would have thought." Lucia looked over at Richie. He was sporting a grimaced look on his face. "You want to take a chance and try to get a room or something?"

"Not 'til we're outta Alabama. Do you know how long that might be?"

She checked on her phone. "Looks like we'll be in Meridian, Mississippi, in about two hours. That will put us well past the state line."

"That'll be a good time to try for a room, but my bladder can't hold out 'til then."

After driving in the enveloping darkness for quite a while, lights finally appeared on the horizon.

Lucia pointed toward the upcoming gas station. "Here, let's try this one."

"Can you reach back in my bag and grab a hat for me, a white shirt, too?"

Lucia unbuckled and turned onto her left side so she could reach back between the narrow space between the two front seats to dig through his bag. Richie got another big whiff of her lovely perfume. It was almost intoxicating to him. He looked over and saw that her shirt was riding up, exposing her light terracotta-colored and toned oblique. It held his attention for just a moment until he realized he was staring. Nonchalantly, he turned his head and focused on the lights of the gas station.

"Here, do you think that this will work?" Lucia slid back into her seat and held out a white tee shirt with the Three Stooges printed on the front side of it and a dark blue baseball cap with a white screening on the back half. "What's this on your hat?"

"It's *Antique Archeology's* logo. That's a weather vane with a rooster on it. You know, those things that are on top of barns or old houses that indicate which way the wind is blowing."

"Oh yeah, I thought it looked kinda familiar. But what is *Antique Archeology?*"

"That show on TV where the two guys go around buying old stuff."

"Yeah, the junk dealers!"

"I guess you could say that. I bought that in one of their stores."

"Hey, what's this?" A shiny, hard object had fallen into her lap.

"That's my cross I wear during my entrance. It's a part of my ring attire."

"That's cool." She draped it over the rear-view mirror where it could dangle just beneath it. "There we go. Hopefully, it will bring us some good luck."

Richie smiled. "Well, here we are." They pulled into the gas station.

"It looks like this place used to be a full-service truck stop at one time."

"It's definitely seen its better days. Anyways, here's the plan. I'm going to go straight to the restrooms while you pump the gas. Check to see if that card from earlier still works. When you're done filling the tank, make sure to get us some food. I definitely need two bottles of water and a Mountain Dew. I'm in desperate need of some caffeine. Oh, and a bag of circus peanuts would be nice."

Her face twisted in disgust. "Do you mean those gross orange thingies?"

"Hey, you better watch it! I love those thingies!"

"Okay, fine then. What if they don't have them?"

"Get some Mallow Cups, I guess. They sure would hit the spot, too."

"What the hell is a Mallow Cup?"

Richie shook his head in disbelief that she didn't know what he was talking about. "It's another one of my favorite candies. Never mind, I'll explain it to ya later." He wadded up the white tee shirt.

She watched with growing curiosity. "What are you going to do with that?"

"I'm going to occasionally hold it up to my nose like a handkerchief to hide my face." He slipped his cap on and pulled it down low on his head. "Okay, let's go."

Minutes later, they were both back in the car.

Richie looked at Lucia. "Please tell me it worked?"

"Yeah! Woo-hoo!" Richie started the ignition. "We got at least one more use out of that card plus I got us a bag full of food!"

With utmost promptness, Richie got back onto the road. "So, how much was the food and drinks?"

"It was going to be twelve something, but I pulled the old 'this is all I got' trick and only gave up seven of our dollars."

A look of displeasure came over Richie's face, then after thinking about their situation, he nodded. "Nice!"

"Did you see their auto tag section?"

"No, I went in and out as fast as I could. I didn't want to chance getting spotted."

"It's not real, of course, but at least it will throw off some suspicion. I figured it was better than having nothing back there at all." Lucia reached into her feathered coat. She pulled out a novelty license plate for the state of North Carolina. It read: Righteous.

CHAPTER 13

The Dead Next Door

"There he is," a young backstage attendant had said to the two young ladies following him as he entered a hallway in the backstage area. *"Hey, Richie, I found some fans of yours."* He smiled, pointing at them.

"Hey, Love Bug, Dottie! How did you like your seats?"

"They were okay." Mary's tone was flat, which meant they were not okay. *"Some idiot kept holding up a sign and blocking our view."*

"Sorry to hear that." Richie slightly chuckled. *"Kevin, can you do me another favor before you run off?"*

"What's that Rich?"

"Take Dottie to meet The Recycler. You'll like him, Dottie. He's a lot of fun to be around. He's got all kinds of crazy jokes and stories he's always telling."

"That sounds awesome!" Dottie excitedly followed Kevin as he led the way.

"Now then, how about a hug!" Richie reached out to grab Mary.

"No! You're all sweaty!" She backed away from him.

"I just finished a wrestling match. What do you expect?" He lunged out and grabbed her.

"Eww, Richie! You're so mischievous, considering that you're supposed to be a priest!"

"Yeah, well, you had me breaking vows a long time ago." He leaned in and kissed her while she was trapped in his arms.

"Funny you say that 'cause that's what I wanted to talk to you about. Those vows aren't just broken, they're shattered."

Richie gave her an intrigued look. She grinned while pointing at her belly. He lit up with excitement at the realization. *"You're pregnant?"* She slowly nodded. Overjoyed, Richie lifted her and twirled her around. *"Who else knows?"*

"No one. I had to tell you first, silly!"

"Do you mind if we run and tell Sherrod and Dottie?"

She responded with a huge smile on her face. *"Let's—"*

∞

"Go! Richie, you have to get up! Let's go! Lucia pleaded, as she was desperate in her attempt to wake him from his near coma state.

He was coming too, looking around the dated, run-down room. "What's going on? Where am I?"

Lucia got in his face and yelled in a loud whisper, "Richie! You're in a motel room somewhere in the backwoods of Mississippi! You have a very fast and very stolen car in the parking lot and now there's a cop coming straight to our door!"

Richie tried to sit up fast, but a sharp stabbing pain in his back took his breath and paralyzed his whole body.

"Oh, God, are you okay? Richie!" She grabbed him by his wide-set shoulders, hoping to help ease his pain. They made her hands look tiny and frail. "Breathe, breathe!"

As his breath finally returned to his body like a long-lost friend, he mumbled, "Get to the bathroom! We'll go out the back window." At that moment, they heard a knocking, but it wasn't at their door. It seemed to be off in the distance.

"Shhh! I think that came from next door." Lucia hoped to be correct on the matter.

Richie was slow getting to his feet, despite trying his best to be quick about it. "Can you bring me my bag?"

Lucia dropped the heavy bag off on Richie's bed with ample speed, then she went to peek out the dusty curtain-covered window. It was a sheriff's deputy accompanied by a female motel worker. "Yeah, they are next door," she mouthed to Richie.

The deputy knocked again. After no answer, the motel worker unlocked the door. She ran over to the wall and pressed her ear to it in hopes of finding out what was going on over there.

Richie slid on a gray pair of workout pants and an old red tee-shirt with the sleeves cut off. Then he walked as fast as he could to the bathroom while he held his back. "Keep listening," he whispered through groans of pain.

Lucia was straining her ears but couldn't hear anything but a low mumble. Then, to her surprise, there was a knock on their door. Panic gripped her. Richie heard it as well and was trying to figure out how to open the fixed window for an escape. Lucia shook her head around and slapped her face a few times, hoping this would help her calm down. Next, she jerked her shirt off and threw it on the bed. *Here we go!* she thought, as she cracked the door open. "Yes, sorry I'm not decent." She covered herself, barely peeking around the door.

The tall and gray-headed deputy spoke slowly and with a blushed face since he was talking to a naked young lady. "Sorry, um, sorry to bother you, ma'am, but it seems we've had a gentleman overdose next door. Did you happen to hear or see anything strange or unusual? Did you notice anyone go in or out since you've been here?"

"No, I haven't been here that long, and I fell asleep right after checking in." Fortunately for Lucia, this was mostly the truth, so she didn't have to worry about being caught in a lie.

The deputy nodded. "Yeah, that's what the workers here told me as well. Sorry to wake you, ma'am. I just had to ask if you saw anything, plus I had to tell you that there's going to be a lot of county officials in and out over here for the better part of the day. There's no need to be alarmed. The victim has had a terrible history of battling with illegal substances. It was just a matter of time before this happened."

Lucia responded without hesitation. "Wow, that's awful. Thanks for informing me, sir."

"You're welcome. Again, I'm sorry to bother you. Try to have a nice day, ma'am." He gave her a slight head nod.

"Thanks, you too." She closed the door with care. Then she put her back against it and slid down in relief, with her hands coned around her mouth. "Okay, he's gone!"

Richie limped out of the bathroom and saw Lucia without her shirt. He shot her a bewildered look and turned away. "What the heck! What did you do? Did you flash him or something?"

"No, I made it seem like he got me outta bed." Then she put her pink vee-neck shirt back on.

Richie made his way back to his bed to lay down. "My head is absolutely killing me. What time is it?"

"9:07. According to what the deputy said, they're going to be over there for quite a while. I wouldn't think we could safely leave 'til they are gone. You should try to get some more sleep since we're pretty much stuck here."

"I can't believe this crap is happening right now. What are the chances of an overdose occurring literally beside us? Man, I hope they don't notice the Camaro."

"You backed it in over by the trees so I don't think they will think anything of it. I put the license plate on it while you were in the shower earlier."

"Gah, my head hurts so bad and now I'm freaking out with them here. I just want some sleep." Richie massaged his temples.

"I'll turn on the TV. Maybe it will be a distraction and help you to fall back to sleep. It works for me sometimes." Lucia picked up the remote control and pressed the worn-out red power button. "Anything in particular you want to watch?"

"How about the news? That's usually boring enough to fall asleep to."

Lucia flipped through several of the motel's cable stations before stopping on a twenty-four-hour news channel. Then she made her way into the bathroom. The news anchor was reporting, "Authorities say if you see Peter Mitchell Simms, do not engage him. Call the police immediately."

"Wow, the poor bastard's initials are P.M.S. No wonder he's a criminal. That would crack Sherrod up." Richie chuckled to himself before eventually nodding off to sleep.

A short time later, Lucia was back in her bed, playing on her phone when the news caught her attention.

"Richie, Richie, wake up for a second. You might want to see this!" Lucia forcefully nudged his arm.

Richie leaned up on his elbows. "What the hell is it now?"

An older gray-headed male news anchor was reporting, "The flight carrying the entire current I.W.L. roster then had to make an emergency landing at Baltimore-Washington International Thurgood Marshall Airport. A news conference on this incident has been scheduled for 1:00 p.m. today. The wrestling leagues owner, Terrance Vaughn, is expected to address this situation. In other news—"

"Give me your phone now!"

CHAPTER 14

Turbulent Tales

"Come on, Sherrod, pick up!" Frustration grew in his voice. "He always answers when it's me calling!"

Lucia looked concerned. "What's wrong?"

Richie vividly pointed at the dated television set. "That flight they just showed on the news was the very one I was supposed to be on and it apparently has made an emergency landing back in the US! I was counting on Vaughn being overseas while I got my ass and that car to Mt. Hood. Now he will most likely realize the Camaro's gone even sooner than he would have before this happened, and I don't even understand why they had to land the plane in the first place. Surely it didn't have something to do with me taking the car, but I can't help but think that it probably did." He grabbed his head. "Man, this is so bad! I really hope that I haven't gotten Sherrod into trouble."

"I doubt you have, Richie. There could have been something wrong with the plane. There are a thousand possible scenarios as to why they came back. I just did a quick search online to try and find out the reason for the emergency landing, but nothing's up yet. You should try and get some sleep since checkout is at twelve." Lucia could see Richie was very concerned, but they couldn't yet leave because of the local authorities working on the drug overdose scene next door. So she calmed him down by getting him to talk about his friend, Sherrod, instead of aimlessly worrying about the possibilities of the situation. With convincing sincerity, she said, "Sherrod, uh, what's his name again?"

"Sherrod Showman."

"You two been friends a long time, I take it?"

"Better part of ten years. We met on the independent circuit. Back then, his gimmick was a Black guy playing a White guy that was trying to be Black. It sounds confusing, I know, but it was so funny and the crowd loved him. His wrestling name was 'Cracka Black' and he was always using phrases similar to what Eminem used during those days and sometimes he even quoted his lyrics during interviews and promos."

"His gimmick? That's like his character, right?"

"Yeah, he got to the I.W.L. a few months after me and they gave him the Showman gimmick. He does it well though, and he got to use his real first name."

"Why did they change him?"

"Mainly because of political correctness. It has run amuck in this country and is sucking the life right out of it. Everybody is offended by everything." His disgust was noticeable. "Plus, the characters have to be as marketable as possible. Funny thing about it though, in the nineties, the more offensive a character could be, the more marketable it was. How times have changed."

"I was born in the nineties."

"Oh, yeah? What year?"

"Nineteen ninety-six."

"So that makes you what, twenty-two?"

"I will be soon."

"Man, to be in my twenties again," Richie shook his head.

"How old are you?"

"Thirty-three. Right now I feel like sixty-three."

Lucia's phone beeped. "I just got a text. It says, *Who dis?*"

Richie sat up on the edge of the flimsy and worn-out bed with excitement. "That's gotta be Sherrod. Tell him I'm busy watching *Barbershop*. It's one of his favorite movies. That way, he'll know for sure that it's me."

Lucia typed the text at lightning speed. "K, it must be him. He's responding back already. The message says, *Been on worst flight of life. 2hr delay led 2 most of guys getting wasted at airport. Finally on plane and open bar made things so much worse. Was like a 10th grade party up there.*"

Richie smirked. "I knew that was a stupid decision by Vaughn."

Lucia continued to read. "*Me and Gino both said that was a stupid decision by Vaughn.*" She shot Richie a look. "*Things really started getting bad when Cannon Ball Chris got on the* p.a. *system. He was trying 2 sing 'Staying Alive' and it was hideous of course. He would not shut up so Mt. Man Jack went up and grabbed mic from him. Chris shoved him onto lap of Devious Denise and she screamed bloody murder. Gino used his authority to dissolve that situation but the peace didn't last. Not long after that the Fantastic Luchadors started sneaking around doing the old shaving cream gag on those trying to sleep.*"

Richie laughed and Lucia patiently watched him for a moment, letting him take in the outlandish story before continuing to read. "*Next Bodacious Brandi came out of the restroom completely wasted and wearing her ring coat with nothing on under it. She went around to some of the guys jerking the coat open and shouting out, 'Boob-ya' instead of 'Booyah', her normal catchphrase of course.*"

Riche laughed even harder and grabbed his side. "Ow, it hurts. Sherrod has to be making this up."

Lucia smiled, amused at Richie's reaction, and continued relaying the message. "*I swear I'm not making this up!*" Once again, she shot Richie a look and cracked a half-grin. *"Apparently she did this to wrong flight att. and he told captain about it. So the cap gets on p.a. and issues warning but before he is even done talking Cannon Ball Chris had stolen scissors from make up crew's bag and chopped off Mt. Man Jack's beard. The 2 of 'em began a brawl right there in plane, took several of us to break them apart. So after that the cap made emergency landing in BWI. TSA got cops involved so now we r all detained and being questioned."*

Richie's face grew serious. He realized this wasn't a laughing matter anymore. "Ask him if Vaughn knows the car is gone."

Lucia sent the message. They sat there for several agonizing minutes, waiting for a response.

With a tilted head, Lucia looked at Richie. "Do you think he's being questioned now?"

"I don't know but I've got a bad feeling about all of this."

Lucia got up to check out the situation next door and pulled the curtain back. "Hey, the coast is clear! No one is out there now. Should we go?"

"Hell yeah!"

Both of them were in a frantic tizzy as they gathered up all of their belongings and dashed off to the car at near lightning speed. "I'll get the stuff put away; you hurry and go turn the key in."

Lucia did just that. On her way back to the Camaro, a different deputy pulled into the parking lot. Richie fired up the Chevrolet so they'd be ready to run, if necessary. The deputy stopped his car beside Lucia and rolled down the passenger window.

The middle-aged deputy called out to her. "Excuse me, miss."

"Yes?" Lucia tried to stay cool and keep her calm.

"Are you getting in that black car over there?"

Her heart pounded. She took a deep breath. "Yes, sir."

"Is that a part of one of those Ghostbuster franchises?"

Confused by the question, Lucia tilted her head. "I'm sorry, what?"

"You know, it's where a group of people dress up like the Ghostbusters, then they go around doing charity work, visiting sick kids and such."

"No, sorry." She shook her head.

"Oh, since it says 'Exorcist' on the side, I thought it might belong to one of those types of organizations. I was hoping to get information on joining. I've always wanted to be in one of those groups some day."

"No, it's some fancy package on my boyfriend's car. Sorry about that, sir."

"Oh, it's okay, ma'am. You have a nice day."

"Thanks. You, too!" She got to the car as fast as she could without it being noticeable that she was in a hurry.

"What was that about? Is he on to us?"

Lucia got into the car. "No, it was nothing. Let's get outta here!"

CHAPTER 15

Interrogation à Gogo

"Look, I already told you guys everything I know. Cannon Ball Chris ain't no terrorist, he's a jackass for sure but not a terrorist. Can you please just give me my phone back now and harass someone else for a while?" Sherrod's discomposure was about to reach a breaking point. The authorities seemed to blow this whole incident way out of proportion, and the entire I.W.L. roster was growing tired of being detained.

The officer in charge responded without the smallest trace of sympathy. "Please, Mr. Showman, just remain patient and do as you're told. It will make this whole process go a lot easier on us all." She was a stern and petite lady that was short in stature and even shorter on compassion.

"That's the problem. I have been doing as I am told. This whole thing can be blamed on excessive alcohol consumption. Some of the competitors here don't know the meaning of the word moderation. They got wasted and acted stupid. Case closed."

An officer brought in a plain manila folder and handed it to the lady in charge. "Here you go, Lieutenant."

"Thank you, Wilcox." She opened the document and scanned it over. "Who was this text message sent to?"

"Which one? That phone is slam full of 'em." Sherrod answered with deliberate contempt for the rude lieutenant.

"Please cooperate with us, Mr. Showman. The text you made right before we confiscated your cell phone, of course. Looks like you gave explicit details of the events that occurred on the plane."

Sherrod grew further agitated. "Yes, yes, I did. The same exact details I gave you. So why are you treating me like this?"

"How do you feel we are treating you, Mr. Showman?" The lieutenant asked, staring at Sherrod over her silver-framed glasses.

"Like a criminal! I was one of the very few people that helped defuse that crazy situation up there and instead of a thank you, I'm being detained, questioned, and continually harassed."

"I assure you, Mr. Showman, that we are treating you all the same. Our job is to keep the public safe and I intend to do so at any cost. I must find out exactly what happened on that flight and why it even happened in the first place. I need every last detail surrounding this entire situation. The FBI will be arriving soon. If you think we're being hard on you, just wait until they get here. Now, please, tell me who was this text message sent to?"

Sherrod was hesitant to answer, but figured he'd better do as he was told. "I assume it's Richie Blackburn. I received a text from an unknown number that I thought could possibly be him."

"Okay. Who, exactly, is Richie Blackburn, and what is your relationship to him? Also, why do you just assume that he is the one that sent the message to your phone?"

"He is my best friend and coworker. I assume that it could be him messaging me because I have his cell phone and I imagine that he would try to contact me from another number." Sherrod felt horrible releasing this potentially incriminating information, but there was nothing else he could do. The authorities had the text messages right there in their hands. The best he could hope for was to spin the story and hope they didn't pick up on the truth of the matter. For the next several minutes, Sherrod told the lieutenant the details leading up to Richie's unexpected departure.

"So then Richie Blackburn stormed out of the building on his way to Oregon? Is that correct, Mr. Showman?"

"Yes, he was so upset that he must have forgotten that I was holding his phone for him. You can ask Gino 'cause he saw me with it."

"Okay then, so tell me what was Mr. Blackburn talking about when he said, *Does Vaughn know the car is gone?*"

Sherrod's heart skipped a beat as he thought, *Oh no, Richie! He must have sent another text after the authorities took my phone.* He stared at the lieutenant with a confused look and said, "What are you talking about? I didn't see that text."

She spoke out sharply while pointing at the message screen. "It's right here."

"Well, I didn't see it and I'm not even sure that's Richie anyways."

"Officer Wilcox, will you bring Mr. Vaughn in here, please?"

Oh no! Richie's ass is grass for sure now! Sherrod thought.

"Yes, ma'am." The stocky uniformed man quickly exited the office, being used as a makeshift interrogation room for the rowdy wrestling roster.

Moments later, Vaughn came strolling in as if he was Prince Charming himself and stood directly in front of the lieutenant. He gazed deep into her eyes and steadily reached out for a handshake. "Hello. Terence Vaughn at your service, ma'am." He never broke his hypnotic gaze on the commanding officer. "It's very nice to meet you."

The lieutenant's ice-cold demeanor seemed to melt just a bit. "Um, you…you, too, Mr. Vaughn."

"So tell me, is your hair naturally that curly Ms—uh, I didn't catch your name."

"Lieutenant Lynn Bach." Color appeared on her emotionless face. "Yes, my hair is naturally this curly and this bright color of orange as well. I'm afraid I inherited it from my mother."

"Well, based on that, your mother is most assuredly a beautiful woman, Lieutenant Bach." Vaughn starred even deeper into her eyes.

"Don't be silly. Please call me Lynn, Mr. Vaughn." The lieutenant's frosty attitude was now a puddle of water.

If Richie was here, he would say, 'Gag a maggot on a meat wagon', Sherrod thought. *This is so absurd. I can't believe she is buying this cheesy spiel. This is what Vaughn does, though, con artist extraordinaire.* He shook his head in disgust as he watched the lieutenant fall for Vaughn's phony act, hook, line, and sinker.

"So what can I do for you, Lynn?"

The lieutenant took a moment to get her mind back on her work. "Well, you see, Mr. Vaughn, we have found an interesting text on Mr. Showman's cellular device."

"Hmm, I see. What exactly did the message say?" Vaughn folded his arms in his usual overconfident manner.

"I'll let you see for yourself, Mr. Vaughn." She handed him the paper from the folder. "Mr. Showman said that these messages are from a Richie Blackburn."

"I did not!" Sherrod's posture was now ramrod straight. "I said it was a possibility that it was Richie. I don't know that for sure."

The lieutenant shot Sherrod a nasty look then continued talking to Vaughn. "We tried tracing the phone down, but the GPS signal seems to have been blocked."

Vaughn gave Sherrod a puzzled look. Then he was very thorough in reading over the sheet. "What the hell is the meaning of this Sherrod?" Belting out in anger, he completely dropped the Don Juan shtick.

"Look, I don't know? It might not even be from Richie."

"Don't give me that crap. You know this is from him. What does he mean by *Does Vaughn know*—" Vaughn suddenly realized what the text most likely meant. His face grew pale at first, then became flushed. He gave Sherrod an intense, scornful look and pointed his finger at him as he yelled out, "That son of a bitch better not have took my car!" Then he promptly apologized to the lieutenant for his harsh language.

"I don't know what you're talking about. All I know for sure is that Richie was going to try to fix his relationship with his daughter's mother."

Vaughn squared his shoulders. "Gino was supposed to have made sure the ring crew packed it onto one of the trucks, so let's see what he has to say about the situation."

The lieutenant looked at her subordinate. "Officer Wilcox, please bring this 'Gino' Mr. Vaughn is taking about in."

Sherrod's heart sank as he thought, *Vaughn will fire Gino over this, and Richie is busted for sure. This is a complete disaster."*

After several minutes passed, Officer Wilcox returned, but he didn't have Gino. Instead, a tall man wearing a very neat and black suit entered the room. A serious and sobering look came across the faces of the lieutenant and Vaughn.

The man looked at the lieutenant. "I'm FBI Agent Omar Jain." He flashed his badge at her. Then he glanced at Vaughn and Sherrod. "Gentlemen, will you please excuse us? Officer Wilcox will take you back to your waiting area."

On the way out of the office, Vaughn looked at Sherrod with great anger in his eyes. "You better tell me where the hell my car is!"

CHAPTER 16

An Oversized Golf Cart in Every Garage

It was 12:54 p.m., on a sunny and beautiful Monday afternoon. Richie and Lucia were about an hour away from the Arkansas state line. The two of them had been quiet for most of the ride. Both were still very tired after driving most of the night and not getting adequate rest at the motel didn't help matters. Richie's music device was now playing one of his favorite classic country songs.

Lucia spoke just above a whisper. "So, what are we going to do for money?"

"Are you sure the card won't work for us again?" Richie's tone was as flat as hers.

"Yes, we're beyond lucky that it worked as long as it did."

"How much cash do we have left?"

Lucia pulled the remaining wad of money from her jean pocket and carefully counted it. "We have a whopping eighteen dollars. After filling up at that last gas station, buying more food, and getting that homeless guy a sandwich, that's all that's left."

The upbeat country song continued to play as Richie sat quietly, thinking about their disheartening situation. "Find the nearest auto parts store or any other business that is related to dealing with cars."

Lucia did as Richie asked. "Just past the state line, there is a Two Tramps Auto Salvage. It's a little ways off of the highway, though. Will that do?"

"Perfect." Richie perked up just a bit.

Lucia was curious about Richie's plan, but she figured she would just wait until he was ready to announce it. In the meantime, she thought a little chit-chat could help kill some time. "So, who's this guy that's marrying your girl?

Richie looked over as if he was waiting for her to add something before he answered. "Nate Rainer."

"Wow, who is he? Like a fancy doctor or something? He would have to be somebody real special to be able to take a woman from you."

Richie looked over at her. "Is that supposed to be a compliment or something?"

"Well, yeah. You're not just some average dude."

He smiled with slightly blushed cheeks. "Gee, thanks." After a pause, he stated dryly, "He's a politician."

"What? A politician? Oh, I think I get the picture now. She likes a man with power."

"No, she just bought into his load of BS," Richie clamored out, to Lucia's surprise. He was very displeased with that comment. "That leach just swept right in and started taking advantage of the situation."

Lucia would proceed with caution, trying not to further upset Richie, but she was dying for more information on his peculiar predicament. "What situation?"

"The situation of me always being gone from home because of my work. He came in and started wooing her, filling her head full of crazy ideas, and just plain ol' muscled in on my territory. Not that I feel like I own Mary, by the way."

"So, why didn't you just kick his ass?"

"I wanted to, believe you me, but I couldn't. That would've just helped to prove that I'm not a fit father. You gotta play it cool with his kind."

"And what is 'His kind' exactly?"

"The kind that uses every possible situation for their own personal gain and benefit at whatever cost. That's one of the reasons he went after Mary. She's got her own Veterinary Clinic, and it's been around for almost a hundred years. She took it over from a prominent family in the region and she knows everybody in the entire Tri-county area, people like and trust her. She was the perfect mark for him to further his political career."

"Oh, I see. So you think he doesn't really love her?"

"Hell no! The only thing that snake in the grass loves is himself and he's a massive hypocrite to boot."

Lucia wanted to understand this man, who was brash enough to steal a woman away from a stud like Richie. "How's he a hypocrite?"

Richie let out a sarcastic chuckle. "Well, for one, he is going to lobby to make all gasoline-powered cars illegal once he gets elected to Congress or whatever the crap it is he's going to be running for after his term as county commissioner is over. He wants the masses to all drive electric cars while he gets to fly all over the world on all kinds of vacations while using tons of jet fuel. Oh, and don't forget about the gas-guzzling limos to get to and from the airport. He took Mary and Josie to Hawaii for two days. Two days! Who flies over the gigantic Pacific Ocean and only stays for two lousy days? He spent most of the time playing golf with some of his fellow politician buddies and left Mary and Josie at the hotel and still managed to convince her she had a good time. Do you know how much fuel that airplane used?"

"No, I imagine it was a lot, though." Lucia watched with copious consideration as Richie continued to describe the person who was stealing his woman from him.

"But the rest of us are supposed to suck it up and make sacrifices for the benefit of the planet while he uses taxpayer money to live it up. It's okay, though, because he's looking out for the little guy. Meanwhile, the little guy's electric bill goes sky high because he can't buy gasoline for his oversized golf cart that the government is making him drive around in, so we can supposedly save the planet. Never mind the fact that somewhere around thirty percent of our electricity still comes from coal and now we'll have to use even more of it to power our "Eco-Friendly Alternative.' Don't get me wrong; I'm all for saving the Earth, too, but robbing Peter to pay Paul doesn't get you anywhere. People, and I use that term loosely, like him want everyone else to foot the bill and make the sacrifices while he lives like a king. That's communism! We used to fight commies in this country, but now we elect them!"

They both set quiet for a moment after Richie's fiery description of Nate Rainer.

"Oh, to answer your question, that's who's taking my girl." Richie laughed. "Sorry that I went off there for a minute."

"No, it's okay. I did ask." Lucia smiled with concern.

The time had passed by relatively quickly, and before they both knew it, they had arrived in Arkansas. After taking multiple winding back roads and almost getting lost on a couple of different occasions, they had finally found themselves at their current destination.

"Mortimer Road is where it is. Should be up here on the left."

Richie's eyes widened. "This has to be it. This is by far the biggest and junkiest junkyard I've ever seen."

It seemed to go on for miles and the surrounding area was completely uninhabited and overgrown, which sent an eerie feeling through both of them. A tall makeshift fence surrounding the junkyard comprised of different pieces of material that included chain-link, rotted flat pieces of wood, long pieces of old tin roofs, and pieces of rusted metal from some of the wrecked cars, all of which barely kept the enormous auto graveyard contained.

"This place is creepy, Richie. I have a weird feeling about it. You sure we should be here?" Lucia folded her arms and a deep look of distress came over her face.

Richie ignored her, as he turned into the main entrance. "Here we go." He gazed at the old, busted-up, rusted, round sign with an arrow below, pointing to the building out front. Two Tramps Salvage Yard had been spray-painted with a now-faded yellow color onto the repurposed antique sign. Richie continued past the sign, driving slowly through a light layer of smoke coming from a small brush fire.

"Do you think anyone's here?"

"I don't know, but I have a feeling we'll find out soon." Richie stopped the car and looked around. He cracked his window and a sour smell wafted into the car along with the smoke.

"You hear that?"

"Sounds like talking. I guess someone is here."

CHAPTER 17

Pink Slip Incident

"I already told you two hours ago, Mr. Vaughn, so why are you still over here bugging me about it? I don't know where your car is and I really don't think Richie would have stolen it." Sherrod stood akimbo, anger dressing his face. "Go ahead and fire me if you feel that strongly about it." At this point, Sherrod honestly didn't care if Vaughn ousted him from the company. Especially after seeing the way he treated Richie, who was a loyal and longtime employee of the Infinity Wrestling League.

Vaughn replied in a feisty, but fiery, tone. "I just got done chewing Gino's ass out for not making sure the car was on one of our trucks. The only reason he's not getting fired is because he was so quick to help stop Milo from tearing the locker room apart and then he selflessly got between those knuckle-dragging mongrels that were fighting on the plane. He's one of the few guys I've got that can actually handle you idiots."

Officer Wilcox returned. "Mr. Vaughn, Agent Jain would like to speak to you and Mr. Showman."

Moments later, they were back in the office.

"Please take a seat, gentleman." Agent Jain pointed to the two chairs across from his makeshift desk.

"Where's the lieutenant?" There was more than a hint of concern in Vaughn's voice.

"She has gotten me up to speed on the current situation, so the lieutenant will now be working on a different part of the case for us."

Sherrod glanced over at Vaughn and could tell he wasn't happy about this decision. *Yeah, you won't be able to woo him over like you did the lady lieutenant, will ya?* he thought as he chuckled to himself.

Agent Jain also noticed Vaughn's displeasure. "I apologize for this taking so long. I know you are a busy man and have places to be. I assure you, we are trying to work through this in a timely manner. I'm a big fan, by the way. My brother and I grew up watching the I.W.L."

Sherrod discretely rolled his eyes upward, thinking, *Oh, great. Vaughn will have you eating out of his hand, too.*

Vaughn's pique disappeared. "Thank you so much, Agent. I'm glad to hear that. Since getting my phone back, I've been on the phone with all my lawyers and advisors and I assure you that you have my full cooperation as well as the rest of the I.W.L. roster."

"Good, that's good news." Agent Jain sat up in his chair with noticeable excitement. Then he leaned on the desk. "We are on the verge of chalking this all up to a matter of excessive consumption of alcohol and poor judgment on the part of some of your employees."

"I assure you that the pink slips are being printed as we speak for those that ignited this fire."

"Rightfully so. Had the plane landed in Europe, this could have been an international incident as well as a black eye for the entire country. The only thing we can't rule out is the text messages Mr. Showman received."

Vaughn sat upright. "Why is that exactly?"

"Because Richie Blackburn just suddenly disappeared a few hours before he was supposed to get on the plane, there's probably nothing to it but we can't yet rule out that he might have helped cause this situation in retaliation to his argument with you, Mr. Vaughn."

Sherrod clamored out, "That's a major load of crap! He was for sure pissed off, but how did he make the plane two hours late? How did he get most of the roster wasted? Better yet, how did he manage to start a fight on a plane that was almost halfway over the Atlantic Ocean when he was never even on it to begin with?"

Agent Jain was calm as he listened to Sherrod. "That's a great point, Mr. Showman, but you see, we just have to rule everything out at this stage. But one thing we can't seem to rule out yet is the fact that Richie Blackburn is gone, along with Mr. Vaughn's car. Add to that, you have his cellphone and we can't locate him anywhere."

"I told you guys a hundred times that he was on his way to Oregon." Sherrod hated lying about Richie taking the car, but he wasn't lying about Oregon. That fact made throwing the authorities off his trail a little easier.

"Here's the thing though, he hasn't used a single credit card, bought an airline ticket, or even a bus ticket. He just disappeared. Apparently, like Mr. Vaughn's car did. How do you explain that?"

Sherrod shrugged. "I don't know, but it doesn't prove that he took it."

"No, it doesn't. But if the police find him in that car, you will most certainly be charged for obstruction of justice. We have every reason to believe you know where he could be and if he did take that car. Why else would you have called his ex and why would she have sent you the address to her wedding?"

Sherrod was relentless in defending himself. "Look, I told you that's where he's going so that doesn't prove anything, and even if you do find him with that car, it doesn't mean I knew he took it."

Agent Jain slowly looked away from Sherrod and placed his main focus on Vaughn. "What's the make and model of the stolen car, Mr. Vaughn?"

"It's a new Chevy Camaro."

Agent Jain gave him a pleased look. "Excellent. All of those are equipped with OnStar, so we should be able to find it relatively easy. Just let me make a few calls."

Sherrod thought, *I hope Richie disabled the OnStar equipment. Otherwise, it's game over.*

CHAPTER 18
Do the Hustle

"The voices don't sound far off. Maybe they're coming from that shed over in the corner." Richie pointed toward an old, rusty beat-up storage building next to the main entrance to the junkyard. He let the car roll slowly toward the well beyond the worn-out shack.

"Richie, I don't think we should go any further. This place is seriously frightening me." Lucia put her hand on Richie's arm. "We should just turn around and leave. I can get us more money."

"You're not going to do that while you're with me. Besides, we'll be fine. What's the worst that could happen? It's just a huge parking lot for wrecked cars. Trust me, I've been in several, and they all seem spooky." Richie tried to calm Lucia, although he had never seen one quite so ominous.

As she gave him a slight headshake in reluctant agreement, a massive brown dog had spotted them coming even closer into his territory. It performed an aggressive and very alarming sound that was a terrifying mixture of beastly growling and baneful barking.

"Holy Moses, look at that thing! It looks like one of those dingoes down in Australia, only a lot bigger."

Lucia's eyes grew as big as tea saucers as she stared in disbelief at the mangy creature recklessly dashing straight to the car. "Ah! Richie, it's coming towards us!"

"Yeah, I can see that." He put the Camaro in reverse and sped backward as he looked over his right shoulder out of the rear window while they exited the salvage yard a lot quicker than they had entered it. Then he stomped on the brake and turned the steering wheel hard to the left, which made the car slide forty degrees to the right. Dry, loose dust fogged up the immediate area around the car, and right as Richie was about to punch the accelerator to escape the demented canine, a small clearing in the dust exposed a large brute of a man with a long black beard. He held the collar of the wicked creature with a long, old, rusty crowbar in his other hand.

"What's that damn dog's problem now?" Another filthy-looking fellow with a bushy red beard and nasty-looking clothes stood in the door of the shed. "Shut him up now!" This man wasn't quite as tall and buff as the one holding back the dog, but he looked equally foul and a little heavier .

Richie strained to see through the dust to get a better look at the second man. As he finally got a good view of him, Lucia let out a sudden scream and grabbed his arm. Richie jerked his head around and discovered a third man standing at Lucia's door. This startled him as well, causing him to jump in his seat at the sight of him eerily staring through the window with his head pressed against the glass. He had a very disturbing grin on his patchy, bearded face. He appeared to be Caucasian, along with the other men. They were so dirty and covered in dirt and grease that it was rather hard to determine their nationality. As he held his hands up beside his unkempt face to see through the dark tinted glass, a slimy fish, hanging from his right hand, smeared up the window. A human-sized bite taken out of the raw scale-covered meat didn't help matters.

The second man, who came from the shed, shouted out while walking toward the Camaro. "Skeeter, get away from that car and go help Otis calm down that stupid Tuco!"

The strange young man did as he was told.

Lucia and Richie gave each other perplexed looks as they watched the second man continue to approach them.

"I'm coming, hold your horses," he bellowed out.

Richie looked the man over. "Hello, I'm, uh, Peter." He lied to conceal his identity, which bewildered Lucia, who gave him a peculiar gaze.

The man bent down and inspected the interior of the car. His stench made its way into the car, and it was almost enough to make them both gag.

"That's nice. We don't have a headlight for this model of car," he barked out through tobacco-stained lips and a puffed-out jaw from his current chew. "You'll have to get it somewhere else. How did you come across us anyways? We ain't exactly on the beaten path."

"Well, it's like this; I'm looking for some competition, not a headlight." Richie's demeanor changed. He put on an heir of cockiness, and gave the man an audacious leer with a raised eyebrow. "We were passing through and found you on the Internet. You see, I got the fastest car east of the Mississippi and I was hoping you guys might know of someone I could race."

The vile man's wrinkled-up forehead rose, causing it to smooth out, as he leaned closer to Richie. "Here's the thing, boy. You ain't east of the Mississippi anymore."

Richie scooted back in his seat a tad bit to escape the stench emitting from him. "No, sir, that's exactly why I'm here. I'm willing to bet that not only do I have the fastest car east of the Mississippi but I'd bet I've got the fastest street-legal car in the entire US!" Then he slapped the top of the steering wheel in an excited and hubristic appearance.

"That's cute." The nasty man released a low chuckle.

"Cute? Hell, it's more than cute, it's the truth!"

"You got any money to back that up, princess?" The man held his head sideways, waiting for a response.

"Damn straight! How's about a thousand dollars? Is that enough to get some competition around here?"

"Let's see it, Cotton McCready."

"Ha, Cotton McCready wishes his car was this fast. You'll see the money after you beat me. If you can beat me, that is." He stared at the nasty man, waiting for an answer.

"All right then, looks like we got ourselves a race. I'm Chester. You'll be racing my baby brother, Otis, over there. We'll have to go out to the old abandoned airstrip on Walker's Gap."

Still playing the cocky character in front of the junkman, he looked at Lucia and pumped his fists in a wild fashion. "Hot damn, baby! We finally got ourselves some action!"

Lucia's eyes widened as she gave him a fake smile. She didn't seem to care for his portrayal of an illegal street racer.

Richie looked back at the man. "So, tell me, Chester, what kind of jalopy am I up against? A Trans Am, Road Runner, Cuda? No wait, I got it, a Fox Body Mustang. That's it, ain't it? Am I right?"

"Well, that's pretty much the right manufacturer, but not exactly the model. Just stay put while I go tell Otis he's got a race."

"Sure thing." Richie watched as Chester turned to walk away. Richie noticed a very large sheathed knife hanging off the backside of his right thigh. Lucia and he breathed a little easier as the stank slowly went away, seeming to follow the heavily soiled individual.

Lucia spoke low to prevent the malodorous junkyard gang from hearing her. "What the hell are you doing, Richie? Are you seriously trying to hustle these hillbillies?"

"Hey, careful throwing that term around. I'm a hillbilly. These guys are something else, something entirely different."

"That's exactly why I'm worried. Are you sure you know what you are doing?"

"Yes, it will be fine. My brother, John, used to go around hustling guys all the time when I was a kid. Anytime we were running low on funds, he would sucker any chump with loud mufflers into a race and separate them from their money, and that's exactly what's about to happen here. I don't feel good about it, but we need some quick cash and besides, I don't know what else to do."

"Why did you tell them your name was Peter?"

"I don't know, probably something I heard on the TV before we left. I didn't think I should tell them my real name since we're in a stolen car." They heard a very loud car startup. "See, just like I said, a loud piece of crap." He smiled at her with overwhelming assurance. Then they both looked in the direction of the roaring automobile.

Skeeter was holding a rotted wooden door open to a different but still rickety old shed. Otis revved the engine as he slowly rolled out. The noise made the now chained-up dog, Tuco, bark with even more ferocity than before.

"Shut your stupid trap!" Chester yelled toward the agitated animal. "I don't know why we keep you around!"

Richie's eyes widened as the loud machine exited the shed, eliminating much of his confidence as he took in the sight of what appeared to be at its essence a heavily modified antique truck.

"What is that Richie?"

"It's what they call a rat rod."

"What's a rat rod?"

"It's usually a car that's been built or customized as cheap as possible, with scrap parts and no-frills. They are rusty, rugged, and it's actually how a lot of cars were first customized way back in the day. A lot of them being built now are just being made to appear that way, but that one looks like the real deal. It's probably a thirty-two Ford pickup. Well, it at least started out as one."

Chester came walking back toward the Camaro. "Whaddaya think of that, boy?"

"She looks pretty mean. Did you guys build it yourselves?"

"Hell yeah, we built it our damn selves. We didn't have Santa Claus drop it off," Chester declared with uncouth bluntness.

Agitated that the rude man completely mistook his attempt at small talk, Richie was quick to say, "What kinda power plant you got in that thing?"

"It's got a built-out blown flathead. We finally got it to stay cool and the damned thing use to vapor lock like a bitch in hot weather, but she runs like a new top now. We've got a 426 Hemi I wanted to put in it, but Otis wouldn't have it."

Richie got a better look at the ragged racer as it approached them. It looked as if it came straight out of a post-apocalyptic movie. It had been lowered to where it barely set off of the ground, and the mud-stained tires and wheels came up to the top of the primer and rust-spotted bed. The top had been chopped a few inches and the hood panels were completely gone, exposing the savage V8. The sound it made was almost unbearable as the exhaust simply ran through handmade and rusty straight pipes that came off of the engine in a very menacing manner.

"Well, if it isn't fast, it's definitely cool. Old school cool to boot."

Chester shook his head to let Richie know he couldn't hear him over the loud engine, so then he motioned to Otis to cut off the car. Right as he killed the engine, Lucia started screaming uncontrollably.

CHAPTER 19
Preaching to the Choir

"What's wrong, Lucia?" Richie shouted, looking her over, unable to figure out what was ailing her. "Why in the hell are you screaming like that? What's going on?"

"Snake! Richie, there's a snake on the car!" Terrified, she pointed toward the hood as her entire arm shook in fear.

"What in the world?" Richie mouthed just above a whisper.

"See, Chester!" Skeeter said in a loud, excited, and shaky voice. He had come up from behind the Camaro on the right side and threw a dead snake onto the hood. "You asked why we keep Tuco around, that's why! He kills all the snakes around this place!"

Richie stared at the serpent. "Is that a rattlesnake?" It was laying belly up and dead from the wounds inflicted by the dog, though its muscles still contracted, making it seem as if it was trying to squirm around.

"Yeah, this damn place is eat up with them. I reckon they like hiding in all the nooks and crannies of the cars and eating the rodents that nest in them."

"Yeah, I thought it was. I just didn't see its rattle at first. I've seen some whoppers in other junkyards myself."

"I didn't figure a pretty boy like you had ever stepped foot in a scrapyard."

Feeling that he was losing respect in the eyes of the junkyard gang and fearing that it could lead to him being exposed as a fraud, he belted, "If taking showers on a regular basis makes me a pretty boy then I guess I'm guilty of being one, and yes, I've been in several auto graveyards, now tell Special Ed there to get that snake off my car before he ends up wearing it around his neck!" Richie now displayed an intense look of aggravation on his face. He had had enough of the junkman talking down to him, and he most assuredly didn't appreciate having a dead reptile thrown so carelessly on the hood of such a rare and valuable car.

Richie's intrepid statements took Chester aback. So much so that he looked at Skeeter. "You heard him, dumbass! Get the snake off his car. Put it in the shed. We'll skin it out after the race." Then he looked back at Richie. "You ever eat any snake, boy?"

Pleased that Chester got the message and dropped the "pretty" off of the "boy," he smiled. "No. I've heard it tastes like chicken."

"Hell, son, it's way better than chicken!"

"We gonna race or what?" Otis demanded to know from the cab of the rat rod. He was noticeably growing impatient.

"Keep your pants on, turd face!" Chester yelled at his brother and turned back to Richie. "Just follow him. We've got a back gate that we'll go through to get to the airfield. Me and Skeeter will follow in our truck."

Richie nodded. "Okay."

Chester told Skeeter to lock the front gate as Richie started up the Exorcist and followed Otis slowly through the junkyard. An ominous song was now playing on the radio and added to the overall creepy vibe that the rusty compound exuded.

Richie looked over at Lucia, who was still a little shaken up from seeing the slithering reptile. "So, I take it that you don't like snakes, huh?"

Annoyed that Richie had even brought up the subject, she rolled her eyes. "Uh, no! I know it's stupid. I just don't like snakes! When I saw that psycho throw that one on the car, it freaked me out."

"No need to feel bad about it. Most people don't like 'em. I'm not overly crazy about them myself. I couldn't imagine eating one. I mean, if I was starving, I guess I would, but it definitely wouldn't be my first choice." Richie took in the astonishing sight of all the decommissioned cars as they slowly drove by them.

"It's a good thing you weren't in the arena the night when my career suddenly took off."

"Oh, yeah? Why's that?"

"Holy crap, there's a sixty-three Corvette! That's a very valuable car. I can't believe some of the vehicles they have here. This place must be ancient."

"Yeah, and that's just this row. It looks like there are countless aisles in this place. It's almost like it's a corn maze of cars."

"For sure." Richie continued to follow the rat rod as if it were a pilot car leading them through a construction site. It was making several turns through the different lanes along the way. "That's odd."

"What is?"

"That huge section of cars over there." Richie pointed to the left. It was a line of SUVs, sports cars, trucks, and all other assortments of newer model automobiles. "They don't look like junked-out cars. Some of them even look like they're almost new."

"Do you think the motors went bad or something, so they ended up here?"

"Nah, I kinda doubt it. They are just in way too good of shape to be here. It doesn't make any sense." Richie stared at the peculiar row of cars until they were out of sight.

"So, what were you saying about the night your career took off?"

"Oh yeah, that's what I was telling ya about. It was at the 'Daze of the Dead'. That's the big event the Infinity Wrestling League puts on around Halloween. You see, I used to have two midget wrestlers that accompanied me for a while when I was a heel."

"Wait, what do you mean by heel?"

"A heel is the 'Bad Guy' that cheats and everyone boos and pulls against."

"Oh, okay. That must have sucked. I would hate people booing me."

"Nah, it's actually kinda fun pissing the crowd off, but anyway, the midgets were still with me at that point. They were called my Choir Boys. They were amazing at getting heat. That's what you call the angry reaction from the crowd and boy oh boy, they sure could get the audience in a tizzy."

"You really should say little people, you know."

"Ha! That's easy for you to say! I made the mistake of calling them little bastards that one time."

"What do you mean? Did it offend them?"

"There's only been less than a handful of times that I truly feared for my life and the time I called them 'little people' was definitely one of them. Rumors circulated around the locker room that they had stabbed some guys outside a bar in Jersey one night, and the fact that they carried switchblades around all the time gave that rumor merit. I thought I was going to be next."

"Why did that offend them? I don't understand."

"I didn't either at first, but they sure made it clear to me that they wouldn't tolerate being called little. They said it was the same as being referred to as petty. You know, like when someone says something like, 'You think that little of me.'"

"Oh, I would never have thought of it in that way."

"Yeah, me neither. Other people with the same condition may be fine with that title, but I never made the mistake of calling those two that again. Later on, I heard that the only reason they didn't slice me up was out of professional courtesy. Apparently, they enjoyed working with me. Part of their gimmick was to carry flasks and occasionally sneak a drink. The commentators called it sneaking a sip of spirits, which added to the whole hypocrite vibe we were putting out, but unbeknownst to Vaughn, those little bastards really kept alcohol in them and stayed drunk all the time."

"What!"

"Oh yeah, it was bad. They were mean drunks, too. Everyone tried to stay away from them. Thankfully, not long after that night, I turned face, which means became a good guy or crowd favorite. Vaughn didn't think they fit in with me anymore, so they got the ax." Richie followed the rat rod through a back gate. "Wow, we finally got to the back of this place."

The mean machine rumbled out as Otis worked through the gears as the three-vehicle convoy gained speed on the rugged back road. He looked in his rearview mirror and saw Chester and Skeeter following close behind in an old tow truck.

"That thing seems like it will be really fast, Richie. Do you think you can beat it?"

"I don't know. It's mad to the max for sure, but it's too late to back out now."

Lucia watched Richie's face as deep concern seemed to overtake it. So she had him get back to his story. "So what did you and your Choir Boys do that was so career-changing that night?"

"Oh, damn, I'm getting worse than Sherrod, telling tales. He takes forever and gets distracted at every little thing. But yeah, the main event at the Halloween show is a match called Horde of Horror. It includes almost the entire locker room all in the ring at once and if you can keep yourself from being tossed out to the floor, you are declared the winner and get rewarded with an oversized plastic pumpkin full of hundred-dollar bills. The commentators love that event 'cause they get to make all kinds of puns and comments like 'How many tricks is it going to take to get the ultimate treat?' and other crap like that."

"Wow, sounds like quite a spectacle."

"Yeah, it's actually one of the events everyone looks forward to. But anyways, that night before the match officially started, the Choir Boys distracted the refs around the ring so that I could crawl under it."

"You actually went under the ring during a match? Is that safe?"

"Yeah, it was safe, loud as crap when guys hit the canvas, but it was okay. So, after forty or so minutes, the majority of the competitors had been tossed out and about fifteen or so wrestlers were still left. So the Choir Boys signaled to me that it was time and we immediately hopped up on the apron of the ring and began dumping bags full of snakes onto the mat. We had placed them under the ring before the event."

"What? Snakes!"

"Yeah, and dozens of 'em, too."

"Were they real?" With panic-stricken eyes, Lucia waited for an answer.

Richie looked directly at her. "Oh yeah, they were very real!"

CHAPTER 20

Because Snakes are Scary

Wide-eyed, Lucia's jaw dropped. "That's insane, Richie! I can't believe you threw live snakes into the ring! Were any of them poisonous?" Shaking her head, Lucia felt like screaming louder than she spoke as they continued their trek on the lonely back road to the abandoned airstrip for the race against Otis.

"I think you mean venomous and no. There were various pythons, corn snakes, king snakes, and other varieties that looked deadly but weren't. We had a professional snake wrangler backstage that they belonged to. He was a really neat guy. He taught us a lot about snakes that night. He said the difference between poisonous reptiles and venomous reptiles was that poisonous reptiles have a substance on the outside of their bodies for defense. Venomous reptiles have a delivery system like fangs or stingers that inject venom directly into the bloodstream."

"I don't care if they were poisonous or whatever, but I would have kicked your ass for pulling a stunt like that."

Richie laughed. "Well, everybody else wanted to as well, but as soon as those snakes hit the mat, all the guys started scattering like crazy. Every single wrestler that was left in the match at that point jumped out, which meant they eliminated themselves. I won without even throwing a single punch or performing a single maneuver."

"No way!"

"Oh yeah. Once the crowd got over the shock of the snakes in the ring they realized that I kind of MacGyvered the situation and they went nuts. They totally appreciated that I won with a cunning plan. It was the trick of all tricks, and in that very instant I became a fan favorite. It was an amazing night. Originally, I was supposed to win and take the money and buy a real fancy watch instead of using it to help the poor, which would have made the fans hate a hypocritical Priest even more, but after Vaughn saw how much the crowd liked the stunt, he dropped that idea."

"Yeah, I can kinda see what he was going for there, a supposed Priest using evil serpents to do his will. That does seem very hypocritical."

"Yeah, it was a very good idea. Vaughn is a conniving asshole for sure, but he does have flashes of brilliance at times and even though that particular scenario didn't work out exactly as planned, it still was a huge hit and we went with it from there."

"Well, I guess in that aspect, throwing snakes around was a good thing, but I still wish that freak hadn't thrown a rattlesnake on the car. I'll have nightmares for a week."

"That reminds me; the snake wrangler told us rattlesnakes are starting to lose their rattles."

"Lose their rattles? That's nuts. How does that even happen? Will they have to eventually call them something else then?"

"I don't know, but he said that the ones with rattles usually end up getting killed by people or eaten by predators. It's almost like an unintentional selective breeding is happening because the ones that don't have a rattle, or at least a good one, are the ones surviving and passing their genes on."

"That's just great. Those little horrors are just getting even more dangerous."

"I know right."

Richie continued to drive. The trail seemed to be endless. Finally, after a great deal of time, he pulled up to the right side of Otis as he had come to a stop. Both drivers turned off their distinctive automobiles. "Looks like we're finally here. That trail was brutal." He rolled down his window so he could hear the gang, and took in the sight of the weeds and crack-ridden pavement.

Chester pulled to the left of Otis, turned off his truck as well, and headed toward the Camaro.

Richie saw him coming. "What exactly is this place? Why was it put here?"

Chester looked out at the weathered tarmac. "I've heard it was a top-secret airstrip during World War II. Supposedly, they could deploy fighter planes into the Gulf in case the Germans tried to attack us from down there. I don't know for sure and don't know anybody else that does either. Damn thing's been abandoned ever since I could remember. Old Man Clyde Harden owned a paving company, and he had two sons that was into racing. They would bring leftover pavement up here and fill in the holes so they could practice on it. That's been many moons ago, though. Me, Otis, and Skeeter are the only ones that come up here anymore. We try to knock the weeds down, but it's about too much to tackle."

Richie was still looking at the rugged surface. "You sure this is safe to race on?"

"What's amatter, boy, you ain't scared, are ya?" Chester cracked a half-grin.

Richie gazed up at the hubris hick. "I think concerned would be the right word for it. I'm not looking to crash this car."

"Hell, son, your fancy little car will be all right. This rides a lot better than it looks. We test and tune-up here all the time."

Unconvinced by Chester's lackadaisical attempt at reassuring him of the safety of the makeshift drag strip, Richie shrugged. "Where do we race to? Where's the finish line?"

"Look real hard, boy. You see that pink dot to the right?"

With his hand over his brow to deflect the sun, Richie strained his eyes. "I think so. Is that a flamingo?"

"Yeah, like in some old lady's yard. We thought it was good enough to use for a reference."

"Looks like it's about an eighth of a mile?"

"Yeah, go fast quick or go home. No time for lollygagging."

Even though Richie was growing increasingly nervous, he kept his poker face and spoke with moderate confidence. "Sounds good. Let's do it!"

"All right then. Hand over your money. I'll hold it 'til after the race."

Richie's nervousness turned to dread, as he feared being caught making a bet he couldn't back up. "Sorry, it's not that I don't trust you, but I don't trust anyone. No offense, but I'll hold my cash myself. I'm good for it."

"Okay then. That means that pretty young thing next to ya stands here with me and Skeeter 'til after the race."

"I don't think so. She stays with me." Richie peered at Lucia. She now had a look of distress planted on her face.

"Now look here, son. She stays here with us or your money stays here with us. It don't make no difference to me which it is." He smirked. "It's not that I don't trust you, but I don't trust anyone, no offense."

Richie's eyes grew big and his heart pounded rapidly. He looked at Lucia once more, and now she was terrified. He glanced up at Chester. "Can you give us a minute?"

"Sure thing." Chester walked over to Otis.

Richie was panicking as he spoke to Lucia. "Look, I don't want you to do something that you're not comfortable doing, but I don't know what to do. I would just take off, but I don't even know where we are, much less how to get us outta here."

Frozen with fear, Lucia sat motionless, staring through the windshield as if Richie wasn't even talking to her.

"It's okay, don't worry, I'll tell them the deal is off." Richie lightly placed his hand on her arm and looked deeply into her wide, blank eyes. "There's no way I'm going to put you in a spot you don't want to be in."

"Well what's it going to be, son?" Chester walked back over to the car.

Disconcerted by the turn of events, Richie called it off. "Look, I'm really sorry but the dea—"

"Let's get this race started!" Lucia slammed her door shut and walked toward Chester.

The loud thud from the closing door jolted Richie and completely caught him off guard. He gazed at her with complete bewilderment.

With a bold attitude, Lucia glanced at Richie. "Are we going to do this sometime today or what?" She took a deep breath and stomped over to Chester.

Richie's eyes stayed glued to Lucia. It shocked him that she was going through with this scheme, even though she seemed extremely frightened by it. *Losing is not an option*, he thought. *Lucia's safety is on the line now. If these crazy kooks find out I wasn't good for the bet. Who knows what they might do to me or her.*

"My, my, this little lady is ready for some action." Chester flashed a disturbing smile as he looked Lucia over from head to toe.

"I am, too." Richie smacked the upper part of the door, trying to distract the apparent superficial pervert from gawking at Lucia. "How we doing this thing?"

Chester was slow to explain the race rules as he continued to drool over the young, beautiful lady. "Well, we keep it simple. Skeeter will hold his hat up in the air above his head. Next, he will swing it in a circle three times, and then he will drop his arm straight down in front of himself to signal the start. The first one to go past the flamingo wins, simple as that. You ready, boy?"

"Yeah, let's do it!" While Richie's voice was deep, his breath was uneasy. He was beyond nervous as Skeeter ran just past the fronts of the mismatched era machines so both drivers could see him signal the start of the race. *God, I wish John was here. It's been a long time since I've done this,* he thought. He started up the sleek Camaro just after Otis turned on his loud and ratty chariot. He wasted no time putting it in track mode as Otis performed a massive burnout that smoked up the entire area so badly Lucia walked several yards away to escape the choking cloud.

"You better heat your tires up, boy!" Chester instructed loudly into the rolled-down window, startling Richie as he seemed to appear out of nowhere in the gray fog.

Richie waved his hand, fanning away the tire smoke and Chester's stink, which was still very potent despite the burned rubber smell that hung thick in the air. "This is a two thousand dollar set of tires. The drive up here was more than enough to get them warm."

Chester's eyebrows rose in apparent shock from the price of the tires, and mumbled, "Suit yourself then," before walking a few feet behind the cars.

Richie mumbled under his breath, "Shows what you know, dumbass. The burnout is also for cleaning off the tires, which won't do any good on this ancient pebble patch."

Skeeter motioned for Otis to back up a bit to line up perfectly beside Richie. Then he raised his hat in the air.

Richie pressed in the clutch and shifted the Camaro into first gear. He revved and held the engine at thirty-five hundred RPMs, hoping to successfully launch the car. His heart was pounding almost as loud as Otis's ear-splitting rod and the Camaro's thunderous engine. With laser-like focus Richie's eyes zeroed in on Skeeter as he waited for him to wave his hat in a circular motion, as Chester had said. Instead, Skeeter forcefully brought his hat down in front of himself and Otis took off in a flash!

CHAPTER 21

Three to Get Ready, and Where'd You Go?

The drag race for one thousand dollars on the abandoned airstrip was now underway. Richie immediately let off the clutch and pressed onto the gas with steady caution, hoping not to spin the tires, which would cause him to lose even more time. He sure didn't have any to spare since Skeeter pulled that despicable, underhanded tactic at the start of the race. Otis was off to a blisteringly fast start and had about three car lengths of a lead, but Richie was making up ground fast. He pegged the red line on the tachometer for every gear as he worked through them with great ferocity. As they closed in on the pink flamingo with near supersonic speed and deafening sounds, Richie muscled past Otis and took the lead by half a car length, and was the first one to cross the finish line.

"Yes!" Richie pumped his clenched fist wildly, overjoyed that he had won the race, and now had plenty of money to get to Mt. Hood despite the fowl starting tactic that was used against him. "Take that, you freaking cheaters! Put that in your pipe and smoke it!" he yelled out, along with some other celebratory whoops and hollers. "Man, I wish John could have seen that."

As the car slowed after his triumphant victory, he turned the winning speed machine around. To his surprise, no one was in sight.

"What the heck? Where did they go?" He scanned the horizon. He looked for Otis and he had disappeared, too. He looked in the rear-view mirror to make sure he hadn't passed by while he was turning around, but he was nowhere to be seen. Richie left the car idling as he hopped out to further examine this strange situation that was now unfolding. Off in the distance, he could hear the loud rat rod. It seemed to be driving away at a hurried pace. Richie used a fair amount of caution as he trotted over to the other side of the worn-out strip and discovered a very rugged trail that Otis must have taken. Richie thought about following him but he wasn't sure if it would be a wise choice since the path looked too treacherous for a car like The Exorcist so he ran as fast as he could, despite his rib pain, back to the Camaro and started driving toward the direction whence they came.

"Where's Lucia?" He drove off of the abandoned airstrip and got back onto the trail that brought them in. He was in a frantic state as he continuously looked left and right, hoping to find his beautiful partner in crime, but she was nowhere to be seen.

Richie's heart beat fast as he sped down the trail. "What have you bastards done? What is going on?"

He worked through the gears and went as fast as the trail would let him go. It felt like it was taking forever; the ride up to the strip went by a lot faster. Richie thought it must have seemed quicker because he was telling Lucia some of his old wrestling stories, just like Gino was always doing with him and his colleagues. Despite how slow it felt, he was making good time getting back to the junkyard, especially on the straights, but a lot of the path was winding and treacherous. It reminded him of his after-school teenage days when he would watch off-road rally racing on the TV's speed station.

"They had to have taken a different way out, like Otis did. That race was over in a flash and now they're nowhere to be seen. They couldn't have gotten far at all if they had taken this same route we used to get up here."

He threw the car into controlled slides to drift through the tight turns to get past them as fast as possible. Dirt and other various rock and stick debris flew wildly behind the expensive racing tires as he made his way back to get Lucia, but he didn't care at this moment. He was certain that she was in imminent danger, and he felt it was entirely his fault.

After several more minutes had passed, which felt like an eternity to Richie, the junkyard had finally come back into his view. It was an ominous sight and seemed even spookier now that he knew the guys running it were definitely up to no good. He looked the rust-ridden field over as he approached the rear entrance. As he made his way through the opening, he noticed they had parked a car in the way further up the path they used coming out.

"The bastards have tried to block me out. Not today!" He made an immediate left turn and headed up a different row. After taking several turns up several aisles, he felt trapped in a labyrinth of junked cars.

"Where are you ass hats at?" Fear and frustration slowly continued to subdue him. After coming to a dead-end, he turned around and headed back up another row, only to discover that they had parked a car in the way, now cutting off that route.

"Come on, you cowards! Stop playing games!" Richie slapped the steering wheel, creating a loud thud. He put the Camaro in reverse and wasted no time going up another aisle. Up ahead, he saw the front of Chester's tow truck come in to view. Richie assumed he was putting another car in his way. "Not this time, stinky pants!" Richie floored the accelerator and barreled down the row. Chester didn't realize Richie was coming up the lane that fast until he was right at him, so he pressed hard on his truck's gas pedal, hoping to prevent Richie from getting by him. However, it was a futile attempt. The Camaro sped by in a black flash and Richie whipped it around in a semi-circle right behind the sheds at the entrance to the junkyard. In a single instant, with a flawless fluid motion, he hopped out of the car, leaving the door wide open and the engine idling. He gave Chester a threatening look and powerfully pointed at him. "Where's Lucia?"

Chester straightened his back and stood in a threatening manner of his own. "It don't matter none to you, pretty boy. You've raced your last race and now you're fixin' to get your last ride."

"So you clowns never cared about the race? This was all just to rob us?"

"Don't go and try to make yourself out to be the victim. You thought you was gonna roll up in here and take advantage of some backwoods bumpkins, but you crapped and fell back in it. That's on you."

Otis stepped out of the shed that housed the rat rod. He had just parked it and now he was hollering out at Chester. "This is your fault. They wouldn't have come here in the first place if you hadn't put the scrapyard on that stupid Internet!"

Chester looked back at Otis. "We have to look like a real business. We can't just keep doing what we do without a cover, you dingleberry!"

Richie chimed in on their family squabble. "Just what is it that you psychos do here?"

"That's none of your concern, pretty boy. Now come here so we can make this quick." Chester removed the large knife from the sheath that hung from his belt.

Riche's eyes widened as he looked around for something to help defend himself with, but it was to no avail. The immediate area where he stood was surprisingly one of the most clutter-free areas of the entire place.

"Go ahead and grab him, Otis." Chester taunted Richie. "It's time to meet back up with your dead relatives. If it makes you feel any better, you are the only person to ever end up winning after Skeeter's false start trick."

"That's comforting." Richie smirked.

"You sure weren't lying about that car. It's damn fast. We're bound to get a ton of money for that thing." Chester and Otis slowly approached Richie, a few steps at a time.

"You bastards ain't getting a damn thing! Now tell me where Lucia is! What did you do with her?"

Chester looked at Otis with a big grin. "Looks like he's gonna be a fighter."

Otis smirked. "That's just the way I like 'em."

Richie motioned him to do so. "Then come and get you some!"

Chester laughed out, then shook his head. "Damn, son, I'm really going to hate killing you."

Otis charged at Richie but he side-stepped the hardy man and grabbed him from behind in a waist lock. Then Richie hoisted the larger Otis up into the air and threw him forcefully to the ground, as he had done to many of his competitors in the past. This made him land hard on his front side while driving his face into the dirt. Richie was pleased with the result, but he regretted making that particular move. It had aggravated his rib injury, and now he was in extreme pain and gasping for air. Before he could continue his defensive assault on Otis, Skeeter had joined the fight, and he was attempting to choke Richie after jumping on his back and wrapping his arm around his throat.

"Dammit, Skeeter, Otis had this under control. You were supposed to watch that girl!" Chester belted out.

All the action that had unfolded riled up the vicious snake-killing dog they called Tuco. He once again was barking and growling uncontrollably toward the ongoing scuffle while pulling against the leash that had him restrained.

Chester eased toward Richie with his knife raised. "There's no need to fight it, just hold still, boy. This will only hurt for a second."

CHAPTER 22

Antenna Waves

Just as Chester lunged the sharpened steel toward Richie's chest, Lucia came out of nowhere and grabbed Chester's arm.

"Damn it, girl, let go of me!"

Otis sat up on his knees and held his injured nose. Lucia noticed his slow ascent and tried even harder to get the knife from Chester. She knew that if she didn't get it before Otis got to his feet, it was going to be all over for the both of them.

Richie finally got a firm hold of Skeeter over his right shoulder and threw him to the ground just as Lucia bit into Chester's nasty right hand like a rabid raccoon.

"Ow, you little bitch!" In shock from both the pain of the bite and that Lucia dared to attack him, Chester dropped the knife.

She wasted no time grabbing it, but just as she did, Tuco's leash finally broke from the constant tugging. Richie saw it from the corner of his eye as he walked toward Otis. "Run, Lucia, the dog!"

She didn't even have to question what he meant. Now, with the knife in hand, she bolted toward the building that most resembled an office of some sort, with Tuco hot on her heels.

Richie lunged for Otis, hoping to keep the big man down, but the grounded Skeeter reached out and grabbed his ankles. This gave Otis and Chester both a chance to take their shots at Richie, and they did so with great force.

After several punches to his head and face, Richie finally fell to the ground. He thought, *I've got to get up. If I don't, they will kill me for sure.*

He was right. The two diabolical men now standing over him unleashed a merciless attack on him, kicking and stomping him while he was down. Skeeter was still holding Richie by his ankles, which was preventing him from being able to get up. Richie put all his effort into freeing his legs first so he could get back to his feet. After a couple of forceful tugs, he freed his right foot and drove the sole of his shoe into Skeeter's face. He finally let go and Richie got to his knees, despite the relentless onslaught of Otis's and Chester's boots.

Now that Richie had a snowball's chance of surviving against these three maniacs, he mounted a counterattack. He waited for Otis to stomp at him again and grabbed his large, filthy boot, twisting his foot, causing his leg to turn awkwardly while getting to his own feet. Now that he was up and vertical, with his right leg, he swept Otis' leg out from under him, causing him to fall like a downed, mighty oak tree. A loud thud clamored out when he hit the ground and Richie placed a firm stomp on Otis' abdomen.

Richie turned his attention to Chester. He made a hard dash toward the plump midsection of the outspoken ringleader, driving his right shoulder hard into him in a spear-like maneuver he had used in the ring occasionally. Like Otis, Chester hit the ground, causing a mighty thud.

Richie looked at the three men on the ground. Skeeter was getting up while holding his face, and the other two gasped for air while trying to catch their breaths. *I've got to get something, anything, to defend myself,* he thought. *I'm outnumbered, and these guys mean to kill us.*

Richie started toward a row of cars as he, too, gasped for air. The pain from the stomps and kicks was setting in, and it was bad. On his way to scavenge for a makeshift weapon, he noticed a few yards over, the mad junkyard dog was jumping and clawing at the door of what appeared to be an outhouse.

"Lucia, are you in there?" Richie's words barely came out as his chest heaved desperately for oxygen.

Before he could listen for a response, Skeeter was on Richie's back again, trying to cut off the air he critically needed.

Lucia was indeed trapped in an outhouse behind the building she was trying to get into. Tuco was too fast, and she had to dart into the stink-filled shed to avoid being mauled by him.

"Get lost, you crazy mutt!" She banged her palm on the door. "What the hell am I supposed to do? How can I get out of here?" She looked around, accessing her unpleasant situation.

Meanwhile, Richie's battle with the brutal blokes had unfortunately resumed. Skeeter had him to his knees, gasping even harder for air while Chester and Otis slowly made their way over.

"You gave it a nice try, boy, but it's over now. I was going to make it easy on you, but that whore of yours ran off with my knife, so now you have to suffer by choking to death." Chester smirked.

Otis got up close to Richie's face, and, with clenched teeth, said, "I'm going to enjoy skinning you out. Your head's gonna make a nice addition to my skull collection. Then I'm going to take that leg bone that you stomped on my gut with and make a shifter rod out of it."

Richie's eyes glazed over as he looked back into the demented ones of Otis. His vision was blurry and fading from the lack of oxygen.

Otis was enjoying torturing his latest victim, watching him die right in front of him. "Oh, and that sweet, sweet girl of yours is going to be so much fun! I can't wait to get my han—"

Otis hollered in pain as Richie chomped down on his nose in a last-ditch effort to free himself from the clutches of the evil trio. Otis had gotten too close to his mouth as he taunted him about Lucia. Otis shoved Richie back to free his nose, which made him land on Skeeter, causing him to break the life-threatening chokehold. Richie now gasped for air and felt immense relief as oxygen filled his lungs once more.

Lucia's only way out of the smelly cell as the relentless dog tried to claw his way in was to push up on the ragged roof. She stood on the bench and pushed up with all her might, pushing the top loose, causing it to crash down behind the ancient structure. Fearing the noise got her noticed, she looked over and saw the three men circling Richie as they held their wounds. They didn't seem to notice her, so she opened the door and leaped up and grabbed onto the top of the shed, and pulled herself up as the dog rushed in to grab her. She narrowly cleared the top right before the canine lunged at her. She landed on her feet and wasted no time getting over to the outhouse door. She pulled it closed and used Chester's giant bowie knife to wedge the door shut, trapping the dog inside. "Finally, how do you like that, you stupid fleabag?"

She looked over and saw the three men now stomping and kicking Richie. "Hang in there handsome, I gotta find some way to help him," she mumbled, as she entered the back of the main building. After stumbling in, she searched around for some sort of weapon but instead, she found an unlocked door to a room that was filled with what appeared to be human bones and multiple boxes with bags of white powder in them. "Oh, my—" She gasped and ran out and headed toward the front of the building.

Richie was in dire straits, as he felt every single stomp and kick from the heavy boots of the heartless attackers. *This is it. I'm going to die,* he thought as white light blurred his vision. Then he whispered, "I'm sorry, Mary. I love you, Josey."

"Did you say something, pretty boy?" Chester hovered over him. "What was your name, anyways? I can't remember."

Otis promptly answered, "Peter!"

"Oh, that's right, Peter Peter Pumpkin Eater," Chester sang in a sarcastic tone. "Well, we're about to squash your head like a damn pumpkin." Then both he and Skeeter sadistically laughed out amid continuous kicks to Richie's battered body.

Richie saw flashes of his life and loved ones, as the white light had all but taken over. Then it was as if everything had paused, and he heard a voice in his right ear. It was completely crystal clear, and it sounded just like his deceased brother, John, saying, *"Get the antenna, dumbass."*

"What antenna?"

"On the Chevelle, the '66 right in front of you. It's not that far. You can do it."

Richie pushed himself up to his knees as the kicks continued to come. He looked up and saw the Chevelle. With everything in him, he got to his feet and sprang toward the car. With a few long strides, he landed on the right fender, grabbed the antenna, and broke it off of the car on his way down to the ground. He landed on his keister and sat with his back against the car. The trio quickly came after him, not realizing he now had a weapon. Skeeter got to him first. He raised his leg to kick Richie in the face, but Richie pushed his leg to the side and, with extreme prejudice, swung the antenna with force, hitting Skeeter in the jaw. In an instant, he grabbed the affected area of his face and turned around, giving Richie the perfect opportunity to get to his feet and strike Skeeter's again, this time across his back. The wiry runt of the three screamed out like a scared child and took off running further into the junkyard. Chester and Otis now closed in on Richie.

"Drop that right now, boy, and I promise we'll go back to killing ya quick." Chester squinted. "This game of cat and mouse is getting old. We need to end this now."

"That's exactly what I plan on doing!" Richie felt a shot of adrenaline hit his battered system as he yelled out and swung the makeshift rod toward Chester's head. He landed a solid blow that put Chester on the ground, moaning in pain. Then he looked toward Otis, who now had a look of concern on his face as he backed a few steps away from Richie. "You're the next asshole! What was it you were going to do with my leg again?" Then he wailed away at Chester without an ounce of mercy. The antenna continuously landed solidly on Chester's body. He screamed in agony as the thin, deadly metal tore away at his already ragged clothes, as blood trickled from his wounds.

"Otis, for God's sake, help me!" Chester cried out.

Otis attempted to move in on Richie, but every time he stepped toward him, Richie would stare directly at him, daring Otis to come closer.

Almost out of breath, Richie continued beating Chester until he was nearly lifeless. Otis picked up on Richie, getting tired, and made his move, lunging toward Richie. Despite being winded, Richie was ready for his opponent. He swung his new best friend, the antenna, straight at the throat of Otis, and he collapsed to the ground and cried out in tremendous pain. Richie got another shot of adrenaline and used the newfound burst of energy to incapacitate the large man.

Richie now thrashed Otis senseless since he had him down. He knew his and Lucia's lives were on the line, so he was going to make sure the junkyard gang would not get the upper hand again. "You ain't so bad now, are ya?" Riche yelled out, along with other taunts between strikes. "Tell me again what you are going to do with my skull!"

Lucia stood at an opening in the fence. "Richie! Over here! We gotta go now!"

He stopped beating Otis for a second and looked up at Lucia. "What are you doing over there? We need to get back in the car."

"We can't, there's no time! The police are on the way! I heard sirens off in the distance. We need to get outta here before they show up!"

Richie looked down at the two beaten men and then he scanned the area, trying to see if Skeeter was nearby. Satisfied he had gotten the upper hand on the unholy trio, he limped toward Lucia. "What about our stuff? We can't leave that behind."

"I got it already, and I found us a way outta here while you beat the crap out of those guys. I was going to help, but when I came by, you had gotten the situation under control. Come on, let's get out of this hellhole!"

Richie stumbled toward the opening in the gate. He turned back and gave The Exorcist an intense look.

"I'm sorry we have to leave it, Richie. If we don't, we'll be caught for sure."

Full of regret, Richie turned away from the stolen substitute for the remainder of his contract payment that Vaughn had cheated him out of and disappeared through the opening in the fence.

CHAPTER 23

Street Smart Tart

"Well, hey there, Sugar. Do you and your friend need a ride?" A scuzzy-looking man who appeared to be somewhere in his late fifties and seemed somewhat intoxicated, hung his arm out of the rolled-down window of the blue Cadillac.

After a quick scan of the car and the driver with her road-traveling-experienced eyes, Lucia answered back in a cold, dead tone. "No, thanks."

"Are you sure? Your friend there looks pretty beat up. I don't mind a bit. I can take y'all anywhere you need to go."

"No, thanks. We're good." She folded her arms over her chest and stared off in the distance, avoiding any further eye contact with the questionable man.

"Suit yourselves then." The man sped off into the early dusk.

"Why didn't—" Richie grabbed his side in pain. His cracked rib was even worse and hurt with every breath now after his battle with the junkyard gang.

"Save your breath. We didn't take his ride offer because something wasn't right. You don't last very long in this kind of life without being well aware of people's intentions. I never deal with anyone who is too eager to give me a lift or accept my advances. They are the ones up to no good or hiding something."

Richie listened while hobbling along. His entire body ached, and he wasn't too sure of how much longer he could walk.

"People that are cautious—they are the ones that I know I can trust. They usually hesitate or get nervous and look around and almost always say no the first time you ask. Those kind are usually not up to no good, they are just going about their day and get an offer out of the blue."

Richie was amazed at Lucia's street smart knowledge. *She really knows how to take care of herself. She's definitely not a damsel in distress,* he thought. "I wish I'd listened to you on your feelings about the junkyard."

She looked over her left shoulder as she paced just in front of Richie on the white line of the lifeless back road. "Your bag weighs a ton."

"I'm sorry I can't carry it at the moment. I might be able to drag it." Richie was in so much pain and so exhausted, he could barely speak above a whisper.

"No, it's okay. I was just saying. You can barely walk, Richie, much less carry this thing." She paused for what seemed like forever. "Thanks."

"Did you just say thanks?"

"Yeah, I did."

"For what?" Confusion masked Richie's beaten face.

"For coming back to get me. You could have went on and just left me there."

"What kind of friend would I have been to leave you there with those psychos?"

"So we're friends?"

Richie gave her a bewildered look. "I wouldn't take an ass whipping like that for someone I didn't consider a friend. Besides, the way you handle yourself, I'm pretty sure you'd have been okay either way."

Lucia's smile turned into a frown. "I'm sorry that you lost the car. It's all my fault. If I hadn't let myself get caught—"

"If you hadn't got caught, the feds would have found us in that car and we would be in jail right now. I was counting on Vaughn being in Europe long enough for me to disable all the tracking devices. That didn't work out like I planned, though. I should have never taken the damned thing to start with."

"Well, to be honest, I'm glad you did, though."

"Why's that?"

"You have been my most interesting client."

"Oh, yeah?"

"Without a doubt!"

Richie chuckled, then coughed. "Ow, don't make me laugh."

Lucia looked over her shoulder, straight into his pain-filled eyes. "I'm serious. This has been an amazing adventure. Plus, it looks like I got a friend out of this. I don't really have any friends." Their eyes locked profoundly. "Look, I see headlights. This might be our ride out of here." She dropped Richie's bag and her suitcase. A mean-sounding El Camino appeared. Lucia threw up her hands and desperately attempted to wave the bright orange-colored hot rod down. The driver of the classic vehicle slowed to a creeping roll as he approached the two of them.

Lucia got a good look at the goateed driver. He seemed to be around Richie's age, perhaps a little older, and was wearing a blue and orange cap. "Excuse me, sir. Could you give us a lift?" Lucia walked beside the vehicle as it continued to roll.

The driver starred through his glasses at Lucia with concerned eyes. "What's going on?" He looked to Richie. "What's a matter with him?"

"He got attacked by three crazy guys in a junkyard."

The driver slammed on the brakes and jerked off his glasses. "You had a run-in with the Tramp family and lived?"

He frantically scanned the area around his car before looking hard into the rear-view mirror. "Are they chasin' you now?"

"Nope, and I don't think they'll be chasing anyone ever again. The cops showed up right as we escaped through a hole in their fence."

"It's about time they busted those damn maniacs. Rumors have circulated for many years about them, but no one could ever prove anything. How in the world did you end up at their place anyways?" he asked.

"It's a very long story. I could explain it to you on the way to a motel, gas station, or anywhere but here. Any safe place at all. We would really appreciate a ride, mister." Lucia smiled.

The man was quiet for a moment as he processed Lucia's story. "Hell, I reckon it's the least I could do for someone who went up against the Tramp clan and survived. Your friend must be one tough sum bitch! My name's Bud, by the way. Hop in!"

∞

Meanwhile, back at BWI, Agent Jain was recently informed of the situation in Arkansas and disclosed the information to Vaughn. "Good news, Mr. Vaughn! Our agents have recovered your car!"

"Excellent! Thank you for prioritizing this issue, Agent Jain. I assume that delinquent Richie Blackburn has been arrested."

"That's where this story gets interesting. Your car was found in the possession of some, well, for lack of a better word, some crazy guys in a junkyard."

Sherrod sat up in his chair to pay close attention to Agent Jain's every word.

"Okay, so he probably sold it to those guys then. Did they mention how they acquired it?"

"I'm sorry, Mr. Vaughn, but that isn't a main priority at the moment. I can't give you all of the details just yet, but I can tell you we've found multiple dead body remains and thousands, if not millions, of dollars in illegal drugs as well as countless other stolen vehicles were found at this compound. The place sounds like a horrific combination of Scarface and Leatherface rolled up into one insane burrito. You see, this is one of those once-in-a-lifetime-style of busts, Mr. Vaughn. It will take months to work through all of this. I'm sure you will be able to learn more about this case once it hits the news media. You and your associates are free to go and Mr. Showman, you can get your phone back."

Vaughn was flabbergasted and replied in a hostile tone. "What about Blackburn? I want him to pay for stealing my car!"

"Look, Mr. Vaughn, I understand your frustration, I really do. But as of now, there is nothing tying Richie Blackburn to this. If we come across something, I can assure you, we will handle this properly. Agent Smith will be with you in a moment and he can give you the details on recovering your car."

Sherrod's mind was racing as he thought, *What the hell is going on, Richie?*

CHAPTER 24

Head Over Heels

"Thanks, Bud! We really appreciate the lift and the help with our bags as well." Lucia smiled at the driver of the hot rod EL Camino.

"It's my pleasure, Ms. Lucy." Bud was on his way out of the motel room. "Good luck getting to Oregon, Rich!"

"Thanks, man," Richie uttered from his bed.

"Oh, if you're needin' to keep a low profile, take Route 66 when you can. There's not much traffic for the most part, just a bunch of grandma and grandpa types out sightseeing usually. I tell ya that road sure saved my ass one night."

Richie shot him a look of bewilderment. *Surely he doesn't know I stole Terrance Vaughn's car*, he thought.

"Not that it's any of my business, but you two didn't stay around to talk to the authorities back at the junkyard. I can't say I blame ya. I just thought I would throw that info out there in case you needed it." Bud tipped his hat at them and closed the door.

Lucia promptly locked it. "What a nice guy. I'm so glad he came along."

"Yeah, me, too. He reminded me a lot of my brother, John. Hey, I gotta ask you a question."

"Yeah, what?"

"Where did you get the money for this room? You weren't holding out on me, were you?"

Lucia smiled from ear to ear. "No. I wasn't holding out. When I first thought that I heard sirens at the junkyard, I ran over to the cash register and robbed it."

Richie smiled. "Your resourcefulness never ceases to amaze me."

"Yeah, I think we make a pretty good team."

"Yes, we do. How much did you get?"

"Just over five hundred bucks!"

Richie was shocked. "What? That's freaking awesome!" He grabbed his body in pain after trying to sit up from the excitement of the news.

"Oh, God, Richie! You're in real bad shape." Lucia rushed over to comfort him. She stroked his hair since she didn't know where she could touch him without causing him more pain. "I'm going to run you a bath. You can soak for a while. Do you want to try that?"

"Yeah. Can you get me some pain medicine?"

"After I run your bath water, I'll head over to that dollar store across the street and get some supplies."

Minutes later, the bath was ready and Lucia made her way over to Richie. "Com'on. Let's get you in the tub." She helped Richie to sit up and pulled off his torn, dirty red shirt. "Your clothes are ruined."

"I know. I'm glad I just had these old workout clothes on." Lucia tugged at his gray pants, attempting to take them off for him. "Damn it, Lucia, I can pull my own pants off!"

"Okay, tough guy, let's see you do it by yourself then."

"Just help me off this bed. I can do the rest myself."

Lucia did just that, and Richie slowly made his way into the bathroom. Lucia stood by the door, listening. Without warning, there was a loud splashing sound.

"Richie, are you okay?" She opened the door in a panic. He was laying halfway in the tub, holding his sides while barely keeping his head out of the water. His legs were outside the tub with his pants around his ankles, fully exposing his backside.

Lucia ran over to him and pulled him out of the water. "Why didn't you just let me help you, Richie? I've seen plenty of naked men before!"

Totally embarrassed from the situation, Riche forcefully spoke, "Not me though, damn it! Get out, I'm fine!"

"Yeah, right! You're obviously not!" Lucia finished pulling Richie's tattered sweat pants off, then grabbed him from behind, under his arms. Next, she hoisted Richie into the tub. The water splashed up and soaked Lucia's clothes. "Ugh! Damn it, Richie! Why did you have to make this so hard?"

"That's what she said," Richie mumbled out a low laugh as he groaned in pain and attempted to cover his lower region with his hands.

"Are you going to be okay? Do we need to get you to an ER?" Her wet shirt was clinging tightly to her firm body.

"No, I'll be fine." He noticed her white top was now more transparent, and he was trying not to stare.

"Are you sure? We probably don't have to worry about getting caught now that we don't have the car." Lucia sat down on the cold tile floor, with her back against the wall, waiting for his answer.

Richie's face went from a pain-filled scour to a sad, somber look. The realization was setting in that he had lost the car. "That sorry piece of crap, Vaughn, won. He destroyed my career, took a large chunk of my earnings, and I forsook my family so that he could do it. I couldn't even give him a jab to his gut by taking his car." He placed both hands over his face and sank lower into the tub.

"He only wins if you let him. There are plenty of other wrestling leagues out there. You could go to Mexico and wrestle luchadores for a while. I could be your interpreter."

"I'm not worried about wrestling right now. I have to get to Oregon and save my relationship."

"How do you know that the both of you wouldn't be better off by going your separate ways?"

"Because we have a daughter together and I have to be there for her. I don't want her to grow up without her father. I know what that's like."

"You can still be a good father to her without being in a relationship with her mom. Always being there doesn't mean you're a perfect dad. I know what that's like." Lucia's response matched Richie's level of intensity.

The two of them were silent for a moment, realizing that they still didn't really know each other and both seemed to have had parental issues growing up. Just as Lucia uttered a few words, her phone rang. She ran out to answer it and came running back into the bathroom. "Do you know who this is?"

Richie adjusted his bruised eyes to the mobile device and then snatched it out of her hands. "That's my number!"

CHAPTER 25

Salty Psychiatrist

"Oh, crap! We shoulda destroyed your phone already." Even though the car was out of his possession, Richie was still paranoid about being tied to it. "What if the feds are trying to track us? Could they have picked up its signal while we were still in the car?"

"I don't think so. I had a techie client for a while; you know, a real geeky type of guy. He blocked the GPS signal and everything else that could possibly make the phone traceable. He thought it would impress me, it didn't. I could have cared less 'til now. We should be fine; he really seemed to know his stuff."

"Okay then, here goes nothing." Richie pressed the answer button. "Hello."

"Richie?"

"Sherrod, what's going on?"

To Lucia, Richie didn't seem that he had an extremely important message, so she whispered, "I'm going to the store, and I'll be back soon." Richie nodded at her as she walked out of the bathroom to change into dry clothes before leaving.

"That's what I was just about to ask you. Where are you at, man? The feds got Vaughn's car back and you, thankfully, were nowhere around. How the hell did you manage that? He just knew he was going to get you busted for taking his Camaro."

"How did he find out I took it?" Richie's eyes widened and a look of panic came over him yet again.

"The text message you sent me. The feds took my phone for a while and they saw it while they had it."

"They did?"

"Yeah, but I lied so hard that my teeth are still hurting. You owe me bigtime, dawg."

"So they don't know that I took it?"

"The feds aren't sure, but Vaughn is, and I got a feeling he's going to make me pay. He knows I was covering for you, but he can't prove it."

"I'm sorry I dragged you into this, man. Do you want me to call Vaughn and admit that I did it? I can explain it all and convince him that you weren't involved."

"No way! I can handle what he throws at me. Worst-case scenario, he fires me, so I'll just go to Japan. Maybe I'll finally learn how they make fortune cookies. I've always wondered how they get the paper inside them."

"Fortune cookies are actually American."

"Nah, they can't be. The things would come in a happy meal or box of cereal if they were American."

Richie laughed. "You're crazy, dude."

"Anyways, they can't prove you took it, so just keep flying below the radar. I still wouldn't use your credit cards or let yourself be seen if I were you, at least 'til you get to Oregon."

The two continued to talk for quite a while. Richie filled Sherrod in on all the details from when he left the arena, leading up to his fight at the junkyard. Sherrod did the same. He told Richie all about the action from the arena and all the happenings on the wild flight. Lucia returned from the store and noticed that the two of them were still catching up. She walked into the bathroom and generously poured bath salts in Richie's water.

"I gotta go for now. Can I call you back tomorrow?" Richie tried to cover his nakedness from Lucia.

"Yeah, call your phone, though, just in case the feds are still monitoring mine."

"So they didn't ask to see mine?"

"No, dawg. Surprised me, too. It's unreal how unorganized they really are at times."

"K, I'll talk to you then. Oh, wait. Did you talk to Mary?"

Sherrod hesitated for a moment. "Yeah, we talked. I'll send you the address to the venue."

"She gave it to ya? That's great!"

"Well, I'm not so sure, Rich. She also said for you to not get your hopes up."

Richie's excitement left as quickly as it came and he hung his head a little. "Thanks for getting the address, Sherrod. I know that had to be awkward for ya."

"Yeah, it was, but I got through it. Talk to you tomorrow, bro."

"'Kay." Richie called out for Lucia to come and get her phone.

She walked back in with a water bottle and pain medicine in her hand. "Here, take these. Are you feeling any better?"

"Somewhat. The salt sure is burning my wounds."

"I noticed you have an accent that seems to come and go. I heard it more when you were talking to Sherrod." She slid back down onto the spot she was sitting on earlier.

"Yeah. I grew up in backwoods Kentucky. It's not as strong as it used to be. All my time on the road and playing a character that doesn't have an accent has caused it to fade out some."

"Is all your family still in Kentucky?"

"No, just the old home place and my brother's garage. Everyone's dead now."

"Everyone?"

"Yeah, my parents died when I was very young and my brother finished raising me."

"I'm so sorry, Richie." Lucia was heartbroken for him. She now understood why he wanted to hold on to his relationship so badly and be in his daughter's life.

"What about your brother?"

"He was killed by a drunk driver one night coming home from a race."

"Oh, that's horrible. Was he a wrestler, too?"

"No, he was a drag racer. Cars were his life."

"So that's why you're such a good driver then."

Richie partially grinned. "Yeah, I guess so. I'm nowhere near as good as he was, though. I hear him talking to me all the time. I never tell anyone, though. I know it sounds crazy."

"It doesn't sound crazy. He was a major part of your life. He will always be with you. When you're that close to someone, they integrate into your being. They become a part of who you are and will be there forever."

"That's pretty deep. You could be a psychiatrist or something." After a long pause, they both chuckled. "What about your accent? What's your story?"

All the remnants of Lucia's smile instantly disappeared, and she looked down. "You don't want to hear my story."

"Sure I do. I wouldn't have asked if I didn't."

She pulled her knees into her chest. "My…my father was American born. He moved down to Mexico because of his business, so he claims. I'm pretty sure he was in trouble with the law. Either way, he ended up outside of Guadalajara and that's where he met my mother. To this day, I'm not exactly sure what he did for work, but it had to be illegal. He was always at home and he made sure to keep us there with him." Lucia stopped talking and wouldn't look up.

Richie could see how uncomfortable she was getting, talking about this, and she hadn't really even said much yet. He didn't like seeing her like this, so he decided he would change the subject. "Hey, sorry to interrupt you, but I'm starving. Was you able to get us some food?"

"Yeah, I got a bag full of snacks out there on the table."

"This is crazy when you think about it. We just survived a real house of horrors and here we are chit-chatting. It must be the adrenaline still pumping."

"I think I'm in denial. Feels like it was all a dream, nightmare, I should say."

"I really thought that was it for me. I thought I was a goner."

"You would have been if you hadn't grabbed that antenna."

Richie hesitated for a second, unsure if he should tell her. "My brother John told me to."

Lucia shot him a look.

"I know, it sounds crazy, but I told ya I heard him talking to me sometimes."

They both stared at each other for a second, then simultaneously started laughing. "Ask him how we can get to Oregon."

Richie placed his hand behind his ear as if he was trying to listen. "He said to ask the psychiatrist."

CHAPTER 26

Truck Load of Bull

Richie came back to consciousness at the sounds of the *Wheel of Fortune*. His entire body ached, and the room was dim. "What? Ow… What time is it?"

Lucia jumped to her feet and ran over to him. "Thank God, you're alive!"

"I don't feel like it."

"I was so worried! I thought you were going to die. I kept checking to see if you were breathing."

"What time is it?"

"It's a little past seven."

"Seven o'clock! How could you let me lie here all day?" Richie tried to sit up.

A look of concern swept over Lucia's face. "I tried to get you up several times. I really thought you were dead at one point. I almost called an ambulance, but I figured you would be pissed if I did."

"It is still Tuesday, at least right?"

Hesitating, she shook her head. "Uh yeah, no, it's actually Wednesday."

"What!" Richie shouted, his voice hoarse and raspy. He groaned in pain.

Lucia grabbed Richie by the shoulders to console him. "Listen, it's Wednesday, but we still have plenty of time to get you there. It will be okay. Every time I tried to wake you up, you wouldn't budge. You did wake up at one point and looked straight at me, then you went back to sleep."

"I sure don't remember that."

"I figured you needed rest, so after that I let you be. You did almost get beat to death, you know. I went ahead and rented the room for another night since I didn't know when you would be getting up."

"Heaven knows I'd love to stay longer, but we don't have time to waste. Oregon is still a long ways off and now we don't have a way to get there."

"Could we get bus tickets?"

"They require an ID and we still need to stay off the radar."

"I saw a billboard for a truck stop when I was out earlier. Maybe we could hitch a ride with a trucker."

"You went out?"

"Yeah, after I realized you wasn't waking up anytime soon, and I was able to convince myself that you weren't going to die, so I went out for some food. I was freaking starving."

"Yeah, I guess you were. I cannot believe I slept that long. How far is the truck stop?"

"I think the sign said that it's about ten miles from here. Maybe we could get a cab or some other driving service to get us there, since you can't walk that far right now."

Richie nodded. "Sounds like a plan to me." He let out a pain-filled groan as he moved to get up.

"Here, let me help you." Lucia jerked the sheets off Richie. Just then, he remembered he wore a towel to bed from his bath so he was stark naked, but he hurt so badly that he didn't even care anymore about Lucia seeing him this way. She got under his left arm, grabbed him by the waist, and stood up with him. Richie continued to groan out from the pain. His ribs felt worse and occasionally took his breath, but at least they didn't seem to be broken, surprisingly enough. Lucia felt so bad for him, but she didn't hate holding on to his hard, athletic body. As they entered the bathroom, Richie caught a glance of his debilitated face in the mirror.

"Geez! I look awful!" Below his left eye was extremely bruised, above his right eye he was sporting a wide deep scratch, and he had a severe abrasion on his chin. He looked lower and saw several more contusions across his upper body. "I've carried plenty of bruises in my day, but nothing to this extent." He raised his left arm and saw a major scrape on his elbow. "That's why my arm is burning. Help me get in the shower." He slowly stepped into the tub while Lucia supported him.

"I can bandage your wounds when you get out. I figured it would be better for them to air out while you slept."

Richie sighed out in pain. "K. Find us a ride to the truck stop while I'm in here."

"Okay, I'll get you some food, too."

A while later, Richie was watching the breathtaking purple and orange sunset through his black sunglasses while leaning against the outside wall of the truck stop. His bandages seemed to blend in with his light-colored blue jeans and white Indian Motorcycles tee shirt. Lucia had patched him up good and got him fed. He was feeling a lot better, but still sore, but he at least felt somewhat rested and was now ready to get going.

Lucia trotted up to him. "I found a lady that might be willing to let us ride with her to Oklahoma City. She wants to see you though. She's nervous about letting one stranger in her truck, let alone two."

"Rightfully so. Where is she at?"

"Over here in the big truck with all the bulls." Lucia picked up Richie's heavy travel bag and he grabbed her pink suitcase. The two of them made their way over to the purple

Peterbilt road tractor-trailer. It stood out like a sore thumb from the shiny metal flake that was embedded in the custom paint job. The metallic finish glistened majestically from the setting sun. "I told her you got beat up in a car crash, so just play along."

"Okay. Whoa, you weren't lying about the bulls." Richie took in the sight of the powerful creatures through the slats of the livestock hauler. "That smell definitely gets your attention."

"It sure does, don't it!" A short, heavyset woman walked around the back of the worn and well-traveled trailer attached to her immaculate rig. "These bad boys are going to Vegas for the Bull Rider's Sin City Invitational this weekend." She walked up to Richie and thoroughly looked him over. "What's your name, cowboy?" She extended her hand.

"I'm Richie." He grabbed her hand that protruded from a green flannel shirt covered by a burgundy fisherman's style vest. He was surprised at how strong her grip was.

"Turn Around Sue at your service. You wasn't lying about how beat up he is, was ya missy?" She looked over at Lucia.

"No, ma'am, he got banged up bad in that wreck. "Why are you called Turn Around, if I may ask?"

"It's my handle. I got it years ago when I would run from one coast to the other, then turn around and come back. Good money, but it wore my ass out."

"What's a handle?"

Richie chimed in. "Her CB radio name." He looked at Sue and smiled. "My grandpa was a trucker."

"Was he a long hauler or did he do short runs?"

"He died when I was really young, but from the stories I've heard, it sounded like he did a good bit of both."

Sue gave a slight nod. "I usually don't give rides, but here's the deal. You seem like good folks, so I'll make an exception this time, so don't try anything funny. I'm a pistol-packing mama and I ain't afraid to give you lead poisoning. My next stop is Oklahoma City and we should get there around mid-morning. Either of you two carrying any weapons?"

Richie wasted no time responding to the serious woman. "No, ma'am."

"Why the hell not?" Sue's pale fleshy cheeks turned a light shade of red under her brown Farmer's Supply cap. "Especially this day and age and out here on the road."

Her response caught Richie off guard. "Uh, I've got guns, ma'am, just not currently on me. I haven't taken the time to get my concealed weapons permit."

"Well, you better take the time when you get home."

"Yes, I sure will, ma'am."

"Good, I'm glad to hear it. We're all filled up and fueled up. If anybody needs to tinkle, you better do it now. We won't be stopping for a long time."

"I'm good," Lucia said.

"I just went," Richie stated.

"Good, let's get rollin' then!" Sue expressed joyful excitement.

A very short time later, they were riding down the highway into the magnificent purple and orange sunset Richie was staring at earlier. Richie watched Sue work through the gears. She was a bona fide pro, and it was a very impressive sight.

"Boy, the sky is beautiful tonight, ain't it?"

"Yeah, it's breathtaking," Lucia said, agreeing with Sue's comment.

"Sorry you have to sit on that hard cooler, missy. They don't make bench seats in these rigs."

"It's okay, I'll be fine on it."

The hours slowly ticked by as Sue drove the semi deep into the night. Her mouth ran almost as much as the diesel engine in the eighteen-wheeler. She wasn't used to having company, so she took full advantage of the extra ears in her workspace. Richie dosed off and on. The jostling of the truck kept him from sleeping solidly. His ribs ached with every hard bump in the road. When Lucia got so tired that she could no longer fight sleep, she sat on the floor and placed her head on Richie's left thigh. It caught him off guard at first, but he delighted in the smell of her perfume. Gazing at her beautiful dark hair from the red glow of Sue's dashboard, it was all he could do to keep from running his fingers through it.

At a few minutes past two in the morning, Sue shouted out, "Okay, you sleepy heads, up and at 'em. This is our one and only stop 'til Oklahoma City, so you better do all your stretching, eating, and bathroom breaking now." The truck rumbled out a menacing howl as Sue flipped on the Jake brake, which released the built-up compression in the engine's cylinders and helped to slow the mighty behemoth as she downshifted through the gears.

"Hey, Ms. Sue, how long will we be here?" Richie inquired.

"This train will be leaving in exactly thirty-five minutes, so don't be late. It don't wait for nobody!"

"Okay, we'll be here," Richie said as he and Lucia were slow to exit the truck. The night air was cool, so Lucia grabbed her black feathered coat and a denim jacket from Richie's bag for him. They began walking toward a fast-food joint beside the truck stop while trying to stretch out their stiff bodies.

"What is going on over there?" Lucia asked.

"Sounds like someone is arguing?"

"Do you see that guy screaming in the drive-thru window?"

"What?"

"That man has gotten out of his car and is literally in the drive-thru window, screaming at the worker."

"That voice sounds familiar." Richie rubbed his eyes to get a better look. "No freaking way!"

CHAPTER 27

Drive-thru

Outfitted with a red polo shirt and gray slacks, a white man with neatly trimmed, dark-colored hair was leaning deep into the drive-thru window of the fast-food restaurant as Richie and Lucia approached. With a bit more effort, he could have possibly entered the building through the opening in the wall. Very agitated and angry, he yelled with extreme disdain at the worker wearing the speaker's headset.

"A prank? This ain't no prank, you stupid bitch!"

"Don't you talk to me like that, you walking turd!" The bold worker yelled back at the almost middle-aged man in self-defense. "Who in the world orders twenty cheeseburgers at two a.m. in the morning, anyways?"

"I'll tell ya who." He adjusted his rather large and outdated gold-framed glasses. "A man with a van full of hungry and pissed-off professional wrestlers, that's who! Why would we have sat here for twenty agonizing minutes if we were pranking you? Hell, apparently, you pranked us!"

As Richie and Lucia got closer to the fast-food establishment, he laughed out loud in disbelief. Then he grabbed his sides as they ached from the explosive vocal sounds he was producing from what he considered a very amusing sight. "That crazy son of a bitch is like that all the time. He doesn't have to get into character, he just has to be his insane self."

"What? You know this lunatic?"

"Yeah, I know him. Probably a little too well. That's Brilliant Jay Benson, also known as The Mouth of Memphis. He's a wrestling promoter, booker, manager, and anything else he needs to be on the independent circuit. He's had several different runs with the big leagues, but his mouth always gets him into trouble."

"Shocking." Lucia's reply held ample sarcasm and a blank expression to match.

The worker looked past Benson and carefully examined the van full of wrestlers and realized the apparent madman was surprisingly telling the truth. "I'm sorry, sir. Look, I really thought that this was a joke being played on us. It happens a lot here. If you'll come in, we'll give everyone in your party free milkshakes while we make your food."

"What other choice do we have? There ain't another blasted grease pit full of damned idiots for miles!"

"Please stop yelling at me, sir. I'm trying to correct our mistake."

"It's about damn time. I guess we're coming in then." He pulled himself out of the drive-thru window "Zac, park the van, we're going in." He then marched in a straight line toward the door.

"Sir, please keep it down or we'll have to call the police," Richie spoke in a phony, proper-sounding voice as he came up behind Benson.

Before the very lively and extremely outspoken man could turn around, he profusely yelled out, "Why don't you mind your own damned business and while you're at it, you can kiss—" Benson turned around to see his former pupil. "Richie, you sly bastard! What the hell are you doing all the way out here?" He grabbed onto him and gave him a big hug.

"Easy, easy. I was about to ask you the same thing."

"God a'mighty, don't even get me started!" Benson shook his head in disgust. "We just put on a show in some God-forbidden town earlier tonight and let me tell ya, we lost our asses! About twenty people showed up, if you can even call them that, and even less teeth. The guy that runs the armory there swore to me that he would have over four hundred people in attendance. So much for that, and then we got our dumb asses lost trying to get out of that hick town."

Richie chuckled lowly as he cordially patted Benson on the back sympathetically. "Dang, man. First, you lost your asses, then you got your asses lost!"

"I know. I guess that just makes us a bunch of dumb asses all around!" Benson burst out in laughter. "Holy hell, what a night it's been. Then after driving all around this crap bowl for hours, we finally found the only damned place open and the crazy bitch running the drive-thru thought we were trying to pull a prank on her."

"Yeah, so I heard."

"I love a good ribbing and I've been known to pull my fair share of them, but that's the last thing I wanted to do tonight." Benson noticed Richie's bruises and looked him over. "What the hell happened to you, son? Did Vaughn send you through a freaking meat grinder or something?"

"Not exactly." Richie slightly grinned and shook his head. "It's a long story."

"Hey, who's this sweet thing you got with ya, Rich? She'd sure make one hell of a valet." Benson's demeanor turned serious, as he looked directly at Lucia. "Hello there, baby doll. Say, your parents must have been beavers? Were they?"

Confused by that question, Lucia's brow furrowed. "No, why?"

"'Cause damn!" Benson laughed loudly and with a good bit of overzealousness at his own cheesy wisecrack.

"This is my friend Lucia," Richie slightly grinned and shook his head.

"Sorry, sweetheart, I couldn't resist. I got a million of 'em." Benson shrugged.

"Lucia, this is Jay Benson. He gave me some work before I got to the big leagues; taught me a lot about the wrestling business."

"Damn straight! Your sorry ass wouldn't have made it all the way to the top if I hadn't took ya under my wing for a while."

"That's probably true." Richie nodded in agreement.

"Here comes the boys. Why don't ya eat with us?"

Richie didn't hesitate. "Sure thing."

Lucia grabbed Richie's arm. "Wait, I need to say something."

"We'll be there in a minute Jay."

The van load of wrestlers made their way into the restaurant. He heard most of the young men whisper to each other, "Is that the Priest? Hey that's the Priest," as they passed by.

Once they were all inside, Richie gave Lucia a confused glance. "What is it? Something wrong?"

"What happened to keeping a low profile?"

Richie's eyes widened. "Oh, crap. I was still partly asleep at first and I couldn't believe what I was seeing. I totally got caught up in the moment." He grabbed his forehead. "I got it! Let's use the restrooms, then you get us some food while I shoot the bull with them for a bit. Then we'll hit the road and hope for the best. Even if Benson runs his mouth, it doesn't mean anything. He's one of the biggest liars in the business."

A few moments later, a very anxious Richie sat at a table beside Benson and the rest of the young wrestlers while Lucia stood at the counter, waiting for their food.

"So, you just up and quit? That's what the rumor is." Benson questioned Richie about his recent happenings at I.W.L.

Richie was disgusted at how fast news traveled in the wrestling industry. "Yeah, I wasn't jobbing out to Timberland. I really didn't mind him going over on me, but to let him bury my career, I just wasn't going to let that happen." The young wrestlers were hanging on to Richie's every word, except one. He was acting somewhat strange and was constantly checking his cell phone. Eager to find out who the young man was, Richie looked at Benson. "Why don't you introduce me to all these young fellas, Jay?"

"Sure thing, Rich. This lively lad is Zac the Heart Attack, that's Terrible Rex…" He went through all the performers' names. Then he finally got to the one acting strange. "That one there is Air Raid Aiden. He is one of your coworker's little brother at I.W.L."

"Oh, yeah? Who's his brother?"

"Overkill."

"Oh, wow, that's neat. Overkill is an awesome guy." Richie forced a fake grin. *Just great*, he thought. *A direct link to Vaughn is sitting here right in front of me.*

Just then, Lucia walked up with their food. "You ready, Richie?"

"Yeah, we better get going."

"You're not going anywhere," Aiden loudly declared in an undaunted tone.

Everyone stared at him with great confusion. Most of the young guys couldn't believe Aiden was talking to The Priest that way.

Benson looked at Aiden with confusion. "What the hell are you talking about, Aiden?"

"I just talked to my brother, Overkill, and he said Terrance Vaughn is offering fifty thousand dollars to anyone that brings The Priest in to him."

Surprised, but not shocked at that information. Richie knew that if Vaughn felt like he was wronged by someone, he would stop at nothing to get revenge. He tried to play it cool in front of the group. "What? That's crazy. What's he want with me? All I did was quit."

"That's not all you did! Not according to my brother! Rumor has it that you stole his car."

Richie played dumb. "What car?"

"The car that you drove out to the ring at Ruckus Among Us!"

Richie looked from Benson to Aiden. "Here I am on the backside of hell, having to hitchhike with truckers across the country. If I'd stolen Vaughn's car, I'd still have it. Do you see it out there in the parking lot anywhere?"

"That's only because he managed to get it back! My brother said he still wants to make an example out of you." Aiden stared at Richie.

"So, let me get this straight. You're going to kidnap me for something that you don't even know if I did or not, which is a felony, by the way, for a lousy fifty thousand dollars?"

"Fifty thousand dollars isn't too lousy to an independent professional wrestler."

"No, it's actually not lousy money to anyone, but it's certainly not worth committing a felony over."

"I ain't worried about getting charged with a felony. We all know Vaughn is above the law anyways. Besides, we also might get a contract with the I.W.L." Aiden stuck his nose up in the air with the cocky response.

Richie was prominent with his reply to Aiden. "So, you really are willing to commit a felony for something that trivial? You're actually risking your freedom just for a chance to work for a guy that would fire you in a heartbeat without a hint of remorse; a guy that would throw you under the bus and not even think twice about it."

Aiden just sat there with an arrogant smirk while his colleagues were simply astonished at the current situation that was unfolding right in front of them, as well as the surprising news from Aiden's older brother. They were now looking around at each other frantically.

Richie could sense things were heading south fast, so he tried reasoning with the young, inexperienced roster. "Look, gang, I get it. I know exactly what it's like being in you guy's shoes. You want to make it all the way to the top in this business and you want it so bad. You want it more than anything. All of you lay awake at night, visualizing being there. I know I did. You would do anything for a chance, anything. Let me tell ya right now, guys, and I'm one hundred percent serious. All that glitters is not gold." He pointed back toward the kitchen of the fast-food building. "You see those people back there? Those hard-working souls are probably happier right now than you would ever be working for Vaughn. Trust me, I know. I sacrificed my family for the chance to be there, and it wasn't worth it. Now I'm praying to God and risking life and limb to get across the country to save what I already had, but was too blinded by supposed success to even see that. I'd rather flip burgers for the rest of my life and go home to my beautiful family than to ever have to kiss the ass of a man like Terrance freaking Vaughn! I know how it is; right now you guys think you're better than everyone else, especially like the people making your food. Just because you perform in front of a crowd once or twice a week and take pictures with little kids doesn't make you better than them. Let me tell you right now, you ain't better than anyone!"

With a blunt response to Richie's heart-felt and informative speech, Aiden huffed. "Hey, that may be true, but I'm willing to find out for myself." He stared at Richie with even greater intensity than before.

Richie looked over at Benson. "Do you believe this kid, Jay?"

"I don't know, fifty thousand dollars is a lot of money, Rich. I lost over eighteen hundred dollars tonight." Benson now held a sinister look on his tired face. "Hey, are you going to cut us in on the money if we help you out, Aiden?"

Without taking his eyes off Richie, Aiden smirked. "You can have all the money. I don't give a damn about that. All I want is a contract with the I.W.L."

"All right then, did you hear that, boys?" Benson said to the rest of the wrestlers with a conniving grin. "We can split the cash amongst ourselves."

Richie was more angry than shocked and he harshly belted out to Benson, "I always knew you were a no good, worthless, backstabbing cutthroat!"

"Hey, it's just business, Rich, no need to get personal about. I always told you to go for the money; the rest is just useless details."

"Okay, I see how it is, then." Richie jumped to his feet without warning, and with lightning speed, he pulled his chair up in front of him and Lucia as if he were a circus lion tamer holding back ferocious animals. "Which one of you greenhorns wants it first? I hope you snot noses realize that it's going to take tougher sons of bitches than you to collect a bounty on me!"

The eager young wrestlers and Benson slowly rose to their feet, inching closer to Richie. Zac was the first one bold enough to attempt to grab him. Richie lunged forward and hit him with great force on his lower forehead, with the metal brace between the legs of the chair.

To Richie's left, Benson attempted to grab him as well, but Lucia planted a well-placed kick straight to Benson's manhood. He let out an ear-shattering scream and fell to his knees while desperately clenching the affected area. Then Lucia dumped a large chocolate milkshake on his head for good measure.

Zac groaned out in pain as well, and blood gushed like a geyser from the wound caused by the chair. "Ow! You busted me open, you asshole!" He was on the floor and some of the other wrestlers came to his side to check on him.

Richie took this opportunity to get to the door while holding the chair up as a shield from the now ravenous group of wrestlers while keeping Lucia behind him. "There's more where that came from!" He and Lucia backed out the door.

To Richie and Lucia's surprise, the distinctive sound of a tractor-trailer horn blasted from the road that was directly in front of the restaurant. Richie wasted no time placing the chair over the rectangle-shaped door handles, hoping to prevent it from being opened.

"Oh, no! Sue, wait, please, we're coming!" Lucia shouted out with great desperation as she ran toward their ride out of there while clenching the bag of food.

From inside the cab of the truck, Sue laughed at the sight of her late passengers scrambling to catch up.

"I told ya, this train don't wait for anyone!" she shouted out the window with a menacing laugh.

Richie was trying to run, but the pain from his injuries prevented him from moving as fast as he wanted to go. The wrestlers finally got the door open and were coming up behind him, and quick, too.

Lucia got to the side of the truck and continued to shout. "Sue, please stop. We're here! Please!"

Sue tapped the brakes on the truck, which caught the beefy bulls she was hauling off guard, making them lose their footing. This caused several members of the prized herd to let out various moans and moos. Even though she had slowed down the road tractor, it was still rolling at a very fast pace. As Lucia approached the passenger side entrance to the truck, she took a mighty jump and landed on the bottom step of the rolling rig, and promptly opened the door.

"Hey! Congratulations! Ya made it, Missy! You better tell ya boyfriend to hurry it up, though. He's falling behind."

Lucia hurriedly climbed into the cab of the semi and held the door open. "Come on, Richie, you're almost here. You got this!"

Richie was reaching down deep, pushing through the terrible pain and gasping for air. Unfortunately, there was no dodging the smell of the bulls' waste, as he breathed it in. One of the faster young wrestlers had pulled away from the pack and was hot on Richie's heels. Sue tapped the brakes and slowed the rig just enough for him to grab the shiny chrome handle on the truck's smokestack. Then he took an enormous leap with his left leg forward, placing his foot firmly on the bottom step.

"He's on go, go, go!" Lucia instructed.

"First you tell me to stop, then you tell me to go. Make up your mind, Missy!"

Before Riche could get all the way in, the speedy wrestler grabbed onto his jacket and was pulling at him with immense desperation. Lucia grabbed Richie's arm and was trying with all her might to pull him into the cab of the big rig, but the young guy had a solid hold on him. Richie's wounds severely ached, and he ewanted to punch the guy off of him, but the near paralyzing pain wouldn't allow him to do so.

Lucia leaned over onto Richie's back and started relentlessly kicking the guy in his face until he finally released his grip on the jacket. The youngster fell to the pavement and yelled out some harsh words toward the truck as she pulled Richie into the cab and closed the door. Sue had the hammer down and continued to gain speed.

"You got spunk, Missy! I like it!" Sue burst into laughter. "What did you do to piss them off?"

"I told them the second amendment wasn't just for hunting," Richie whispered out through his seemingly endless agony while trying to catch his breath.

Sue rolled her window down and yelled back at the gang of wrestlers. "Take that, you butt hurt commies!" She laughed out loud as they rolled into the night.

CHAPTER 28

Fanny Pack

"*So, how're things going with the veterinarian chick?*" The voice had come from John, who was underneath a small pewter-colored pickup truck. The loud clicking of a hand ratchet echoed throughout the garage. "*She's a real hottie.*"

Richie had stood, looking around the garage. "*It's going good. Where did you say the new filter was at again?*"

"*It's on top of my toolbox.*"

"*Oh yeah, got it.*" Richie grabbed the oil filter off of the large, red chest.

"*Don't forget to put a little oil on the new gasket.*"

"*Seriously, John, I know how to do that. You first taught me that when I was about seven. Plus, I've only done it a hundred thousand times since then.*" Richie did as his older brother asked, then handed the filter down to him.

"*Yeah, yeah. So, you going to marry her or what?*"

"*I had thought about it.*"

"*Is she okay with your career choice?*"

"*Well, she's not crazy about it.*"

"*I guess that's understandable. Does she know how hard you've worked to get to this point in your career?*"

"*Yeah, she totally gets it. She just doesn't want me to get hurt and be gone all the time.*"

"*That's all well and dandy, but you need to ride out this run to the max. Do it while you can. You never know when it will end."*

"Oh, don't worry about that. I'll stay at I.W.L. 'til they kick me out or I wear out."

"You're too tough to wear out." John came out from under the truck and stood up off his creeper.

"I don't know, man. They throw a lot of taters in the big leagues. Cameras are close and a lot more eyes watching. Gotta make it look good."

Just as Richie finished that statement, a car horn blew from outside.

"Sounds like your ride to the airport is here. Hey, listen, I'm real sorry I couldn't take you this time. I'm just way too busy today."

"Hey, I told ya it's no problem, man. I'm sorry I can't stay and help you out."

"Don't sweat it, little brother."

"I guess I'd better get going then."

"Hey, you do what you think is right. If you want to marry her, then go for it. I just want you to be happy. She seems like a real nice girl."

"She is." Richie picked up his bag.

"She'd have to be, to put up with your crazy ass." John punched him in the arm, then hugged him. *"See ya next—"*

∞

"Time to get up, kiddos. This ride is almost over. It's sure been fun having some company for once. You two are quite the troopers for listening to me all night. You even laughed at all my bad jokes."

Lucia rubbed her tired and dry eyes. "Wow, we're here already?"

"Almost, Missy, about five more minutes."

Richie groaned and tried to stretch out his aching muscles the best he could while still sitting down in the rigid passenger seat. "You always drive at night, Ms. Sue?"

"Sure do. Lot less traffic and I make way better time. I gotta be more careful though. The freaks come out at night."

"Yeah, I bet so." Richie shot Lucia a half-grin.

"I think it was on this very same stretch of road back in the early to mid-nineties; I had an incident with a real nut job."

Lucia's face developed a look of concern.

Richie's eyes widened. "Wow, what happened?"

"Well, ya see, it was a rainy beginning to my night. The sun was down, but there was still just a little bit of light left. I hadn't been driving commercially long at that point. I was still wet behind my ears."

Lucia's facial expression turned quizzical. "Why were your ears wet? Was the roof of your truck leaking or something?"

Sue and Richie burst into thunderous laughter, which confused Lucia.

"What? What's so funny?"

"*Ow*, my ribs." Richie painfully laughed at Lucia's lack of knowledge on this idiom. "It's an expression. Being wet behind the ears means you're new at something or haven't been doing it long."

"I didn't know! Stop laughing at me!"

"Calm down, Missy, we ain't making fun of ya. It was just a cute misunderstanding." Sue patted Lucia's arm. "Anyways, I hadn't been driving eighteen wheelers long, and it was cold that November night and pouring down rain. Just like in the song. I happened to see a young guy out walking in that mess on the road just up ahead of me. I felt horrible for him having to be out in such miserable conditions, especially at night. The company I worked for at the time had a strict no passengers rule, same as most companies, but I just couldn't do it. I couldn't leave that poor bastard out there that night. So, against my better judgment, I stopped and let him in. He was soaked to the bone and so appreciative, at first anyways."

"Had his car broken down?" Lucia asked.

"He didn't say. We got up the road a bit and he just sat there. Like I said earlier, it was the nineties, and fanny packs were popular and he had one, a black leather one."

Richie looked at Lucia. "Fanny packs were these bags you wore around your waist."

Lucia rolled her eyes and sucked her teeth. "I know what a fanny pack is."

Sue chuckled at the two and continued to tell her story. "Anyways, we were riding along and he was being quiet. I mean, real quiet. He just sat there, staring out the windshield, while playing with the zipper on his fanny pack. He kept unzipping it open a little ways then he would zip it back closed. He did it kinda slow, but real deliberate like. After a while of that, it started making me feel uneasy. He wouldn't really say much, just played with that zipper, back and forth, back and forth. Then, to make matters worse, the *Twilight Zone* song came on the radio. I usually love that song, but it ain't exactly what ya wanna hear when you think you might have actually entered the twilight zone."

Richie's and Lucia's eyes were glued to Sue. She had their complete attention.

"At first, I kinda felt that maybe my imagination was just getting away from me, so I thought I would try to break the tension just a little. So, I looked over at him and said, 'So, what ya got in the bag there, fella?' He sat there cool as a cucumber and said, 'Nunya damn business.'"

"What! That ungrateful ass!" Lucia yelled out. "What did you say back to him?"

"I didn't know what to say. I was floored by that comment. So, I decided to let it be for a minute or two, hoping the tension would ease up some. So, then I said, 'Look, I'm not going to judge ya or anything, but I could be held responsible for anything you have on ya, so I'd really appreciate it if you would tell me. What's in the bag?' He sat there for a second then looked at me and said, 'Nunya damn business.'"

"You've got to be kidding me!" Lucia exclaimed.

Sue looked at her. "That's exactly what I thought, too. I started praying and wishing I had a gun. That's the very reason I carry one now and always will, for that matter. I was all but panicking at this point. I thought, *What have I got myself into? What am I going to do?* I said to him, 'Look, mister, I didn't have to pick your ass up, you know. I'm going to ask you one more time and you'd better answer me! What is in the bag?' I said it real slow and forceful just like that and that bastard had the nerve to look at me dead in the eyes and say, 'Nunya damn business!'"

Lucia's eyes widened. The suspense was killing her and Richie.

"Oh hell, I was beyond pissed now, so I slammed on the brakes, and I hit them hard, too. I didn't know what else to do. The truck started going sideways as it began to jackknife. He almost flew into the windshield. My stuff came flying out of the back, and amid all the chaos that was breaking loose, I remembered that I had a screwdriver in my door panel next to me. So, I hit the go pedal hard and straightened the truck out before I brought it to a stop. Then I grabbed that screwdriver and I pointed it in his face and screamed, 'Get the hell out, now!' You shoulda seen his face. He was scared stiff, and he wasn't acting so tough now. After he got out, I went about my business. Took me a while to calm down, of course, but I did. The next morning, I was gathering up all my stuff from where it flew out of the back and there was that damned fanny pack! He was in such a hurry to get out that he forgot the thing!"

Sue turned on her turn signal along with the Jake brake once again and began downshifting. "Here we are, kiddos. This is our stop. I hope you've had fun. I know I have."

Richie and Lucia gave each other a look of disappointment from the quick and unsatisfying ending to Sue's story.

Richie smiled. "Thanks so much for the ride. We really appreciate it."

"And thanks for not leaving us behind last night," Lucia added.

"That was funny as all get out!" Sue laughed.

Richie and Lucia got out of the truck with their stuff and were standing beside it, looking in at Sue through the open door.

Lucia tilted her head. "Hey, Ms. Sue."

"Yeah?"

"What was in that guy's fanny pack?"

Sue looked down at her curious passenger with a very serious face and said, "Nunya damn business!" and broke out into tremendous laughter.

CHAPTER 29

A Stroll Through Hell

"It's going to be a scorcher today, folks. Record-breaking heat headed your way, so be sure to stay hydrated and keep yourself cool!" said the overzealous D.J. from the radio of a car that was getting filled up with gas. "In other news, the Word Meteorological Organization has released the list of names for the 2018 Atlantic Hurricane Season, which starts in less than a month. Among the names, some of the more notable ones are Alberto, Helene, Michael, Debby, and Florence. Aw man, we better watch out for Florence. I dated a girl by that name once and man, she was a real ball-buster, if you know what I mean. She was just so cruel, indecisive, and full of hot air."

"Ugh, what are we going to do? Of the few people that are here, they won't even consider giving us a ride or they are going east." Lucia sat down next to Richie on a metal bench in front of the gas station that Turn Around Sue had left them.

"I don't know. What time is it?"

"Eleven-fifteen. We've been here for almost an hour already."

"Good grief! And it's already Thursday! We are losing so much time." Richie placed his elbows on his knees and buried his face into his hands. His frustration was growing along with the outside temperature, which was making their matters continually worse.

"Maybe this isn't supposed to happen."

Richie sat back up and looked over at Lucia. "What are you talking about?"

"Maybe Mary doesn't need you to save her. Have you ever thought about that?"

A scowl-filled look came over Richie's face, and he stared intensely at Lucia. "This was never about saving Mary."

"What's it about then?"

Again, Richie buried his face into his hands. "I guess it's about saving me."

"Saving you? From what, Richie?"

He sat quietly, not wanting to answer, but Lucia wouldn't let the matter go.

"What is this saving you from?"

"From a life of loneliness and regret, okay! A life of watching a crooked politician raise my child. A life where I watch the only woman I've ever loved do all the things we planned to do together with someone else. There's your answer. Are you happy now?"

Lucia wanted to give Richie a shot of encouragement, but his detailed response left her speechless.

"Maybe you're right. Maybe this ain't meant to be. Maybe I should just stay away from Josie and keep her from having to go through that whole divorced parents' back-and-forth drama. It isn't fair for her to have to pay for my mistakes. Maybe I should just walk away."

"You don't have to be with Mary in order to be a good father, Richie. You deserve to be a part of Josie's life, and she deserves to know you. As bad as things were with my father, and as much as I hate him, at least I know. I know who he is. I know I don't want to be like him. I know where I came from. Josie deserves to know, too. Even if you walk away now, a time will come when she will find out this 'crooked politician' isn't her real dad. She will wonder who you are and why you weren't in her life. She will wonder if it was something about her you didn't like, or you regretted having her. You don't seem like the kind of guy that would want your baby girl to think or feel that way."

"Hell no, I don't want her to think like that. She's the best thing in my life. I've never loved anyone or anything as much as I love her."

"Well then, you can't walk away. But if things don't work out and Mary does move on, at least it doesn't mean you can't still have a wonderful relationship with Josie."

Richie sat there and thought with serious intensity. "You're right, but—"

A short, overweight man came out of the front door of the gas station, making his way over to them. "You drifters are going to have to beat it!"

Lucia said, "Excuse me?" as she and Richie gave him a baffled look.

"There ain't no excuse for ya! You two been harassing my customers by begging for rides and I ain't goin' to put up with it no more. Now get outta here now!"

"I'm sorry, sir, but we don't have anywhere to go at the moment." As hard as it was, Richie tried to show the contemptible man some respect.

"I don't give a damn. Leave here now!"

Richie tried to reason with him. "It's already in the eighties and getting hotter. Just let us call a cab or something and we'll be gone."

"Damn straight you'll be gone. They ain't no cabs around here, so beat your feet!"

"This is ridiculous!" Lucia exclaimed. "We're customers. I bought some items from you earlier!"

The rude man spoke loudly. "Well, you're costing me money now. If you ain't gone by the time I get back inside, I'm calling the sheriff!"

They both got up from the bench and grabbed their belongings.

Lucia shouted, "Thank you for your kind hospitality, sir!"

"Just start walking. We don't need him to call the police."

"This is total crap!" Lucia yelled out as they started walking west.

"What part of Oklahoma City is this? It sure is quiet. There's next to no traffic on this road."

Lucia shrugged. "We actually went past Oklahoma City. You were asleep when we did. Sue said she had to meet a guy out this way to do something with the bulls while she got some rest."

"Well, that's just great. Hopefully, someone will come along and give us a lift. Here, let's do this." Richie got out his Antique Archaeology cap and round sunglasses he wore to the ring and put them on. He gave Lucia his other sunglasses and handed her a cap with the I.W.L. logo. "Better put those on. This sun is brutal today." He secured her pink suitcase on top of his bag. "We can walk single file and carry our stuff front to back. I feel horrible making you help carry my heavy bag, but my injuries won't allow me to carry it by myself."

"It's okay. Maybe we won't have to carry it for too long. Thanks for lending me your sunglasses. I lost mine back at the junkyard." Richie gave her a nod, and they continued walking down the quiet, two-lane road. A while later, they stopped to take a break.

"Gah, it's so hot. What time is it now?"

Lucia looked at her watch. "Almost one o'clock. I'm glad I bought us some water before that asshole ran us off."

"I'd had you get us a lot more if I had known we'd end up out here. It's hard to believe that grass can even grow in this place." Richie stared out at the infinitely flat landscape. There was nothing but patchy brown and light green grass surrounding the sunbaked highway. "Does your phone have service?"

"Not at the moment. What are we going to do if no one stops?"

"Someone's bound to stop sooner or later. Have you ever been in a situation like this before?"

"Not exactly. My customers will at least drop me off at a rest area or something."

"Why do you think no one would give us a ride? Was it because of me?"

"Probably. They might have thought you were pretending to be beat up in hopes of getting sympathy. Then we would rob them after getting down the road."

"Makes sense, especially if they're like their fellow neighbor that was running the gas station. That clown woulda ran off baby Jesus." Richie reached into his bag and grabbed Three Stooges shirt he used earlier that week and stuffed some of it under the back of his hat and the rest hung down like a thin curtain, helping to protect his neck from getting burned by the blazing sun. "Do you need one?"

"No, I'm good."

"If you change your mind, let me know. I got so badly sunburned one time when I was a kid that my shoulders and back were covered in giant blisters. It was one of the most painful and agonizing times in my life."

Lucia's face snarled up. "That's horrible."

"Yes, it was. Nighttime was the worst. I couldn't lie down to sleep from the pain. When I would finally get exhausted enough, I would eventually sleep through it only to wake up stuck to the sheets from where the blisters had busted open at night. Every morning was a new fresh hell to go through detaching myself."

"My God, Richie! It sounds like you should have been in the hospital."

"Probably. I definitely had a new respect for the sun after that."

They continued their slow-paced walk in the staggering heat.

Something about this situation made Richie think of one of his favorite slow country songs. He let it play in his head and hummed along, trying not to think about how hot he was.

"Here comes someone!" Lucia dropped her side of the bag and desperately waved her arms as she walked out onto the road toward the vehicle.

It was a blue and white eighteen-wheeler coming up behind them. "Lucia, be careful." He was concerned for her safety as he watched the truck. It seemed to be coming up on them very quickly.

"Hey, hey, over here!" She walked out further to get close to the semi.

"Lucia, back up. That guy's going really fast."

The truck was approaching at a high rate of speed as it got closer to her.

She continued to wave her arms frantically. "Hey, slow down!"

The truck was barreling down toward her and showed no signs of stopping.

"Lucia! Get out of the road!" Richie ran toward her, causing his injuries to ache even worse.

The truck wasn't stopping or moving over. Just as it was going to hit Lucia, she dashed to the side of the road and fell into Richie's arms. "You freaking idiot!" She shook her fist at the speeding semi, then she yelled vigorously in Spanish.

Richie clenched her in a tight bear hug, as he was sure he would almost watch her die. "Lucia! Lucia, stop. He's gone."

"Can you believe that asshole?"

"You scared me to death! I thought you were dead."

She snapped out of her angered mindset and realized Richie was holding onto her in a panicked state. "I'm okay. I wasn't going to let that jerk hit me." She hugged him, since she was already in his arms. "I'm okay."

"K, good." Richie awkwardly broke their embrace. He wished he had held on for a moment longer. "I'm not sure if I am." He rubbed some of his wounds. "We better get going."

"Yeah." Lucia hung her head as she caught her breath, then began walking.

Richie tried to calm down from the potentially life-threatening incident and went back to humming the country song that was stuck in his head.

After almost two hours of traversing the shoulder of the burning blacktop, Richie's bruised body ached badly. He let go of his side of the bag and fell to his knees almost as fast as the luggage, and Lucia immediately did the same.

CHAPTER 30

A Groovy Mirage

"This is crazy," Richie muttered through his extremely dry lips. "I feel like we're in a spaghetti western, only we're not in a desert surrounded by sand."

"My feet are killing me."

"I can't believe we've only seen three vehicles this whole time. I really don't wanna die on a back road in Oklahoma." Richie tried to get up onto his knees.

"We have to be close to something. My feet hurt so bad that I—. Hey, look!" "There, coming toward us! Is it a mirage? Please tell me you see it, too."

An antique Volkswagen van, often called a VW Microbus, was driving east on the terribly hot two-lane road, coming straight toward them. Richie got to his feet as fast as his bruised and overheated body would allow and stumbled out onto the road, waving his arms in a slow but desperate fashion. The teal and white classic vehicle slowed, coming to a halt. The driver showed ample caution as he rolled down his window while peering with intensity through wire-framed glasses.

Richie pleaded with the somewhat older man. "Please, mister, can you give us some water and a ride? We have money, we can pay you. Please don't leave us out here. We've only seen three other people in I don't know how many hours now and they wouldn't stop."

Using his hand to shield the sun from his eyes, the slim gentleman could tell Richie had been out in the heat for a while and he watched Lucia struggle to get to her feet. His light apricot-colored hair was shining brightly. "Yeah, I can give you a lift. What are you two doing out here on a day like this, anyways?"

The driver then opened his door and the sounds of a classic love song rang out along with the cool air from the air conditioner.

Richie was quick in explaining how the grumpy old guy at the gas station had run them off and how the eighteen-wheeler almost ran over Lucia. After getting their stuff in the van, the driver gave them each a bottle of water from a cooler he had in the back. Richie sat next to the driver, sipping on his water, and Lucia was behind them, chugging hers down.

The man peered at Lucia in the rearview mirror. "Not so fast there, sweetheart. I've heard drinking too much water too fast can be bad for you, even fatal."

Richie glanced back at her. "He's right. There was a guy in the old west that actually managed to survive walking through Death Valley on one of its hottest days of the year. Then the poor man ended up dying by drinking too much water once he got back to civilization."

The driver looked at Richie. "Yeah, I read about that somewhere. Hell of a bad joke, isn't it? Survive one of the hottest places on Earth only to die from drinking water. I'm Howard, by the way."

"I'm Richie." He extended his hand and shook Howard's hand. "And that's Lucia."

"I can't believe that gas station attendant ran you guys off. Especially as hot as it is today."

"I can understand that he didn't want us harassing his customers, but he wouldn't even give us a chance to figure something out."

"Yeah, that's not very neighbor-like at all. Where are you two headed?"

"Originally, the plan was to get to Mt. Hood, Oregon, but I'm not sure where to go now." Richie looked back at Lucia.

"Well, my next stop is the Heart of Route 66 Auto Museum in Tulsa. I'd be happy to drop you off anywhere on the way."

"Okay, we really appreciate the lift and the water. Just please don't leave us at that gas station!"

"Don't worry, I won't." Howard chuckled as he shook his head.

Richie gazed out the window for a while as Lucia and Howard talked. He was watching them pass by where they had been trekking for the past couple of hours in the grueling heat. "I ain't gonna lie. It's terrible to watch us zoom right past where we were just walking."

"I bet so!" Howard responded.

"I ain't complaining, though. Your vee dub is awesome, by the way."

"Thanks. It's a sixty-seven Samba. It's had a Subaru engine conversion done on it along with upgraded suspension and brakes, and added A/C of course."

"It's damn nice, that's for sure. Did you do the work yourself?"

"Some of it. It was originally supposed to be a present to my mom and dad. They wanted to travel the U.S. in their golden years, but my father absolutely refused to accept it."

"How come? You did a fantastic job with it. You know, I've seen where some of these can go for over a hundred thousand dollars. If you ever tried to give me the keys, I probably would take your arm off with them."

Howard chuckled at Richie's statement. "Oh, it didn't have anything to do with the bus. He disowned me decades ago for, what's the best way to put it, adopting an alternative lifestyle."

"What? That's crazy," Lucia uttered.

"Yeah. He disowned me the second I made my announcement. For decades he went without speaking to me."

Richie spoke just above a whisper. "Wow, I'm sorry to hear that, man."

"Mom didn't mind at all. I was her only child, so she loved me to the moon and back, but not Dad. Anytime I would come over, he would lock himself in the bedroom 'til I left. So I finally stopped going over. I didn't want to make him feel uncomfortable in his own house. Besides, it really hurt my mother, being stuck in the middle. I didn't mean to cause them any problems, so after all the years of radio silence, so to say, that went by, I finally came up with a plan. A surefire plan that would get me back in their good graces. I decided that I would give my mom this very bus for her birthday that year. My dad had a lot of destinations he always talked about wanting to see and my mom loved these old VW vans, so I thought maybe I could make up for being such a disappointment to them by gifting them a way to follow their lifelong dreams; a way for them to have fun in their old age, a chance to get out and live a little. I had it all pictured in my mind. They would be so proud of me and so thankful for giving them something they always wanted, but boy did that bubble get burst."

"Geez, that's tough," Richie said.

"Yeah, that's awful," Lucia added.

"The thing that really got me about it all was that I didn't ask him for anything when it came to this decision. I didn't ask him to come to a wedding, change his outlook on life, nothing. I was still his son that tinkered out in the garage with him when I was younger. We watched ballgames together, but just because I had a different romantic preference, I was dead to him." Howard choked up a little, and a tear ran down his cheek. "God, I'm sorry, guys. You all just wanted a ride, not my life story." He nervously laughed and wiped his eye. "You two are just so easy to talk to; you're such a lovely couple. It feels like I've known you a long time."

Richie looked at Lucia and she was staring back, giving him a half-grin and looking down before saying, "You don't have anything to be sorry about, but your dad sure does."

"Yeah, he sure missed out," Richie said.

"It feels like I'm the one that missed out, though."

Richie sat quietly for a moment, thinking about Josie. He couldn't imagine disowning her. Especially over something so trivial. *Howard's father has to be a heartless bastard,* he thought.

Lucia leaned forward. "So you don't think there is any possible way to change his mind?"

Howard shook his head. "Unfortunately not. He's dead now."

"Man, I'm really sorry," Richie said.

Lucia reached up and patted Howard's arm. "So sorry for your loss."

"That's why I'm taking this trip. I'm spreading his ashes in all the places he wanted to see."

"Wow, you're a really good person for doing that. I don't know that I could have done that for my father. As a matter of fact, I know I couldn't."

"Well, Lucia, I figured that if I never forgave him, it would only hurt me and I'm dog tired of hurting, so I guess this is my way of getting over all this mess."

"How's your mom doing?" Richie asked.

"Not so good. She got sick and went into a nursing home not long after Dad died, so when I'm done with this trip, I'm going to go help with her and try to get her back home if possible. I don't want her to be in that place any longer than she has to be."

"You're a class act, Howard. I hope my daughter cares for me the way you have cared for your parents."

"Well, I appreciate that."

They rode in silence for some time after the heart-wrenching conversation.

"Wow, look at that sky. Looks like we got a big storm coming in," Howard pointed out.

Dark and threatening-looking clouds started forming in front of the blazing and, until now, relentless sun. Up ahead was a westbound car pulled off onto the shoulder of the worn-out road with a huge amount of white steam pouring out from underneath the hood. Two intimidating-looking strangers were standing next to it and they stared without faltering at the van as it approached. The shorter of the two men, dressed in a white tank top and dirty jeans, started waving down Howard.

CHAPTER 31

Going My Way?

"What is it, National Hitchhiker's Day?" Howard snickered.

Richie replied in a slow, low tone as he scanned over the men. "These guys look like they could be rough company."

"Yeah, that they do, but we can't leave 'em stranded out here in this heat. We'll at least see what they have to say." Howard slowed the van down and pulled up next to the broken-down sedan.

The taller and older of the two men approached the van first. He was wearing a black slim-fitting tee-shirt with tattooed covered arms protruding from the sleeves and beige cargo pants. He was a stocky Caucasian man that looked to be in excellent shape for his older age.

Richie looked back at Lucia. She had dozed off.

Howard rolled down the window. "Looks like you got some car trouble."

Richie observed the man. He had a powerful, no-nonsense presence about him.

"Yeah, just too hot out here today."

"I'm on my way to Tulsa. I'd be happy to drop you off somewhere on the way there."

The man took a long, hard look toward the east. Richie got an even better look at his face. He had a strong jawline with a cleft chin that molded up to a salt-and-pepper-colored crew cut that was heavy on the salt. His dark eyebrows sat over even darker and somewhat familiar eyes. He looked back at Howard with an even more intense look. "No, that won't work. I'm headed west."

"Oh, well, I'm sorry to hear that, but it's a long way before you get anywhere going west on this road. You should just let me drop you off at a gas station that shouldn't be too much farther up this way." Howard pointed east.

"Are you deaf or just plain stupid? I said that won't work. I'm headed west!" Veins protruded from his forehead and neck area as he grew increasingly aggravated at Howard.

Suddenly, Howard had a very concerned look on his face as he glanced over at Richie. "Okay, then. Good luck to ya."

The now angered man pulled a massive chrome-colored pistol from behind his back and pointed it at Howard's head. "Get out!"

Dumbfounded at what was now transpiring, Richie looked back at Lucia, who was beginning to stir.

Howard was hesitant but started slowly moving from the van. "You don't have to do anything crazy. I can take you wherever you want to go."

The angered man grabbed Howard before he had fully exited the van and threw him to the ground without the slightest signs of compassion.

Richie thought, *I can't let this happen*, and dove through the driver's door, grabbing the gunman, ensuring a scuffle.

The younger guy, seeming to be of Latino descent, now had pulled out a handgun as well and had the black weapon pointed at Richie, but he couldn't get a clear shot as the two fought for the gun. Howard got back to his feet and grabbed the man's gun, attempting to pull it from his hands.

Richie tried desperately to get the gun from the older guy and almost had it, but he connected with a well-placed punch to his injured ribs. This allowed him to push Richie up against the van and he placed his pistol to his forehead.

This is it, I'm dead, Richie thought.

Then a deafening shot rang out and, to Richie's surprise, the older guy screamed profusely. The gun from the younger man in the white tank top had gone off from the struggle with Howard and fortunately for Richie, this seemed to have saved his life. The bullet landed in the older guy's right thigh, which he grabbed in pain. This allowed Richie to plant a haymaker on his left cheek, sending him flying to the ground.

Caught off-guard from the discharge of the gun, this gave the guy in the tank top a chance to overtake Howard, so he performed a reckless headbutt to his nose. As Howard went staggering backward, his attacker pointed his gun straight at his head and pulled the trigger. Another deafening shot rang out, and Howard's body went limp, collapsing to the ground.

"No!" Richie yelled as he lunged toward the younger guy. He nailed him in the neck with a clothesline as if he was an opponent in the wrestling ring. The guy in the tank top landed hard on his back. Richie looked at Howard's lifeless body and went into a complete fit of rage. He stomped and kicked the young guy. Wanting him to pay for the senseless act of killing Howard, he grabbed the guy's legs and stepped over one, then crossed the other leg back over his own, tucked his feet up under his right arm, and rolled him over onto his stomach. Richie sat on the guy's lower back while pulling his legs toward his head, placing him firmly in a scorpion hold. Richie had performed this move on several occasions in various matches, but never with such an intent as to inflict real and damaging pain. The guy in the tank top screamed as his lower back felt as if it could snap in half at any moment. Simultaneously, the scorching hot pavement burned his arms and chest.

Just as Richie thought he was going to feel the bones of the young guy break beneath him, without any warning, he felt a pistol pressed against his temple with extreme force.

"Adios, asshole." The older guy had made it to his feet and snuck up on Richie.

"Papa, no!" Lucia came running from in front of the van.

"Papa?" Richie mumbled. Completely bewildered by Lucia's remark, Richie let go of the guy that was trapped in his clutches.

The older guy backed off Richie while keeping his gun pointed at him. "Lucia!" A look of shock enveloped his face. "I've spent the better part of three years searching for you! Three Years! Where the hell have you been?"

"Avoiding you!" she cried out with ferventness. Then, with noticeable caution, took a few steps back.

"Why? I'm your father. Why would you run from me?" He lowered his gun and grabbed his leg wound.

"Because of that!" She waved her left hand at Howard. "Death follows you like a loyal shadow and I just couldn't take it anymore!"

Flabbergasted, it was too much for Richie to take in all at once. A perfectly nice man who helped him was just murdered right before his very eyes, and his new friend's father was responsible. *This isn't real. It can't be*, he thought. The young guy that he had beaten senseless was starting to stir, so Richie resumed brutally kicking him.

The older guy lifted his gun toward Richie. "Papa, no! He's famous. If you kill him, you're sure to get caught."

"Why? Who is he?"

"He's a famous wrestler. He works for Terrence Vaughn. You can't kill him."

Seeing the gun pointed at him, Richie held his arms out and stood still, staring at the man. After hearing Lucia say that he'd be caught, it dawned on him who the wanted man could be. "Oh, I think I know who you are." He leaned toward Lucia's father and gave his face another hard look. "You're the P.M.S. guy that's been on the run since the eighties. I saw you on TV. I knew you looked familiar. I can't believe this is your father, Lucia. No wonder you didn't want to talk about him."

The angered man went over to Richie with an air of great determination, dragging his injured right leg behind him. Once again, but with even more force, he put his large chrome-colored gun up to Richie's head. "My name is Peter Mitchell Simms! Call me P.M.S. again and I'll blow your damn brains out of that sorry bucket you call a head regardless of who you are!"

Richie stared into his eyes. The urge to take the gun from the wanted man was massive, but he was just too close. An almost angelic image of Josie came into his head, so he figured he would play it safe this time and do as the desperate criminal told him to.

"Please, don't, Papa. All he wants is to get back to his family!"

He lowered his gun. "Look what you've done to poor Chico! Get him in the van! Lucia, get those bags from the trunk."

"Why should I? What in the blue hell makes you think we're going with you?"

Richie tossed Chico into the van as if he were tossing an opponent out of the ring. Something he had done countless times in his wrestling career. There was a muffled moaning sound that followed a deep thud.

"Look, Lucia, we're taking the van. What other choice do you have?"

"I'd rather die out here than go anywhere with you, you murdering monster!"

Her statement seemed to have struck a nerve with Simms. He stared straight into her eyes and spoke through his now clenched teeth. "Get in the damn van now or you'll watch me kill at least one more worthless bastard!" He menacingly peered over at Richie. He bent over, getting ready to grab Chico's 9-millimeter. "Hold it right there, Billy Badass." Simms aimed the gun at him.

CHAPTER 32

Two's Company, Four's a Crowd

"So, where's your family at, uh, what was your name?" Simms asked with heavy insincerity from behind the driver's seat of the van with his pistol on his lap at the ready.

"Richie." He had a deep feeling of repugnance while driving west, past where they were walking in the staggering heat, yet again. He did notice, though, that he really liked driving Howard's van, but certainly not like this. Not under these circumstances, especially not when his dead body lay just off the road after being senselessly murdered by a couple of maniacs.

"Ah, Richard. I knew a guy named Richard once. He was a real Dick." Simms sarcastically laughed. "Bet you never heard that one before, have ya, Richard."

Richie ignored his half-witted comment and thought, *Hey, at least my initials ain't P.M.S., you stupid asshole.*

Then Lucia answered for him. "Mt. Hood, Oregon, is where he's going."

"Mt. Hood? That's perfect 'cause I'm on my way to Seattle. You can drive 'til then, Richard. Especially since I've got a bullet in my right leg and probably can't press the gas pedal anyways. As a matter of fact, I know I can't."

Guess I'm bound for Mt. Hood after all, Richie thought. *I can't believe I even thought about not going. Doesn't matter much now anyways. It will probably take nothing less than a miracle to come out of this alive.*

Lucia turned around and looked at Simms' leg. His right pant leg was no longer beige, but blood-soaked from his lower thigh to his ankle. "You can't go that far without getting your leg fixed first."

"It's not that bad. Hurts like hell, but it missed the femoral artery, so I should be okay. I'm glad it was a 9-millimeter and not my Desert Eagle that hit me. I wouldn't have a leg left if it would have been. Have you ever shot a .50-caliber handgun, Richard?"

"No."

"Then you don't know your guns. It's a man's weapon." Simms remarked with a cocky smirk.

"Why are you going to Seattle?" Lucia asked.

"I've got some official business to take care of. I've had a lot of that this year. That's why I'm back on TV. Some ol' hag that saw me on *America's Most Wanted* thirty-something years ago just happened to recognize my face at a juice bar and notified the cops. Damn that John Walsh!"

Lucia rolled her eyes back in disgust. "Then why didn't you just go back home for a while? Why be out here, risking getting caught?"

"Because certain individuals tried to screw me and my business over, so now they are being taught an important lesson. The bastards have to be put in their place. Speaking of business, what the hell have you been doing this whole time? And where? I've been worried sick about you."

"What does it matter? I'm no longer one of your concerns."

"You're my daughter, my flesh and blood. Of course, you're my concern!"

"Words, words, just words that don't mean anything! You throw them around like you do your blood money and corrupt power."

"That's not true! All I ever did was try to take care of you and your mother."

"All you ever did was keep us locked away because of all the enemies you made! And you couldn't even do it right or, or—" Lucia stopped talking.

Simms leaned up closer to the front of the van and yelled, "Or what? Or your mother would still be alive?"

"Yes!" she hollered, flinging her arms.

"Your mother stopped doing as I said. It's a miracle you're still alive!"

"She was tired of being a prisoner in her own home. She couldn't take the kind of life you forced on us anymore! She said she would rather be dead than continue to live that kind of life!"

"Well, she got her wish! You two ingrates didn't appreciate anything I did for you. I gave you everything and you couldn't care less. I grew up with nothing! My mother was a nobody from Jersey that moved to Hollywood, hoping to become a movie star and she ended up becoming a crack whore! Guess who paid the price for that? I was bounced around every foster home and went through every orphanage in Southern California."

Lucia's demeanor changed, and she grew quiet for a moment. "I never knew that."

"I didn't have time to tell ya 'cause I was too busy clawing and scraping so that you didn't have to grow up like I did!"

Lucia sat quietly and stared out the window for a moment. She was truly shocked by Simms' last statement. "I'm sorry you grew up like that, but look what you've done since then. Look at how many people you've killed. How can I be grateful knowing how much pain you've inflicted on the world?"

Simms shook his head, and then he now stared out of the window. "What about him?" He nodded toward Richie. "What are you doing with him? Is he your boyfriend?"

Richie looked at Lucia, curious what she was going to say.

Chico blurted out before she could answer, "He's a punk-ass bitch."

"Really?" Simms looked over at Chico. "He beat your sorry ass like a bass drum. Is that what you're going to tell everyone? I got my ass beat by a punk-ass bitch?"

Chico looked down in embarrassment and shrugged.

"Keep your mouth shut, Chico. I don't pay you to talk." Simms looked forward. "Judging from the way he's bandaged and bruised, I'd hate to see the other guy."

"Three. Three other guys."

Simms looked from Lucia to Richie with a look of astonishment on his face. "Wow, impressive. I guess you really are a Billy Badass." He returned his gaze to his daughter. "So, are you going to tell me why you're with him or what?"

Richie looked over at Lucia. "Go ahead. It doesn't matter much now. We're all headed in the same direction."

Lucia filled her father in on all the details as they continued west. The sky was slowly growing darker as the storm continued to roll in at a slow and menacing pace.

Moments later, after being brought up to speed on their story, Simms looked out of the window. "Wow, I'm impressed. A man that can take matters into his own hands. You remind me of me."

Richie's face turned into a scowl. "I'm nothing like you."

"You might be right because I wouldn't have lost the car."

Richie tightly gripped the steering wheel and clenched his teeth. *It's no wonder people want to kill you,* he thought.

"The feds were crawling all over the place. What else were we supposed to do?" Lucia explained.

"You should have already had any tracking devices disabled by then," Simms spoke in a condescending tone.

Lucia continued to defend their actions. "He thought Vaughn would still be in Europ—"

"It's okay, you don't owe him an explanation."

"He's right." Simms nodded. "I guess it's a good thing he didn't know what he was doing or we might not have been picked up back there. Howard, was that his name? Probably wouldn't have stopped to talk to us if he hadn't had you two with him."

Richie gripped the steering wheel even tighter.

"We've got to get rid of this stupid mystery machine soon. We stick out like a nun in a strip club in this thing. I don't know why anyone would want a piece of old crap like this."

Richie looked at Simms in the rear-view mirror. "Some of these old vans can go for over a hundred thousand dollars. You don't know your cars, do you?"

CHAPTER 33

Kickin' It On 66

The foursome continued driving west into the early signs of dusk, and they were now on Route 66, just as Lucia and Richie's friend Bud had suggested. It was pretty much like he said, little to no traffic, with a few exceptions. They had been passing by old buildings, antique gas stations, and many other historical landmarks as they drove through several dried-up ghost towns.

Richie took his eyes off the road for a split second, to glimpse Lucia. "John woulda loved this. He always wanted to travel on Route 66 and check out all the sights."

"Haven't you ever been on it? I figured with all the traveling you do, you'd seen just about everything there is to see by now."

"The insides and outsides of airports, arenas, motel and hotel rooms is about the extent of it. The schedule just keeps you too busy to enjoy much of the surroundings. It sounds like we are always on vacation, but nothing could be further from the truth. Sometimes we can squeeze in a little sightseeing, but it's not that often."

"All this nostalgic crap is so stupid. Every bit of it should be bulldozed down and done away with," Simms said in a presumptuous tone.

Lucia frowned. "Why?"

"It doesn't do anybody any good. It just romanticizes a crappy past and makes people delusional of the real truth."

Richie shook his head. "What truth are you talking about? Besides, how are we supposed to know where we are going if we don't know where we've been?" Richie asked.

Simms sat up in his seat and continued to talk haughtily. "First off, the only place we are really going is a hole in the ground or a furnace to be burned. Second, when we hold on to stupid traditions and ways, we only get further from the blunt truth of that. People go around saying this is how Granny done it or this is how Grandpa believed. Doing something or believing a certain way just because it's always been that way doesn't make it magical, or even right, for that matter. Take this antiquated road, for example. Do you think the poor folks that were forced to travel this road in order to escape the dust bowl thought this place was so great? To them, it was a damned alleyway that took them from one crappy existence to another as they left all their dreams and farms that they had all worked so hard on behind. But you think we should preserve that and say how neat it all is."

Richie looked at Simms in the rearview mirror. "Wow, you really know your history."

"Just because I don't like something doesn't mean I don't know about it."

"Those examples you just gave are the very reason we shouldn't forget the past. We need to know how things were and how people believed in the past so we can make a better future."

"It's impossible to make things better in this godforsaken place. We are thrown to the wolves, then thrown into a hole. There is simply no need to glorify this insanity."

Richie kept his eyes on the road, as he figured there was no need to further that conversation with him.

Lucia looked over her shoulder, into the backseat. "Are we going to get a room or something? I'm starving and your leg needs bandaged."

Simms looked down at his leg and nodded. "Yeah, find us a room close to a restaurant."

Chico looked over at Simms. "How do you know she won't text the cops or something?"

"Because her new boyfriend is dodging the police as well. If she brings the heat on us, then she brings it on him. Did you two hear that? We're all in this together for the moment, so we might as well work as a team for now. Do you have any problems with that, Richard?"

"No, but I do have a problem with your boy, Chico. I don't like the way he has been eyeing me and I'm telling you right now, if he tries something stupid, I won't hesitate to break his murdering ass in half."

Simms looked at Chico. "Knock it off, dumbass. If you do try to pull a stupid stunt, I'll let him have at ya. Is that clear?"

Chico looked down and barely nodded his head.

Tilting his head, Simms was unsatisfied with his response. "I said, is that clear?"

"Yes, sir!"

Moments later, they pulled into the parking lot of a motel in McLean, Texas, marked with a large cactus sign that read: The Cactus Motel.

Chico looked up at the sign. "The Cactus Motel? Looks more like the Apocalypse Inn. Is this place even open?"

Lucia looked up from her phone. "Yeah, the instructions on the website said to get a key from the box and someone will come by soon to take our money."

"Grab the key for this room upfront. What's the number, is that a 7?" Simms said.

Lucia nodded. "Yes."

Running the show, Simms barked out orders. "Okay, Chico, stay here in room 7 and pay with your fake I.D. and credit card when the people come. Lucia, also grab the key for that room at the very back corner."

Lucia squinted. "Looks like room 22."

"K, grab it, too. We'll be back with food soon, Chico. Let's get rolling, Richard."

Chico exited the van and headed to the room.

Richie looked in the rearview mirror. "Where am I going?"

"Let's go back to that Red Rock River Steakhouse, or whatever it was called, that we passed a short ways back."

Moments later, Richie pulled into the steakhouse's parking lot. Simms handed Lucia a wad of cash. "Here, get Chico a burger with steak fries, and I'll have a Caesar salad with no croutons or chicken and get whatever you two want."

"Well, what do you want?" Lucia looked over at Richie.

"A burger will be fine."

"K, I'll be back." She opened the door to exit.

"Hey, wait! Give me your cell phone."

Lucia shot Simms a frustrated look.

"Just in case you get a little too anxious, I'll hold it for you."

Aggravated, Lucia handed it to him, slammed the van door close, and headed toward the restaurant entrance.

"Just like her mother. Always doubting my intentions."

"Just what are your intentions?"

"To keep us all from getting caught by the police at the moment."

"Then what, though? After I get off this crazy train in Mt. Hood, assuming you let me, what are you going to do with Lucia?"

"I'm going to see that she is taken care of. Why? Do you think I won't hold up my end of the bargain and let you go?"

"Is that what you call kidnapping someone? A bargain?"

"This isn't so much a kidnapping now as it is a partnership. There's absolutely no good reason that we shouldn't work together for the common good of us all."

"I stole a car from a man that ripped me off. This is the worst thing I've ever done and by no means should I be working with you towards a common goal. You're a hardened criminal and a murderer."

"That is the very reason you need me. You're on the lam, or at least very well could be! Who better than me to help you get to where you're going?"

Richie pointed his finger at the rearview mirror. "No, I ain't agreeing to any kind of partnership. If we do get busted, I ain't going down as your accomplice."

"Look, for one, we're not going to get busted. I've done this far too long and I know exactly what I'm doing. For two, if by some freakish strange luck the cops do manage to get their hands on us, why would I take my baby girl and her associate down with me? I've done unspeakable things in order to provide her with a life that I didn't have. The last thing on the face of the Earth that I would ever want to do is see her put behind bars."

"Her sure, but why wouldn't you take me down with you?"

"It would kill her if I did that. I see the way she looks at you. I've only ever seen her look at one other person like that." Simms looked out the window, watching the rain finally fall after threatening to rain all evening. "Anyways, just chill out and trust me. I understand that's a lot to ask, but you will get to Oregon and you won't go down with me."

CHAPTER 34

I Will Rock You

Sometime later, they sat in room 22 of the Cactus Motel, finishing up their meals in the dark.

Lucia shoved a fry into her mouth. "So, why can't we turn on the lights or the TV again?"

Simms swallowed a forkful of Caesar salad. "Because that van is now a lightning rod for attracting the cops. I'm sure they have found the body of the guy that Chico shot and there will be an APB out for it. They won't expect us to be back here. They will think whoever stole it took off."

Richie shot an ill look at Chico. "How do you know they don't have cameras?"

"'Cause they are so cheap here that they don't even have a full-time worker for the office, much less cameras. Plus, I checked when we first pulled up. Everyone hurry and do what you need to in the bathroom and get some sleep. We'll be leaving around four-thirty a.m. Chico, did you get all of our bags out of the van?"

"Yes, sir."

"What about you two? Did you get all your stuff?" Simms looked at Lucia.

"Yes, but what about your DNA? I'm sure your blood is all in the back seat."

"Chico will take care of it first thing tomorrow if they don't come before then. We'll just have to chance it for now."

At 5:23 a.m., Simms was now waking everyone up on the early Friday morning. He cracked the bathroom door open and turned on the light so everyone could see. Richie was still sore and ached from his wounds. Now added to that was an annoying sunburn on his forearms and face below where his sunglasses sat. Before they lay down to sleep the night before, Lucia had changed his bandages for him after wrapping up Simms' leg. Richie slipped into a dark blue pair of jeans and a black shirt that had a black-and-white picture of his face, wearing his trademark glasses that had red reflections and a white cross in them. The words "The Priest" were below his face, and on the back, in red letters outlined in white, it read: "Mercy is not an option," one of his famous catchphrases. Now that Simms had basically kidnapped Lucia and him, he was hoping to be noticed. He didn't trust Simms for a second, and he thought if he was recognized by someone, they could notify the authorities.

"Hurry up! My alarm didn't go off! Get the beds made. We have to make it seem as if no one was in here!"

Making up the beds, Lucia slapped the pillow. "Where are we going?"

"A few streets over to that old Phillips 66 gas station. There's a blue sedan for us there. Chico, don't forget those bloody towels. Make sure they get put in the van and don't forget to put the key back in the box."

"On it." Chico slipped out the door. He still had a noticeable limp from the beating Richie had given him.

Richie turned and stared at Simms, barely able to make out his face from the bathroom light. "What's he going to do with that van?"

"What's it to you?" Simms returned a stare of his own. "Now get your crap. We have to be ready to bolt out of here once he's done."

Richie grabbed his bag and stormed past Simms on his way out. At that point, he dropped his bag and went toward the van. Chico had a small bottle and was squirting the contents all over the inside from the side cargo door.

"What the hell are you doing?" Richie shouted at Simms' henchman.

Surprised, Chico looked up at him, flicked a chrome lighter, and with caution, tossed it into the van. After an intense whoosh , the van engulfed into a raging inferno.

"No! You idiot!" Richie was now sprinting toward the fiery sight. Once he got to Chico, he punched him with a glancing blow, causing him to stumble back a few feet before falling onto his backside. Richie was frantic as he scanned the van, then the surrounding area. He spotted a rather large landscaping stone and wasted no time grabbing it.

Caught off guard by the entire incident, Simms made his way over to the van and Lucia was right on his heels. "Knock it off now! We gotta go!"

Richie finally spotted what he was after in the van. He hoisted the rock up over his head and threw it directly against the back glass. It bounced off after cracking the glass and almost landed on his feet.

"Come on, Richie! What are you doing?" Lucia cried out to him.

He picked up the heavy stone and, once more, hoisted it up, and, with all his might, threw it at the cracked back glass, sending it flying inside the van, as shards of the glass exploded. With the van engulfed in flames, Richie was quick and careful as he reached in to grab a shiny gray-colored brass urn. After two failed attempts, he finally got a good enough hold on it and pulled it out as the flames completely consumed the vehicle and black smoke blanketed the surrounding area.

"You freaking idiot! If you try something else like that again, I won't hesitate to shoot you on the spot where you stand!" Simms ran away from the intense flames, stopping only to grab their bags.

As they approached the gas station, while trying to catch their breaths, Lucia touched Richie's arm. "Is that the ashes of Howard's father?"

"Yes."

"Why did you risk getting hurt to get them? He sounded like a terrible man from what Howard told us."

"I didn't get them for him. I got them for Howard. He was on a mission to spread his dead father's ashes, so it's the least I can do for him."

Simms looked up at the sky, with clenched teeth, showing his frustration. "You have got to be kidding me! You are risking getting us caught and putting us further behind schedule for that? That's so stupid."

Richie cut his eyes at him. "No, what's stupid is killing a man for no good reason then topping it off by burning down his beautiful antique van he built for his parents!"

"I'm only going to tell you this once: keep your mouth shut and do exactly what I say or I will shoot you!"

Richie got into Simms' face. "You ain't going to shoot me! You woulda already done it if you were going to. Now that you're injured, you need me to help you to Oregon, 'cause your boy Chico there is too incompetent to get the job done!"

Simms pulled out his massive handgun and hit Richie across the face with it.

"Papa, no!" Lucia shouted as Richie hit the ground.

Simms bent down and got into Richie's face. "You're right. Chico is a little too young and incompetent for my liking. And I get that you're a badass, but you ain't ever went up against anyone like me. No, I don't want to shoot you, but that is your absolute last warning. I will literally blow your brains out of your head if you don't do as I say. Please don't make me do that in front of my little girl. Now get up and drive us to our destination. Is that clear?"

The left side of Richie's lip was trickling a small amount of blood and swelling up. He was still seeing a few stars as he sat up and thought, *Okay, he's pissed off, but I still don't think he will shoot me. I better play along though, so I can hopefully get him caught at some point. I can't risk getting killed while trying to take him out by myself, as long as Chico is still in the picture.* "Only on one condition."

"I don't think you're in a position to be making conditions."

"A request then."

"What?"

"I have to be in charge of the radio if I'm driving."

With a look of disapproval and annoyance, Simms shrugged. "Fine, now let's go! I hear sirens off in the distance."

CHAPTER 35

"Dyeing" for Success

*"A*re you sure you want to do this?" Mary had a look of concern on her face.

Richie handed her a box of black hair dye. *"Well, not really, but I have to if I'm going to work for Vaughn."*

"So, you're going to be like a mean preacher? I don't get it." She opened the box and looked over the instructions that were packed inside.

"A priest that's kinda evil. It's like he's self-righteous and judges others for their shortcomings. Instead of letting God do His work, he tries to do it for Him; a spiritual vigilante of sorts."

"Sounds like a hypocrite to me."

"Yeah, I guess you could put it that way. I'm not crazy about this gimmick either, but if I want to work in the big leagues, I'll just have to deal with it."

Mary handed him a towel. *"Here, put this around your neck."* She put on a pair of rubber gloves that came with the hair dye kit. *"Have you told John about this yet?"*

"Oh yeah, he's excited to death. He's not been this happy since he got his new leg."

Mary began working the dye into his hair. *"This is going to be kinda weird."* She laughed.

"What, are you going to break up with me if you don't like it?"

"Probably." She laughed again.

"Gee, thanks. That's okay. I hear there's all kinds of groupies lurking around backstage once you get on TV."

Mary punched this shoulder. *"You better watch it, mister."*

"So, what, we're exclusive to each other now?"

"I hope so. Don't you want to be?"

"Depends on how bad you screw up my hair." He let out a big laugh.

"You better be nice or I'll shave it all off."

About thirty minutes later, she tapped him on the shoulder. *"Let's go over to the sink. It's time to rinse it out."*

Richie bent over the large lavatory. *"Is this where the dogs get washed?"*

"Yep, so you're right where you belong."

"Very funny. Is old man Sheppard still going to sell you this place when he retires?"

"That's what he says, but I hope it's not for a long time. This is the biggest and oldest veterinary clinic around. There's so much to learn. I'm not sure I can handle it."

"Sure, you can. You're the smartest chic I know."

Mary handed him a towel. *"All done. Let's see how it turned out."*

Richie wasted no time drying his hair, then he rose from the sink. *"Well, how does it look?"*

"Oh my, it's hideous!" She grabbed her cheeks.

Richie looked worried. *"No, come on, Mary. Stop screwing around. Tell the truth."*

"It's awful!" She tried not to smile.

"Give me a mirror, Mary."

Mary handed him a mirror.

He carefully looked the new dye job over. *"It's not that bad, just a little darker. You had me scared to death!"*

Not able to hold it back any longer, she busted out in laughter. *"Yeah, I guess we can still date."* Richie dashed toward her. She let out a half scream and started running from him while uncontrollably laughing. He was hot on her heels as she cried out, *"Not so fast! Slow—"*

∞

"Down Richard. I know what you're up to," Simms said.

The foursome was still driving in the low-key blue sedan that Simms had ordered from one of his associates. When it was possible, or feasible, they stayed on Route 66 like their friend Bud had suggested to them earlier, but Interstate 40 had replaced most of the historic highway through Texas. The sun was creeping up on them from behind as the miles ticked away.

Richie looked in the rearview mirror. "What are you talking about?"

"You are wearing a shirt with your face printed on it while driving twenty-five miles an hour over the speed limit. You're hoping to get us caught, but I think you've forgotten your own goal. If you did manage to get us caught, any chances of getting to Oregon to stop that wedding are over. Even if they don't bust you for taking Vaughn's car, you will be detained for questioning. We're still a long way out, and that would obliterate any chance of getting there in time. I know you want justice for that guy Chico shot, but you're going to have to choose which is more important. If you choose justice, I hope you realize there will be many more deaths. I assure you that I will not go down without a fight."

Richie thought about what he said for a moment and he didn't want to get anyone else killed so he let up off the accelerator.

Feeling the car slow down, Simms smiled. "I like you, Richard. You are a wise individual."

Richie clenched his teeth as he thought, *This ain't over, you piece of crap. We will get justice for Howard.*

A few miles later, Lucia pointed up ahead. "Hey, look! That water tower is leaning."

"Whoa, cool," Richie said, as they passed the iconic sight. "I think there is a huge cross somewhere around here, too."

"That would be a good spot to spread some of Howard's father's ashes.." She turned and looked at Simms. "Can I have my phone back? I'm not going to contact the police. I don't want anyone else killed, either."

Simms handed it to her. "We ain't got time for this crap. You get one stop for spreading ashes and that's it!"

"Fine!" Lucia boldly stared at her father.

"You better make it quick!" He turned his attention out the window.

She looked at Richie after searching on her phone. "You're right. Exit 113 will take us to a nineteen-story cross."

"I think I might see it up there on the left."

"I can't tell. It's still a little too dark. Here's the exit."

As they closed in on the massive structure, it came clearly into view. The low rising sun reflected off the white steel and made it shine out in bright yellow brilliance. So bright that it almost hurt their eyes in the dawn of the new day.

Lucia's eyes widened. "Wow, that's amazing!"

Richie pulled the blue sedan up to the statues that surrounded the cross. They thoroughly looked at the sculpted figures that depicted the story of the crucifixion of Jesus Christ as they exited the car.

As Simms shut his door, he said, "Wow. Somebody went to extreme measures just to propagate a ridiculous fairy tale."

"It wasn't a fairy tale to Mom!" Lucia gave him a nasty look as they walked toward the cross.

"Might as well have been. She had all that faith, and where did it get her?"

"It got her away from you! Towards the end, that's all she wanted! So you can stand there and call this fake all you want, but to me it's not." She mumbled something in Spanish.

Simms looked up at the large attraction, then looked at Richie. "You don't buy into all this crap, too, do ya?"

Richie looked at Simms, then looked at the cross. "I have no doubt there is some truth in the Bible as well as possible falsehoods, but as a whole I feel like it's largely misinterpreted."

"Misinterpreted? How's it misinterpreted?"

"Well, for one, I think we take parts of it as literal when it could just be an analogy. For instance, when it talks about God sitting on his throne, we automatically picture a king sitting on a throne like in medieval times, at least I do. When a lot of the Bible was written, they might not have known how to describe what they were telling, so they based it off of things they knew everyone understood at that time.

"For two, my grandfather on my mother's side was a snake handler from West Virginia."

Simms smiled. "So, your grandfather was Alice Cooper. That's awesome."

Richie gave him a slight look of disapproval from the lame joke. "He justified that practice from one of the verses from Mark, I believe. It basically says something like the followers of Christ can pick up deadly serpents and not be harmed. Those people that practice snake handling, like my grandfather did, for example, most likely have misunderstood or misinterpreted that particular scripture. They have taken it to mean that they should play with snakes to prove they love Jesus, but the verse most likely meant that if you are in a situation where you need to pick up a deadly creature then you can do so without getting harmed."

Lucia chimed in. "That makes a lot more sense than just bringing a box of snakes to Sunday services."

Richie nodded. "I personally could see that God is some kind of force, a power that is beyond our understanding. It's in control, holding this crazy ride together for some collective good, I hope. But who really knows for sure?"

Simms stood quietly for a moment. "Nah, it's all a load of crap."

Richie shrugged. "It very well could be. But I personally just can't see how all this is an accident, a chance creation. Too many things point to us being created somehow. Just like this humongous sight. Someone had to build it. So, who or what built us?"

Simms had a look of aggravation come over his face, then he started walking back to the car. "Okay, enough wasting time! Dump the damned ashes and let's go!"

Lucia and Richie walked up next to the cross. She handed him the urn. He was careful as he spread the ashes around.

"Thanks for not leaving me back at the steakhouse."

Richie looked at her, then back down at the ashes.

"You could have run away from Papa while I was inside."

"Yeah, I know. He couldn't have done anything about it right there amongst the other customers. I did think about it, but after hearing that you've been running from him for over three years, I just couldn't chance not getting back to you with the authorities in time before he ran off with you. He needs to be captured. We need to make that happen."

"Yeah. It's such a screwed up situation. I hate seeing him hurt from that gunshot wound, but, at the same time, I get satisfaction from it. It's so weird to love and hate someone at the same time. I have had a few chances when I could have texted the cops, but I was afraid if I did it would keep you from getting to Oregon."

"Getting to Oregon at this rate is probably out of the question."

"Let's go now!" Simms yelled out from the car.

Minutes later, they were back in the sedan and traveling down the interstate. A popular song about being best friends with Jesus was now playing on the radio.

The sun was continuing to rise higher into the vast sky, and darkness was swiftly disappearing from the landscape. Up ahead was a black car on the shoulder of the road with the driver door wide open, almost extending over the white line. Richie slowed down a bit as he approached it. The vehicle came into perfect view as he passed by it, then he yelled out, "No freaking way!"

CHAPTER 36

Serendipity Strikes

"That's it, you stupid son of a bitch! I told you no more games. Now I'm going to kill you!" Simms shouted, reaching under Richie's seat for his gun. It had flown out of his lap as Richie slammed on the brakes after passing the black car.

"Wait, please don't! This isn't a stunt, I swear! That Camaro back there is the one I took from Terence Vaughn!"

The black machine was a marvelous sight, sitting beside the road as the morning sun shone down on it.

"What's it doing here? Better yet, why should I care?"

An eighteen-wheeler blew its horn as it narrowly missed the blue sedan sitting in the right lane and slightly sideways from the sudden stop.

Simms slammed his palm against Richie's headrest. "Get out of the road before you get us killed!"

Richie pulled off onto the dusty shoulder of the road and excitedly backed up to The Exorcist. "I just can't believe this! What is it doing here?"

"It doesn't matter. We ain't taking it anywhere. It's not like we can turn it in for a reward. We're on the run here, you idiot!"

Usually, being called an idiot would have infuriated Richie, but he could have cared less at that moment as he stared at the vehicle in the rear-view mirror. He was beyond astonished that the most amazing car he had ever driven, plus the only car he had ever stolen, was just sitting on the side of the road hundreds of miles from where he last saw it. *I mean, what are the chances of this happening?*

The radio continued playing the friendly Jesus song while the four sat in quiet.

Then Lucia broke the silence. "Is it possible that someone else stole the car, then left it here after running it out of gas?"

Richie looked at her, still in disbelief, and shrugged. *I can't just leave it here*, he thought. *If I can get it back to Vaughn, it could possibly save Sherrod's job.*

"Doesn't matter. Let's get going," Simms barked.

"Okay, sure is a shame, though. That's a hundred and thirty thousand dollar car. Rumor has it that there will only ever be one hundred or possibly even less of them made." Richie glanced over his right shoulder, and put the blue sedan in drive and started rolling forward.

"Wait." Simms stared out the window. Then he looked out the back window and gave the Camaro a long and thorough look. "I know a guy who would appreciate that car. I need to bury the hatchet with him, and that might be the perfect olive branch."

Richie bit his lip to keep from smiling as he was pleased Simms took the bait. He shifted the gear into park and turned off his music device. "You want me to see if it will start?"

"No, give me the keys to this car while Chico and I go check it out."

The two men exited the sedan and Lucia started talking as soon as the doors shut, turned to Richie, and grabbed his arm in excitement. "Can you believe this? I can't!"

Richie looked back at her with a huge smile on his face. "No. This is nuts! Has Sherrod sent any messages?"

"No, I just checked a few minutes ago. You would think if Vaughn knew it was gone again, Sherrod would have notified us."

"That's exactly why I asked. Someone must have stolen it between here and the junkyard. Maybe we can use this opportunity to get your dad busted."

Lucia had a look of concern on her face. "I hope so. I really don't want to go back home with him."

"Do you think he is planning on killing me?"

"It's a good probability. He won't for a while, though. I don't think Chico can drive, so he needs you to get him to Oregon, at least."

Richie nodded in agreement. "Here he comes."

Simms knocked on the window, and Lucia opened the door. He bent down and looked into the car. "Okay, here's the deal. Fortunately, the key fob was left in it, but it's out of gas. You three are going to go get some while I stay here and disable the OnStar device so we can't be tracked. Lucia, give me your phone." Then he looked directly at Richie. "If you don't come back or try to pull a stupid stunt, I will make an anonymous phone call to the police and tell them I saw the famous wrestler, The Priest, leave this thing here. Is that clear?"

Richie nodded. "Yeah, you better tell your boy not to try something stupid, either."

"Don't worry, he won't. Also, we need a headlight. Stop by an auto store and pick one up. Last thing we need is to bring more attention to ourselves. Running around with a headlight out will be a beacon to the cops." He handed Richie the keys to the sedan. "Hurry back!"

Chico got into the backseat and Simms got a small kit of some sort out of one of his bags in the trunk. Richie watched him in the rear-view mirror limping toward the Camaro as he drove off.

A good while later, they made it back to Simms. They pulled up behind the Exorcist and he started walking toward them, as they got out of the sedan.

Simms and Richie walked around to the right side of the car and began fueling it up. "I was starting to think you weren't coming back."

"The gas station was pretty far, and we had a hard time finding an auto store."

Simms nodded. "Figures. We'll get the headlight installed later, as long as it's in before nightfall. Chico, come here."

Chico trotted over to Simms. "Yeah, Jefe?"

"You're going to be riding with my baby girl."

"What? Why do I have to ride with him?" Lucia peered at Simms.

"'Cause he can't drive very good and I just can't leave the sedan out here. I have to at least leave it in a safe place to be picked up."

Lucia folded her arms and looked away, not pleased with this news.

"You can still drive, right? I know you didn't have a ton of experience, but you should be able to follow Richard and me. You can manage that, can't you?"

Annoyed by his condescending tone, her response was aggressive. "Yes, I can still drive." She stomped over to the sedan and slammed the door closed after she flopped down in it.

Richie closed the fuel tank door. "K, it's all in. We can finish filling it up at the gas station. That will be enough to get us there."

Simms took the gas can and chucked it to the side of the road. "Let's get going!"

Lucia exited the sedan and ran up to Richie. "Here, figured you would want this." She handed him his music device.

"Thanks!" He beamed.

Richie was pumping the gas pedal to prime the fuel line. He pressed the start button and the beast almost roared back to life. He let it sit for a second and plugged in his music device while he waited.

"What was that?" Richie looked down at his feet.

"What?" Simms looked over at Richie, then looked down at the floorboard.

"I thought I felt something rub up against my foot. Did you guys check this thing out for any critters? Who knows how long the door was left open on this thing."

"Yeah, I looked it over, and Chico checked under the seats. There's nothing there. Let's get moving already. We've wasted enough time."

Richie shrugged, pressed the clutch in, and pushed the start button once more. After a slight hesitation, the engine fired to life.

"Damn, listen to that!" Simms had a pleasantly surprised look on his face. "This thing must be absolutely wicked."

"You have no idea. Funny thing, this car got its modification into The Exorcist here in Texas, and here it is yet again."

"It won't be for long."

Richie had fallen into a slight trance. He thought he would never see the car again, but here he was, behind the wheel once more. The sound of the engine was still very mesmerizing to him as he buckled in. His music player picked up where it left off with the Jesus song.

"That's enough of this hippie crap! Play something that rocks."

Feeling fortunate to be behind the wheel of the Camaro, equipped with his favorite tunes, and most of all, still alive, he pressed the skip button on the device. Next, he slowly pulled out onto the road while watching in the rear-view mirror for Lucia. His silver cross was still hanging from it and shimmered brightly as it jostled around. Lucia pulled out onto the road as well and followed close behind him. The radio began playing Henry Rollins' cover of "Lonesome, On'ry, and Mean" by Waylon Jennings.

"Now that's what I'm talking about!" With ample excitement, Simms bobbed his head to the rhythm of the upbeat song.

Richie was working through the gears, then glanced over at Simms as he rocked out. He couldn't help but crack a smile as they continued west.

CHAPTER 37

Smile for the Cameras

A pudgy and pale Caucasian man sporting a gray-colored crew cut sat in front of a computer at his cluttered desk in a state-of-the-art federal building. He had a raspberry filling stain on his wrinkled white button-up shirt and donut glaze caked in the corners of his mouth. He scrutinized the only security footage that captured images of Terrence Vaughn's Camaro being stolen.

"Well, well, well, what do we have here?" he mumbled. "Jain is going to want to hear about this."

He picked up his phone and awkwardly dialed the numbers that were on a scratch pad beside his computer.

"Jain here, make it quick."

"Agent Jain, Burridge here, sir. Thanks again for putting me on this case, sir."

"Yeah, no problem. You seem like the man for the job. Your credentials are superb."

"Thank you. I'm so sorry to bother you, sir. I know you're up to your eyeballs down there in Arkansas, but I have some very interesting information for you."

"Okay, what do you have for me?"

"Two things. I was going over footage from the Tallahassee arena where Terrence Vaughn's car was stolen." Burridge paused, waiting for a response from Jain.

"And?"

"Oh, right." Burridge cleared his throat. "I've got a glimpse of a man getting into the car. He just opens the door; he didn't have to jimmy it or anything, so he must have had a key fob on him."

"Okay, that does sound interesting. Were you able to zoom in on the man's face?"

"I was able to zoom in from the left side. Unfortunately for us, he was wearing a black mask?"

"Like a ski mask?"

"Not exactly, sir. It looked more like a wrestler's mask. It was shiny and tight-fitting. The bulkiness of a ski mask wasn't present. Along with that, I noticed that he had an American flag coat on as well. I couldn't discern any of his features, but judging from his hands and nose that was protruding from the mask, he was apparently white, definitely male, and well-built too."

"Sounds like that very well could have been a professional wrestler. Like maybe Richie Blackburn, for instance."

"That's what I thought too, sir. That's why I called you."

"Has he popped up anywhere? Used his cards or triggered any facial recognition cameras?"

Burridge shook his head. "No, sir. He's still flying well beneath the radar."

"Hmm, I find that very strange for a guy that just wanted to get to Oregon. What's he hiding?"

"I don't know, sir, but it is suspicious for sure."

"Anything else, Burridge?"

"Surprisingly enough, there is more, sir. Right before I found the footage of Vaughn's car thief, one of my assistants dropped off a report of a stolen car in Texas." Burridge paused, waiting for a response.

"And?"

"It uh, I really hate to tell you this, but it was Terrence Vaughn's Camaro, sir."

"Another one of Mr. Vaughn's cars was stolen? Is that what you're telling me?"

"Well, sort of, sir, but not exactly. It was the same Camaro as before. The one that was just recovered has been stolen again."

Jain giggled in disbelief. "There's no way, Burridge."

"I'm sorry, sir, but it's true. We've officially confirmed it."

"You have got to be kidding me!"

"No, sir. I wish I was. The tow truck driver reported it stolen this morning. Apparently, Vaughn had hired him to transport it to his estate in Vegas. He had picked it up at the police impound lot there in Arkansas and stopped for the night just across the state line. He said when he got up the next morning, the car was gone. It was as if it just disappeared." Burridge read from the report with his head tilted back, as if he was straining to read.

"Disappeared?"

"Yes, sir. Here it says he backed the flatbed car hauler right up to his motel door so he could keep a close eye on it. 'This was a huge customer for me so I was taking extra precautions' he says. The report goes on to say that the hauler was never moved, the driver never heard any noises, and the cameras by the entrance never show the car leave. There was only one way in and one way out. Also, the key fob was missing from his shirt pocket. Goes on to say the tow truck driver seemed to be visibly shaken from the incident."

"What's his back story? Who is this guy?"

"My assistants had already looked into him. He's squeaky clean, sir. Runs a legitimate business, pays his taxes, he's a class A citizen."

"So, you're telling me this damned car just disappeared right out of thin air?"

"No, sir, I'm telling you the tow truck driver said it disappeared out of thin air. This is crazy, I know, but I felt like I had to fill you in on the latest developments. Was I wrong in calling you, sir?"

"We found it through the OnStar device the first time. Did you try that?"

"Yes, sir, we did. It seems the OnStar has been disabled. We couldn't find a signal anywhere for it."

Jain looked down and massaged the bridge of his nose. "No, you're doing a fine job, Burridge. I just can't believe this car has been stolen again. Has Vaughn been notified?"

"I assume the tow truck driver would have contacted him or the local police he reported to, but I'm not certain on that."

"Okay, contact him and make sure that he gives any and all information that could possibly help with this."

"On it, sir!"

"Also, monitor Sherrod Showman's phone very closely. They said that is Blackburn's best friend, so we may find something out there."

"Of course, sir."

"One more thing."

"Yes?"

Jain cleared his throat. "Put out an all-points bulletin for everywhere west of Texas, especially on all roads leading into Oregon. Notify the governor there as well and let him in on the details of the possibility of an out-of-control pro wrestler headed to Mt. Hood so that he can prepare appropriately with all the local authorities."

"Right away, sir. Anything else?" But there was no response. "Sir, are you there? He musta hung up already." He mumbled, then he called over his assistants and started belting out orders.

CHAPTER 38

A Worthy Challenger

It was approaching two o'clock in the afternoon as the pair of cars entered Aztec, New Mexico. Richie hated leaving Route 66 behind as they had done so a couple of hours ago, but they gained an hour, fortunately, as they entered the Mountain Time zone after leaving Texas. He took great delight in the vintage sights and constant reminders of yesteryear that still clung to life along the highway, even though he just got a glance as they sped by. Most notably was the Cadillac Ranch—ten cars buried nose-first into the dirt, which protruded out while covered in graffiti, making an unusual work of art along the side of the road. They now approached slightly more green terrain as the trek was now headed in the northwest direction on a mostly straight stretch of highway with very few winding curves.

Not taking his eyes off the road, Simms turned his head toward Richie. "So, what's your plan, exactly? What are you going to do if your woman takes you back but you no longer have a job to support her? Better yet, what are you going to do if she doesn't take you back, and now, on top of that, you're jobless?"

Richie hesitated to speak, as if in thought. "Why do you care? Why do you want me to get there in time?"

"My beautiful daughter and you have a deal. I will do what I can to help her hold up her end. Despite all I've done for her, I've apparently failed as a father in her eyes. So I figured maybe I can make things right before I leave."

"Before you leave? Where are you going?" Richie looked over at Simms with a bewildered look.

Simms gazed outside his window. "My plan is to flee the country. My reign in Mexico has come to an abrupt end. I've been tying up loose ends before I leave. Finally, by chance, I found Lucia. I've spent thousands of dollars trying to find her and by some stupid dumb luck, I stumbled across her when I least expected it."

"So you're not taking her back to Mexico? That's the impression she's under, you know."

"No, I just wanted to tell her goodbye. I would have left a long time ago if I could have found her sooner."

"Why haven't you told her this yet?"

"I'm waiting 'til Seattle. I'm going to tell her goodbye there then head towards Asia. I'd appreciate it if you wouldn't tell her."

Simms' statement surprised Richie. From the way Lucia talked, he was convinced he would drag her back to old Mexico, kicking and screaming. He looked over at Simms. "Don't worry, I won't."

"I answered your questions, so now answer mine."

Richie glanced at him, then shifted gears. "I guess, regardless of Mary's answer, I'll turn my brother's old garage into an auto detailing business."

Simms sat quietly as he processed Riche's comment. "I take it he worked on cars. Is he dead now?"

Richie's face grew noticeably sad. "Yeah, he's deceased, unfortunately. He left me his building and all of his automotive tools. He was a genius with cars. He could paint them, fix them, build them, race them; there was nothing he couldn't do. I'm nowhere near the level he was, but I do know what it takes to make a car look its best. Plus, if I'm self-employed, I can go see my daughter anytime I want. There will be no one to answer to but myself."

"I can't help but like you, Richard. You are your own man. I can really appreciate that." Simms nodded.

Richie was unsure of how to answer. "Thanks, I think." His eyebrows furrowed.

"No, seriously, you are in charge of your own destiny." Simms pointed his index finger at Richie. "I know you hate my guts, but you really do remind me of me. You're always thinking one step ahead and aren't searching for anyone's approval. That seems to be a rare trait, especially these days. That's also why I have to ask a favor from you."

A perplexed look formed on Richie's face. "A favor?" A hair-raising metal song was playing on the radio.

"Yeah. I want you to look after Lucia. From one concerned father to another, I'd be beyond—"

"No way!" Something caught his eye in the rear-view mirror, then he quickly looked over his right shoulder as he brought the car to a sudden halt on the side of the road.

"What is it?" Simms looked back as well. "God, no!" He shouted as the blue sedan driven by Lucia was flipping over, causing a minor sandstorm to envelope the area while pieces of the car and shards of glass scattered about the roadside before the car finally came to a staggering stop on its top.

Looking over his right shoulder, Richie backed the Camaro up on the side of the road. A dark green Dodge Challenger SRT caught his eye as it passed by.

The lead singer sang out from the speakers as if they were introducing a villain to Richie's situation.

He twisted his head to get a better look and saw a ferocious-looking devil face emblem on the fender. "It's a Demon! That's the fastest production car ever built in America!"

Simms gave the car a hard look as it passed. "It must be Needham's men." He looked back at the wrecked car.

"Who's Needham?" Richie asked as he brought The Exorcist to a stop.

Simms bolted out of the car and ran as fast as he could on his wounded leg to the upside-down sedan, and Richie followed him in a flash.

"Lucia! Are you okay?" Simms fell to his knees and looked into the broken window of the now destroyed car.

Richie pried open the severely dented door. "Watch out!"

Simms shifted his body out of the way of the door, then lunged in to check on Lucia. "Oh, my baby, are you okay?"

She moaned out in pain and tried to lift her arms.

Richie saw that he couldn't get to Lucia with Simms in the way, so he ran over to the passenger side to check on Chico. He bent down to look inside the car and saw the lifeless body of Simms' henchman hanging from the seat belt. After a closer look, he saw blood trickling from a bullet hole in Chico's temple.

"Richard! Come help me get Lucia up!"

He rushed around the car. "Bad news. Chico is dead." His tone was grim as he helped lift Lucia.

"They thought it was me, I'm sure. Come on, let's hurry and get her to the car."

Richie stopped in his tracks. "Are you crazy? We need to get her in an ambulance."

Before Simms could refute Richie's statement, a man in a dirty t-shirt and torn jeans approached behind them with a young boy at his side from a rusty pickup truck.

"Are you all okay? I've called 911 already, so they should be here soon. Is there anything we can do to help y'all 'til they get here?"

"Hey, Dad, it's The Priest!" The boy excitedly pointed at Richie. "Can I get his autograph?"

Simms gently but hurriedly pushed Lucia fully over to Richie and pulled his pistol from his pants.

Richie realized what he was about to do. "No, Simms!" Then he quickly lay Lucia on the ground and grabbed Simms's gun before he could fire any shots. "Run! Get out of here!" Richie screamed out to the father and son. They did just that, and immediately after they got back into the pickup, the father began recording Simms trying to fight Richie off of his gun with his cell phone.

"We can't leave any witnesses!"

"It's too late to worry about that. We should get Lucia to a hospital."

With a last-ditch effort, Simms jabbed his thumb into Richie's right eye, forcing him to release the gun and grab at his wounded orbital area. Now that Simms had freed his gun from Richie's grasp, he pointed the oversized pistol at his head once again.

Richie moaned out in pain. "Remind me to show you how to do that without actually blinding someone."

More cars with concerned drivers stopped at the crash scene, angering Simms even further. "Just great. There are too many people here now. Let's get her in the car and if she needs medical attention, we will take her ourselves. It's not safe anyways. One of my enemies might try to harm her to get at me. We need to get outta here now."

"Okay, just don't shoot anybody," Richie said with his injured eye clenched shut. A small trickle of blood ran down the bridge of his nose where Simms' fingernail punctured his skin. They placed Lucia in the back seat of the Camaro as fast as possible and returned to the road.

"Burn rubber, Richard! We need to make a lot of distance between ourselves and the scene of the accident."

As Richie gained speed, they approached the next interchange on the highway. "Look! Sitting there on the exit ramp. It's the Demon!" Richie shouted. The vision in his injured eye was blurred, but thankfully, not gone.

Lucia lifted her head to look at the car. "Yeah, that looks like the maniac that wrecked us, I think. Is it green?"

"F8 Green with satin black hood, roof, and deck lid. That's definitely the car I saw drive past us."

"Has to be Needham's man." Simms pulled out a pair of binoculars to get a better view of the driver of the Dodge.

"He shot Chico, then I lost control. Scared me to death!"

Richie looked back at her. "Are you okay?"

"I will be."

He looked over at Simms. "Who is this Needham?"

Simms now watched out the back window, waiting for the Demon to return. "One of my biggest enemies. He's the one I wanted to give this car to as a peace offering. We've tried to knock each other off several times over the years. He must know about my plans to—" Simms realized he almost revealed his plans to flee the continent in front of Lucia and stopped talking.

"What plans?"

Simms ignored Lucia and stuffed the binoculars into his black bag. He had grown pale and very somber.

"What plans?" His silence worried her. "What's wrong? What's going on?"

"It's The Heat Seeker." Simms barely spoke above a whisper. "Back there in the green car. My enemy Needham has apparently hired a hitman known as The Heat Seeker.

He's the most notorious hitman there is. Nobody ever escapes The Heat Seeker."

"Hence the name I take it?"

Simms looked at Richie and uttered, "Yes. He is so good that he won't even consider doing a job for less than two hundred and fifty thousand. I know because I tried to hire him myself one time. I told him for a quarter of a million dollars I'd do it myself."

Richie was occasionally looking in the driver's side-view mirror, anticipating the return of the Challenger. Off in the distance, he glimpsed a dark car that appeared to be approaching fast. "Oh crap, he here he comes!" Richie downshifted to gain speed and swiftly made the sign of the cross for good measure.

CHAPTER 39

Good Feeling About Bad News

Squinting with his head tilted back, Burridge dialed Terrance Vaughn's number. Before he pressed the last number on the phone, Katie, his assistant, approached his desk.

"Excuse me, sir, but you need to see this immediately. We have found some security footage of Richie Blackburn at a truck stop and fast-food restaurant next to it, close to the same time that Mr. Vaughn's car was stolen the second time in Texas."

Burridge hung up the phone and looked up at the young, enthusiastic lady holding a black laptop computer. "Show me what you got, Katie."

The dark-skinned young lady did as he asked, as the video played. "Right here. This camera shows him getting out of a semi."

"Where is this? He looks hurt."

"Somewhere outside Searcy, Arkansas, and yes, he looks injured. He keeps holding his ribs and walks slow with a limp." She clicked on a different tab. "Now, here, inside the fast-food restaurant, he's talking to this group of men that later turn on him and try to attack him."

"What was that about?"

"After a quick search, I found out that the men are wrestlers. I'm not sure why they attacked him. Could it be they thought he had Vaughn's car?"

"But he got out of a road tractor. Wait a minute. If he was here, then who stole the car the second time? There's no way it coulda been him."

"Exactly! Who stole the car?"

"Hold up!" The nerdy young man was all but running to Burridge with his laptop in hand.

"What is it, Harris?" Burridge looked aggravated yet confused.

"If you think that the fact Richie Blackburn didn't steal the car is interesting, then get a load of this!" He was giddily excited as he placed his computer on the desk for his superior and colleague to see. "This report just came in that a young boy and his father saw Richie Blackburn and a young Hispanic lady are apparently being held hostage by Peter Mitchell Simms!"

Burridge's head tilted back, then leaned in to Harris. "What? Peter Mitchell Simms? The same Simms that has evaded capture since the eighties?" Shaking his head, he was in total disbelief.

Harris nodded. "Yes! Can you believe it?"

"No, I can't. Where did you get this information from?"

"New Mexico Highway Patrol. They took the statement from the man and his son just a short time ago. They were stopping to assist a wreck, and Simms almost shot them. Blackburn stepped in and grabbed Simms' gun, and they ran back to their vehicle. Simms managed to hold onto the weapon and made Blackburn help him load the injured lady into the car."

"How did they know it was Blackburn and Simms?"

"The kid, I believe Travis is his name, is a huge wrestling fan and recognized him right away and his dad was adamant that the man holding them hostage was Simms, but that's not all."

Burridge's eyes widened. "What else?"

"It, uh, this is huge. It seems they drove off in Terrance Vaughn's Camaro." Harris looked straight into Burridge's eyes with his arms held out, waiting for his response. "Mind-blowing, isn't it?"

Burridge seemed to check out for a moment as he tried to make sense of the situation. "Are you certain of this? I mean absolutely certain?" He held his hands up close to his subordinate's face, as if he was blocking out any distractions so he could receive a straight answer.

"Yes. Simms was limping as if he had a leg injury and he was forcing Richie Blackburn, The Priest, to drive at gunpoint. They sped off in a black Chevy Camaro that had red stripes on the side. It had to be Vaughn's car. Plus, Travis, the kid, recognized the vehicle from the Pay-Per-View that aired this past Sunday."

Burridge rubbed his face. "So, let's get this straight. Katie brings me footage that proves Richie Blackburn, The Priest, didn't steal his boss' car. Then you get notified that the same man is being held hostage by Simms. A drug lord that has been on the run for over thirty years and he is now forcing Richie Blackburn, The Priest, to drive the car he didn't steal."

Harris grinned. "Bingo! The Priest is being forced to drive the car that he's accused of stealing!"

Katie looked at Burridge. "Wait, was it Simms that stole the car then?"

Harris chimed in. "And somewhere along the way he kidnaped The Priest and the Latino girl that's with him now?"

"That's a real possibility. Holy cow, this whole thing is nuts. Let me tell Jain. I have to call him right now." Still amazed by the turn of events, Burridge picked up the phone.

After Burridge had completely brought Agent Jain up to speed on the new developments, Jain wasn't sure if he should have been more frustrated or surprised at the information. He made his way to an empty patrol car to call Vaughn, so he could disclose the news to Vaughn and hoped to make sense of it all. Vaughn answered on the third ring.

"Hello, this is Terrance Vaughn speaking." He sounded robotic, as he often did, trying to be beyond professional and make himself seem very important.

"Mr. Vaughn, this is Agent Jain of the FBI. We spoke a few days ago, if you remember." Jain sounded subservient, which wasn't a surprise for an FBI agent.

"Agent Jain, of course. What can I do for you? Are you already in need of some backstage passes or front row seats?"

Jain sensed Vaughn's pretentious smirk on the phone. "Well, that would be nice, but I'm afraid I must have a moment of your time." Jain dreaded being the messenger of a troublesome situation to a high-profile individual. "From the sounds of it, I feel you haven't received any unfortunate information in the past several hours."

"No, what is it, Agent? Is it about Richie Blackburn? Do you finally have him in custody? Did that lowlife admit to stealing my car? Speaking of which, it should be arriving at my estate in Vegas right about now."

Jain cleared his throat. "Well, sir, it is about Richie and your car, but here's a bit of bad news I must deliver to you first."

"Okay."

Jain gripped the bridge of his nose and closed his eyes. "There's no easy way to say this, but your car has been stolen again."

"Surely, you're joking, Agent. It should literally be arriving in Las Vegas anytime now. You must be mistaken."

"No, sir. I'm sorry, but it's not a mistake. It was stolen off the rollback carrier it was on and is now being piloted by Richie Blackburn."

Taken aback, Vaughn's eyes widened and his jaw dropped. "Ha! See? I told you Blackburn stole it! How was he able to do it a second time?"

"Well, sir, I know this sounds crazy, but we have proof that he didn't steal it the second time. The first time is still questionable, but we have him on video in an entirely different place when it happened."

"Well, what are you going to do about it?"

"This is where the proverbial plot thickens. Are you familiar with the name Peter Mitchell Simms, Mr. Vaughn?"

"Of course, he's the infamous drug lord that's evaded police for decades. His face has been everywhere the past couple of weeks."

"Yes, and we have reason to believe he is holding Richie Blackburn as a hostage in your stolen car, forcing him to drive it at gunpoint."

Vaughn's face went blank from the surprising information. Then, after mere seconds, a devious smile formed and his eyes lit up like a Christmas tree.

"I know this is somewhat shocking news, sir."

Vaughn was giddy with excitement. "Please forgive me, Agent, for always being a shameless promoter, but this is like winning the lottery, the press lottery, that is!"

"I'm not sure I follow you, sir."

"Well, you see, if by some chance you could make Blackburn out to be the hero of this situation it would almost completely erase the terrible airline incident and the Infinity Wrestling League could instantly save face and even profit greatly from this current situation."

Jain was relieved Vaughn was taking the news so well, but his curiosity was growing greatly. "How do you think I could make that happen and, better yet, why would I? Why would I falsify a situation and risk this career that has taken many, many years to achieve?"

"I'm not sure about the how, but I believe I have enough resources to help you want to come up with something. Instead of saying why, you'll be saying why not." Vaughn reclined in his chair with a sinister grin plastered on his face.

CHAPTER 40

Vanishing Checkpoint

Pulling out his colossal pistol, Simms checked the chamber for a bullet. He looked back over his shoulder, through the rear window, to check on the approaching Challenger.

"He's almost caught up to us!"

"I know!" Richie piloted the Camaro faster and faster through northbound traffic on the four-lane highway. The green and black Demon had caught up to The Exorcist and filled its rear-view mirror up completely. "Oh crap, he's here already." Richie had a death grip on the steering wheel. His knuckles shone white with his hands at the ten and two positions. He now approached an eighteen-wheeler from behind at breakneck speed.

Simms' eyes widened, as he leaned back in the seat. "Watch it!"

"I know what I'm doing." Richie jerked the steering wheel to the left, narrowly avoiding crashing into the semi. In that instant, he passed the big commercial truck, and the Dodge came barreling around the right side of the rig and was, once again, glued to Richie's back bumper with dust still boiling off the vehicle where The Heat Seeker had boldly taken to the shoulder of the road to avoid colliding with the large hauler.

Simms was watching the Demon, not taking his eyes off of it for even a second. "Nice try. But he is still on us."

In the back seat, Lucia held on for dear life. "Do you think if we stop and offered to give him such a rare car that he would consider letting us go?"

Simms shook his head. "No, when he's paid to do a job, he sees it through. Even if I hired him to kill Needham now, he'd still kill me first."

"He's starting to overtake us." Richie pointed out as his new automotive foe crept up on the left side of the Camaro.

"I thought this was one of the baddest cars ever made!" Simms smirked at Richie and raised his pistol as he looked over his left shoulder.

"It is! But here's the thing, so is that one! It's like the announcers at the shows are always saying, the preverbal unmovable object versus an irresistible force. Only this ain't a show."

"Damn straight it isn't! Roll your window down!" Simms leaned over to Richie and pointed his pistol at the driver's side window.

Richie rolled down the window, filling the car with a deafening sound from the wind noise. Lucia's hair flew all about as if it were a black forest in a tornado, and Richie's face squinted as he tried to keep the wind out of his eyes so he could still see the road. The Dodge kept coming, and now its passenger side window was halfway down, revealing a gun barrel pointed directly at them. Right as it got beside the Chevrolet, Simms reached as far past Richie as he could and fired his hand cannon.

The shot rang out, and the bullet hit the side mirror on the door, causing it to explode into countless green pieces, and the Dodge Charger slowed immediately to get out of harm's way. Simms' attempt at getting rid of the Demon's gunman had failed.

Richie had a look of anger plastered on his face as he rolled up the window. "Don't try that again!" He buried his left ear into his left shoulder, trying to get the painful ringing to stop. Even with all the wind noise, the gunfire was deafening.

Simms looked back through the rear window for the Demon. "I'll do whatever it takes to escape that killer!"

"Looks like our problems just got worse." Richie nodded toward a police helicopter up ahead.

"Fantastic! I guess we popped up on their radar after racing through all this traffic." Simms looked back and the black and green Dodge Demon was nowhere to be seen.

Richie looked at Simms and could tell he was perplexed. "What is it? Where is he?"

"He, he just vanished."

"I guess he didn't like our new company." Richie looked up at the helicopter and then rubbed his right eye. It was still blurry, but not as bad as before.

"Lose this guy!"

"It will be hard on the long, straight road. I can put some distance between us, but I imagine their cameras can zoom in for a long way."

"Do what you can."

They continued their frantic drive through traffic. After several close calls, swerving around the vehicles, and almost losing control after dodging a van that switched lanes without using its turn signal, Richie had put some distance between them and the helicopter.

"Looks like we're starting to lose him, Richard."

Richie still had a death grip on the steering wheel as he cut his eyes at Simms, then to the rear-view mirror to check on Lucia. "You okay back there?"

"Yeah, I'm fine. The crash happened so fast I didn't even realize what was going on 'til Papa showed up at the door. Sorry about Chico." She looked at Simms.

"I'm sure Richard is glad he is dead." Simms looked out the window.

"Hey, I take no joy in someone losing their life. I wanted justice for Howard, but I didn't want Chico to be shot by another criminal."

Simms stared at Richie for a moment, then looked back at the road. "Chico had no business being with me in the first place. He wasn't cut out for this kind of life."

"Is anybody?" Richie quickly realized he sounded like a hypocrite for judging Simms when his own line of work had sometimes caused those who loved him most a lot of suffering and heartache as well.

"No, probably not. Chico's father was one of my best men. His dying request was that I watch out for his only son. I failed at that as well."

For just a split second, Richie felt sorry for Simms, but then he noticed a huge roadblock with many state police cars up ahead and countless flashing lights. He slammed on the brakes and eventually brought the speeding car to a halt. The three of them looked at the obstacle in awe from about fifty yards away. "What do we do now?" Richie stared ahead, his heart pounding. He was confident the bystanders at the scene of Lucia's wreck could verify he was a hostage of the most wanted man in America, but he was still concerned about possibly being wanted himself for stealing Vaughn's car. Either way, there was nothing he could do about it right now.

"I'm not sure because if we try to turn around, they will set up another roadblock and all these assholes will be on our tail. Maybe there is a side road we can lose them on." He frantically looked on his phone for an alternate route. "I had a feeling that we shouldn't have taken this road. It's too long and straight and too far from other major roads."

"Isn't this a bit extreme for a speeding car that just left the scene of an accident?" Lucia shook her head as the helicopter hovered overhead.

"They know who we are. America's most wanted, holding a minor celebrity hostage."

Richie cut his eyes at him.

"That father and son eyed us back at the crash scene. Now we have the entire United States on our asses. Damn you, Needham! Damn you to hell!" Simms slapped the dash of the Camaro as the realization set in of how unlikely it was for him to escape to Asia. Then he grabbed his leg in pain.

Richie watched him as he clenched his thigh, then looked back at the roadblock. "What's this? What are they doing?"

The patrol cars parked beside the desert highway, clearing the road. On foot, an officer slowly approached with a cell phone, his hands in the air and wearing his uniform pants and white tee shirt, to show Simms that he was not armed.

CHAPTER 41

A Not-So-Excellent Execution

Richie sat in amazement at all the police officers and patrol cars that were on the scene. The flashing blue lights were almost hypnotic, and the situation didn't even seem real to him. Although Simms' ability to stay calm impressed him, he was considering the amount of trouble he was facing.

I guess that's it, he thought. *There's no way I can get to Oregon now. I've lost Mary to a worthless scum-sucking politician and my daughter will grow up without me in her life.* He looked back at Lucia for a moment and thought about how she must be feeling. *Her father will go to prison forever if by some chance he doesn't get himself killed first trying to escape this mess.*

"What the hell do you want? Who is this?" Simms shouted into the cell phone as he held his gun and eyes on the officer that had brought it to him.

"This is Agent Jain of the FBI. I assume I'm talking to Peter Mitchell Simms. Is that correct?"

"I'm known by many names. What's it to ya?"

Jain tilted his head and rolled his eyes from behind a desk that was hundreds of miles away from the scene. "Do you realize who you have as a hostage, sir?"

"Yeah, a meathead wrestler. So what?"

"Well, you see, Mr. Simms, that meathead wrestler is worth a lot of money to his boss."

"So what? I have plenty of money."

"You don't have a way out of this, though."

Simms sat quietly, thinking about Jain's comment. "Okay, what's your point? What do you want?"

"It's not so much as what I want, it's what Richie Blackburn's boss wants."

"Which is?" Simms was growing annoyed with Agent Jain.

"Richie Blackburn's boss, Terrance Vaughn, also known as The King of Professional Wrestling, needs him to look like the hero of this situation. If you can let Blackburn overtake you right here and now in front of the cameras, we will eventually find you asylum abroad so that you can live the rest of your life comfortably and not on the run."

Simms looked over at Richie with a grin of disbelief. "What kind of stupid joke is this? Besides, what makes you think Richard wants to participate in this little charade of yours, anyway?"

Richie watched Simms talk on the cell phone, now curious about said charade, then he looked back at Lucia and caught her staring at him this time. She seemed embarrassed and looked away.

"Screw that! I've been on the run for over thirty years! Do you really think I've managed to do that by trusting anyone in an authoritative position such as yourself?"

"Mr. Simms, please, please listen to me. This is a golden opportunity for you."

"Anytime anyone says it's a 'golden opportunity,' it usually is only golden for them." Simms spoke with an air of self-assurance, along with ample anger.

Agent Jain was becoming increasingly frustrated as well. "Mr. Simms, if you're not willing to listen, then may I please speak to Mr. Blackburn?"

"Sure thing, douchebag." Simms carelessly handed the phone to Richie.

Richie grabbed the phone. "Yes?"

"Mr. Blackburn, this is Federal Agent Jain with the FBI."

Richie looked at Simms, then back out the window. "What uh, what can I do for you, Agent?"

"Firstly, are you okay? Has Simms harmed you in any manner?" Jain's tone was overwhelmingly insincere, as if programmed to repeat the lines from a poorly written hostage manual.

Richie slightly chuckled. "Well, he has harmed me in one manner and threatened to kill me on several occasions, but so far he has managed to not do so."

Simms looked over at Richie and got a meaningless grin from him in the process.

"Good, good. Now listen carefully. Your boss, Mr. Vaughn, is willing to drop the charges against you if you play along with this cover story we're about to perform." Jain spoke slightly bent over at the shoulders with his hand up to the phone like a teenager trying to convince their parents of a scheme they had just concocted.

"Charges? What charges? I'm the one that's been kidnapped by America's most wanted here." He figured he'd better at least try to defend himself.

Jain stood up straight from behind the desk. "The charges of you stealing his car."

Richie's heart jumped into his throat, as it had done so a lot over the past several days. He sat quietly, not knowing how to respond.

"Mr. Blackburn, are you there? Hello."

"Yeah, I'm here. Look, all I want to do is get to Oregon by Saturday afternoon. That's it."

"I see, Mr. Blackburn, but that is a bit of an impossibility now, so you might as well help us out along with yourself."

Curious about the plan and not knowing what else to say, Richie played along. "Okay, what do I need to do, then?"

"First off, can Simms hear you?"

Richie looked over at him. He was still holding his gun on the officer and scanning the surrounding area. "Negative."

"Ok, good. Do you see the officer that brought the cell phone to the car?"

"Yes."

"Good, that's Officer Bullseye. He's a crack shot and I can assure you he gained that nickname honestly. I need you to get into an altercation with Simms just long enough for Bullseye to reach his weapon and fire a shot into Simms. He has a pistol tucked into the back of his pants. Don't worry, he won't miss. He never misses. You are perfectly safe."

Richie sat quietly once again.

"Are you there, Mr. Blackburn? Do I need to give you better directions? Simply distract Simms with a punch, shout, or anything that will allow us to execute our plan."

Richie imagined Officer Bullseye shooting Simms in the head and his blood splattering all over his baby girl in the back seat. *Simms deserves that, but Lucia doesn't. No one deserves to see that happen to their father.* He couldn't bear the thought of his precious little Josie seeing that happen to him. He couldn't let that happen to Lucia, either.

Richie looked back at Lucia, then to Simms, before speaking into the phone. "I don't think that will work."

"Why not?"

"'Cause that requires Simms' daughter to witness his execution without a trial."

"Simms' daughter? What do you mean? Is that young lady with you his family member?"

Hearing this caused Simms to spin his head around and stare at Richie with an intense look. It got Lucia's attention as well.

"I've got a better plan."

"Yes, what is it?"

"I'm going to leave Simms tied up for you somewhere safe, as long as you can assure me he gets a fair trial."

Simms cut his eyes at Richie and had a look of shock at his bold statement.

"That monster doesn't deserve a fair trial!"

"You're exactly right. He doesn't. But his daughter doesn't deserve to watch the FBI waste her father right before her very eyes either, just because a rich egomaniac like Terrence Vaughn thinks it's good for business. So, if you can guarantee me that he will get a fair trial, I will tell you where I left him at."

Agent Jain looked up and closed his eyes, then hung his head and sighed. "Please don't do this! It is a huge mistake! Mr. Vaughn has big plans for you after this. The publicity alone will make you a very rich man."

"Oh, that's nice. Be sure to tell Vaughn that he can kiss my ass!" Richie flung the phone out the passenger side window right past Simms and then put the Camaro into gear and popped the clutch, causing the machine to burn some serious rubber as he drove past the police cars sitting along the road. Officer Bullseye pulled his pistol from his pants and pointed it toward Simms, but he wasn't able to get a clear shot because of the excessive tire smoke as The Exorcist sped away.

The commanding officer at the roadblock radioed Agent Jain. "What happened? Do we pursue them?"

Jain began shouting instructions that instant. "Negative, stand down right now! I repeat, stand down! Do not pursue them openly! We can't force Simms' hand. That might lead to Richie Blackburn getting hurt or killed, and we can't risk that happening. That's the very reason I had you pull the patrol cars off the road. I want you to put an unmarked car on their tail so we can keep an eye on them. We are going to have to do this covertly. Since Simms wouldn't listen to reason, we are going to have to take him out by surprise."

CHAPTER 42

Lost at a Drive-in

"It's going to be dark soon, so pull into the drive-in theater that's up here on the right." Simms had seen a roadside billboard for it a few miles back. "It should be a good place to get this headlight fixed, as well as some food and a bathroom break, of course. Then we can get back on the road."

"Finally!" Lucia let out a giant breath of relief.

Richie turned into the aged but exuberant facility and drove by a faded turquoise pointed arrow sign that was greatly accentuated against the pastel pink and peachy yellow sunset. The first line of the marque section read: Double Feature Friday. The second line listed the movies they would show: *Corvette Summer* and *Vanishing Point*. Next, he paid the young girl at the window and parked at the far right side toward the back, hoping not to draw any unwanted attention while they fixed the car's headlight. The three of them had been driving for several hours since their run-in with authorities back in New Mexico. It was now late Friday evening, and they were somewhere around the Mt. Pleasant area in Utah. Right after parking, all three of them made an immediate and hobbling beeline for the restrooms.

Richie had a hard time walking. He was very stiff from being in the car for so long and his injuries from the junkyard fight didn't help matters for him. He looked over to his right and noticed Simms limping from his bullet wound. To his left, he watched Lucia gingerly walking because of her minor injuries from the car crash she was involved in earlier that day. "So much for keeping a low profile." Richie chuckled. "We're all a damn mess."

Richie and Simms were in the only two tightly placed toilet stalls of the men's rundown restroom, taking care of their respective businesses.

"I'm in a tough spot here, Richard."

Richie looked over toward the neighboring stall. "Sorry, dude, I can't help you with that." He flushed the toilet and went over to the hard, water-stained sink.

"Very funny, asshole! I'm talking about that comment you made about leaving me tied up somewhere."

"Yeah, so?" Richie washed his hands.

"I've killed pricks for making comments like that in the past."

Richie turned around and looked at the stall Simms was in, while slinging water off his hands.

"But you also kept me from getting my head blown off."

"I couldn't let Lucia see that. Even though you probably deserve such a fate as that, Lucia doesn't deserve to watch it."

Simms stepped out and went to the sink, staring at Richie while doing so.

"What are you getting at Simms? What's the point you're trying to make?"

Simms was quiet as he washed his hands. Once he was done, he got up close in Richie's face. "I know you want me to pay for the murder of the guy in the hippie van, along with all my other crimes. And I know you want to save your relationship with your baby momma, as they say. But what I don't know is which one you want worse. That's the point I'm trying to make. I'm tired of wondering about this subject. You just can't have both, you just can't."

Richie didn't know how to respond, so he just stared into the cold eyes of the hardened criminal.

"I knew you were having a hard time deciding which was more important, so I decided to help you out with that."

Richie got a sinking feeling in his gut. "What are you talking about?"

"My longtime enemy isn't the only one that can contact The Heat Seeker."

The sinking feeling in Richie's stomach immediately worsened. He was afraid to ask, but dying to know. "What do you mean?" Then his face grew red. "What have you done?"

"It's more like what you have done." Simms arrogantly smirked. "I tried to reason with you in the beginning. I tried to make you see we were allies in this situation, but you just wouldn't have it, so I took out a little insurance policy on our drive here. I couldn't risk you actually leaving me tied up somewhere for the feds."

Richie thought back to the previous hours, and he had noticed that Simms was texting on his phone a lot on the last stretch of highway leading to the drive-in theater. "Well, spill it, you creep. What have you done?"

Simms had an impervious, snarky smile. "I contacted The Heat Seeker. I tried my very best to counter the contract that had been placed on me, but he is a strict man of principle. He would not budge, no matter what. So, I made a different deal with him. A completely separate offer, out of the norm of things, but, nonetheless, a viable offer, and fortunately for me, he accepted. You see, the deal states that if I were to die, in any fashion whatsoever, before he can kill me himself, then he will kill you."

Richie stood quietly as he thought about that scenario. Then he thought, *I can still get you caught, though.*

Simms continued his spiel in the same arrogant manner. "I also told him that if I were to get apprehended by the authorities because of you, or someone like you, helping them out then he will pay a certain beautiful Misses and her lovely little daughter a visit."

Richie's face now turned pale, and he almost vomited.

Simms continued to display his arrogant grin as he talked. "Like I said, I took out an insurance policy. So, to simplify this whole thing, if you get me killed, you die. If I get captured, your lovely family dies."

Richie's queasiness transformed into pure rage. He grabbed Simms by the upper part of his shirt and wadded two fistfuls of it up in his hands as he got up in his face.

"What are you going to do? Kill me?"

"I'd die for my family, so why wouldn't I just kill you now?"

"I have no doubt you would die for them. You are the eternal hero, never doing any wrong and willing to sacrifice it all for someone who doesn't even care about you. But the main reason you won't kill me is because of Lucia. If you wouldn't let some pig-headed cop waste me, why would you do it yourself?"

Richie's rage now turned into shock. *He's right*, he thought. *I can't kill him because of Lucia. That would make me as big of a monster as him.* He regretfully looked down at the cracked gray concrete of the restroom floor in complete defeat.

Smugness oozed off of Simms as if it were an enveloping morning mist. He took great delight in being able to take total control of the situation they all were in. "Let's see. How do ya say it? Oh, yeah, checkmate, bitch, you just lost," Simms said with great intensity as he pointed his index finger in Richie's face. "That's right. I beat you, asshole, so deal with it. Oh yeah, there's one more angle that's covered that I almost forgot to tell ya about."

Richie looked straight at Simms, waiting for yet another devastating blow.

"I also told The Heat Seeker that if he did manage to kill me, while I'm still with you, and if he felt that you didn't do everything in your power to prevent it then he has orders to kill all three of you. So, if you think you can just rest on your haunches and let him kill me, then you and your family will all die!"

Richie's lip curled up, and he clenched his fists. The many emotions he went through on this simple bathroom break were almost more than he could take.

Simms got up close to Richie's face once more. "You don't make it in this kind of life without covering all the angles. I'm always one…ha, more like three steps ahead of everyone else around me. You see, I have it all covered. I'm always thinking ahead, playing out every scenario, and figuring out every possible angle. I can't be beat. It's impossible." Then, at the top of his lungs, he shouted in Richie's face, "I am God!"

We'll see about that, Richie thought.

A somber Richie and gloating Simms were changing out the broken headlight while Lucia was in line for some much-needed food like cheeseburgers, shoestring French fries, and cold fountain sodas. The first movie hadn't started yet, but golden oldies tunes played through the speakers, setting a nostalgic mood among the cheerful moviegoers.

"You're a lucky son of a bitch to hit a deer like that and only lose a headlight."

Still distraught from the conversation in the bathroom, Richie responded in a somber and sarcastic tone. "Yeah, apparently I'm a walking four-leaf clover."

"I knew it! I knew we were being tailed."

Richie looked up. "What are you talking about?"

"That black Dodge Charger that just pulled in. Over there to the far left." Simms pointed out. "It's an unmarked patrol car. I knew they wouldn't just let us drive off from a roadblock like that."

"What are we going to do about it?"

"Well, in the meantime, I'm going to keep my ass outta sight just in case they are going to try and pop me. Here, finish putting this new headlight in."

Richie painfully bent down and took over the job while Simms snuck into the passenger side of the Camaro. He reclined the seat, keeping it up just enough to keep an eye on the unmarked Charger.

After making a few adjustments, the new headlight was in and, as Richie painfully got to his feet, Lucia walked up with her arms full of food and drinks.

"Here, let me help you with that." Richie unloaded some of the food off of her. As he did so, he got in Simms' view of the Charger.

"Move, dumbass!" Simms waved to the right, trying to get Richie to move over in the same direction.

Feeling that Simms' attitude toward him was eventually going to get out of hand, especially after the bathroom conversation, Richie turned and shot him a look of contempt before walking over to the right side of the Camaro. He reached into the white bag holding the food and grabbed a cheeseburger. He then bent down and shoved the greasy meat sandwich hard against Simms' chest. "Here's your food," he said through clenched teeth.

This show of aggression angered Simms, of course, and he immediately reached for his pistol, which he conveniently placed on top of one of his smaller bags that was sitting between his legs on the floorboard of the car. Just as he went to point it at Richie and put him in his place, a voice seemingly came out of nowhere.

"Excuse me. I'm really sorry to bother y'all, but I was wondering, are you the wrestler they call The Priest?" The curious man was now standing next to the Camaro.

Seeming to ignore the man at first, Richie continued staring down Simms. It appeared as if he was daring him to retaliate against his show of aggression through the open window, but he eventually slowly turned his head toward the unexpected person so that he could address him. Once his eyes fully locked onto the very familiar man, and he fully comprehended who he was looking at, he was totally shocked.

CHAPTER 43

Cotton McCready

"Oh, wow, this is amazing!" With an infectious smile, Richie sped straight up to the interested man like a small, excited child on Christmas. "Is it really you? It can't be."

"Cotton McCready at your service." The light-complexion-skinned man looked to be about fifty years old or so and had dark-colored hair protruding out from underneath a plain black baseball-style cap. He seemed eager to shake Richie's hand as he extended his own out to him.

Richie wasted no time receiving his hand for a firm shake. "Man, this is a huge honor! I always thought I'd meet you at a racetrack or a big car show somewhere, never a place like this."

"Yeah, I'm here with some friends of mine." Cotton pointed over to several four-wheel-drive vehicles in the back row. "We came out here for a Jeep convention that's happening this weekend. One of my pals has a brother that lives here and he suggested we check this place out."

"It's my first time here as well. I love *Corvette Summer*, it's one of my all-time favorites."

"I've always liked it, too. My pal said they played *American Graffiti* and *Dirty Mary, Crazy Larry* last week."

"Wow, those are some great classics as well. I'm sorry if I'm geeking out too much. It's just so awesome finally getting to meet you. I'm a huge fan of yours, always have been. Some of the best parts of my teenage years were when I was pulling for you in that ol' number forty-four Chevrolet. I was completely bummed out for months when you retired a few years ago."

Cotton gave Richie a modest smile. "Well, I appreciate that. I really do. Ever since I've quit driving stock cars constantly, I've actually had time to be a spectator for various things myself and I gotta tell ya, I'm a huge fan of yours as well. Professional wrestling was one of the first things I got into. I hadn't watched it since I was a kid and it sucked me right back in just after watching it one night."

"Excellent! That means we were doing our jobs." Richie smiled.

"Oh yeah, you definitely earned your money that night. It was when you had that Mass Death Match with Voodoo Larue."

"The Battle of Beliefs with Ragin Cajun himself. That match was brutal."

"I loved that part of the match when you broke that bottle of sacramental wine over his head, then yelled out, 'The power of Christ compels you!' I about fell out of my recliner, laughing. I thought to myself, *Dang this guy is awesome!*"

Richie chuckled, then disclosed an unknown inside fact. "Larue wanted us to hang him on a cross at the end of the match and our boss, Terrence Vaughn, liked the idea, but he didn't let us do it, of course. He was afraid that would have pushed the envelope a little too far and in that instance, I'm sure he was right."

"Hey, Richard," Simms called out, but Richie was star-stuck at the moment and didn't even hear him.

After a couple more failed attempts at trying to get Richie to notice him as he talked to his idol, the now-retired race car driver, Simms instructed Lucia to walk up to him and get his attention.

Perturbed that her demanding father couldn't just let Richie enjoy this moment, she walked up to him with regret. "Richie, he needs to talk to you," Lucia said just above a whisper. Then she gave Cotton a simper-like smile.

"He can wait a minute," Richie blurted out. "I've looked up to this man for most of my life and I seriously doubt anything he's got to say is important enough to interrupt us." Then Richie glanced over at the black, unmarked police Charger, just to make sure Simms wasn't trying to warn him about the cops.

"Look, Richie, if I'm interrupting something, we can do this some other time. I've got box seats at Charlotte. We can watch a race there together." Cotton felt the tension in the air and didn't want to add to it by keeping Richie occupied.

"Box seats at Charlotte? Sweet man! We have to do that for sure!" Richie noticed the worried look was still on Cotton's face. "Oh no, man, don't sweat it, you ain't interrupting anything. I'm just kinda in a jam here, but that's something we can talk about another time."

Richie's boldness aggravated Simms greatly and the fact that he was now blowing him off completely infuriated him, and, to make it even worse, there wasn't a single thing he could do about it. He just had to lay low and hope not to draw any attention from the Charger or any other patrons at the drive-in.

Cotton turned away from the car and lowered his head a bit to avoid being seen by Simms. "Hey, Rich, if you're in trouble or something, I might be able to help. What's going on here, you can tell me."

"Nah, everything's fine." Richie's tone was unconvincing. He was trying to play it cool, but it seemed to be to no avail.

"You're supposed to be in Europe kicking off a huge tour, but here you are in the middle of nowhere, covered in bruises.

I know wrestling's not fake, at least in the manner everyone says, but I saw your last match with Milo Jones and I know he couldn't have beaten on you that bad."

It flattered Richie that The Cotton McCready, one of the greatest stock car drivers ever, was actually a fan of his and apparently a big one. "Look, I'm uh, I'm kinda in a predicament that I can't fully explain at the moment, but I have to prevent that sack of crap in the passenger seat getting captured by the police. My family's life as well as my own is on the line."

Cotton's eyes got as big as softballs and his jaw dropped. "Do you want me to call someone? Someone besides the cops, of course."

Richie's demeanor noticeably changed, and he hung his head. "There's really no one to call. He claims that if I get him as far as Mt. Hood, Oregon, where my family is, that he'll let me go. I really doubt he'll stick to that promise, though."

"Dang, I'm sorry, Richie. I originally was just going to come over to look at this car, but then I realized it was you driving it. I was kinda shocked and confused because I just saw you drive it to the ring this past Sunday. I had no idea you were going to tell me you were being held hostage."

"Like I said, it's a long and very complicated story. I need you to trust me and keep this on the down-low."

"Yeah, sure, that's no problem, Rich. I got your back." Fearing that he was going to get Richie in further trouble with his captor, he talked about the car right quick before heading back to his Jeep. "So, is this your car?"

"Not exactly. I sure wish it was. It's the most amazing thing I've ever been in."

Cotton looked surprised at the fact that it wasn't Richie's car, but then he figured it probably had something to do with the complicated story he was talking about. "Oh, I bet his thing is a real monster, ain't it? I saw some videos of it on the Internet."

"Man, you have no idea." Then he looked at Cotton. "Well, maybe you do, being a professional racer and all." They both chuckled. "This thing has more horsepower than your stock car did, and it's street legal!"

"Whoa! That's unbelievable, Rich. Sadly though, in another ten years, it will probably have twice as much horsepower than a stock car."

Richie looked disappointed. "Yeah, that was something I wanted to ask you about. What the hell happened to that sport? It's nothing like it was fifteen or so years ago."

Cotton shook his head. "Somewhere along the way, it became wrong to be Southern for some reason. And after the powers that be in the sport got wind of that fallacious fact, it was all downhill from there. Huge changes to the rules, point system, and the way the sport was marketed as a whole was put into effect and the fans, the real and true fans, absolutely hated it."

Richie nodded in agreement. "That's exactly what I've noticed as well. The old fan base's opinions and feelings got cast aside. It felt like we all got left behind."

"You did. It's kinda like…" Cotton paused, getting his thoughts together. "You could put It this way, I guess. Football is like chicken wings and baseball is like hotdogs. Racing was like gravy and biscuits, but it's been replaced with raisins and orange slices. They took the Southern flavor right out of it and it's not been the same since."

"Wow, that's a perfect way of putting it."

Replacing the oldies' music echoing through the parked cars were big exciting movie sounds that were now broadcasting through the antique speakers as the classic film played on the big white screen up ahead. It was now completely dark, and a hush came over the crowd as they settled in to watch the movie under the shining stars on such a clear and beautiful night.

Cotton leaned toward Richie. "I better get going, but before I do, though, are you sure there ain't something I can do to help you out? Is there anything you can think of?"

Richie scanned the drive-in, his eyes settling on the black unmarked police Charger. "Well, there is one thing you could do."

CHAPTER 44

Good Ol' Number 44

Sitting behind the wheel of the Camaro, Richie pinched his nose as warm blood trickled out of it. Looking at the cheeseburger in his other hand, he desperately wanted to eat, but couldn't because of dealing with yet another wound to his already battered and bruised body.

"Why did you do that, Papa? He has enough injuries to deal with as it is! How do you expect him to drive you around if you keep hurting him? Put that stupid gun away! He kept you from getting shot just hours ago and he's doing all he can to keep you from getting caught!"

"I don't care what he's done. Nobody ignores me like that or disrespects me either and gets away with it! I'm fully in charge here and I demand to be treated as such or there will be severe consequences. He's lucky I only hit him in the nose with it."

"Gah, you're such an idiot. I don't know how you've actually managed to elude capture for so long." Richie imagined taking that beloved handgun of Simms and pistol-whipping him into next week.

Simms stared Richie down with a strong look of pure anger.

"You've already got me between a rock and a hard place, but that's not good enough for you, though. You just have to keep getting that ego stroked."

"He's right, you know. Enough is never enough with you."

Simms turned around and looked directly at Lucia. "You shut your damn mouth! I didn't put up with your mother giving me lip and I sure as hell am not going to put up with you doing it either!"

Richie shook his head in disgust as he thought about how long Simms had searched for her and now that he had her back for a few days, before leaving her forever, that's how he talked to her. His only baby girl. To make matters worse, he constantly reminded her of how unapprovingly her deceased mother was to him. *This guy is a complete monster. There's no hope for him*, Richie thought. *If only Lucia hadn't been in the car back at the roadblock. That's all that saved you, asshole.*

Simms continued to watch the unmarked police Charger like a hawk. He still had a scowl on his face from feeling disrespected by Richie's actions. "You took a huge chance getting us caught by chatting with that hillbilly fan of yours."

"That hillbilly fan was Cotton McCready. Before you say anything, I realize that name doesn't mean anything to you, especially since you've been down in Mexico for decades, but he is a five-time stock car racing champion. The only athlete more popular than him back in the nineties was Michael Jordan. He's actually gracious enough that he is going to try and help us out with our uninvited friends over there. He said he would do what he could to help us lose them. Besides, how was I going to get us caught when we're already being watched?" Richie sat quietly, staring straight at the movie screen with a blank expression on his face.

"How do you know he will help? What makes you think he's not over there on the phone with the cops right now?"

Richie looked directly into Simms's eyes. "He knows what's on the line for me, so he decided to help out instead of calling the police. If he was going to call them, they would be here already. He's working on a way to help us, I'm sure of it."

Simms smirked. "Well, wasn't that very nice of him? What is the plan and when is it supposed to unfold?"

"He said he would let me know as soon as he figured it out."

"Well, in the meantime, I have to go change this bandage in the restroom. I've bled straight through it." Simms was referring to the still untreated bullet wound on his leg. "Give me the key fob."

Baffled by that statement, Richie looked at him. "What, are you crazy? Just change it here in the car. How do you know the cops in that Charger won't rush you while you're in there?"

"I already thought about that. If they were going to take me here, they would have done so while you had that make-out session with your go-kart buddy. Plus, this is a public place. They know how dangerous I am and they probably don't want to risk getting anyone hurt. It would appear they are going to stay in surveillance mode until they think the time is right to strike. Then again, they might charge right in as soon as I pass the doorway, but I've got an offering for the porcelain throne that just won't wait. Hopefully, they won't see me go in now that the lights are off. If they do, I will just shoot my way out."

Richie reluctantly handed him the car's key fob, then unwrapped his cheeseburger. Surprisingly enough, it was still slightly warm.

Lucia watched Simms limp toward the restrooms with one of his small black bags, staying low and moving as quickly as his injury would allow. "He's never going to change. He's never going to be sorry. He is a complete lost cause. An evil monster forever, it appears."

Richie chewed away at his burger while holding his injured nose. He felt horrible that Lucia had a father that was so terrible. *I can't imagine being so bad that Josie thinks that way of me,* he thought. He sipped his drink. "I had a conversation one time with Mary about what evil really is."

"Oh yeah? Did you come to the conclusion that it's named Peter Mitchell Simms?"

Richie snickered. "No, I didn't have that revelation 'til yesterday, I think. This whole thing has gotten my days completely out of whack. It feels like an eternity ago that I left Tallahassee. Anyway, the conclusion Mary and I came to was that being evil clearly boils down to selfishness."

"That sounds a little too simple. How did you two come to that conclusion?" Lucia turned her head so she could clearly hear his response over the sound of the cult classic film that was fully underway at this point.

"Well, let's see…I got it. Take a bank robber, for instance."

"Okay?"

"A person decides to go into a bank to take someone else's money. At that point, they don't care about anything but his or her own wants. They may need money for a good reason, but if they infringe on someone else's property, that's wrong. If they shoot the guard on the way out, they have infringed on the guard's right to life for their own selfish reasons. Being evil boils down to being selfish. Being evil means you only care about your position and have no regard for anyone else's. It's the very opposite of being good. If you see a kid hold the door open for an elderly person, then the kid sacrifices a few seconds of their life because they care about helping someone out. Willing to sacrifice or give equals good. Being overly selfish or wrongfully taking equals evil. That's my take on it at least."

Lucia nodded in understanding. "That makes a lot of sense. I guess you're a saint for giving up your career for your family."

Richie stopped chewing his burger. "No, I'm definitely not a saint. I took away Vaughn's right to own this car."

"But you did so because he cheated you out of your contract money."

"Still doesn't make it right. Look what a mess I've ended up in for being selfish."

"Richie, you weren't being selfish. You were fighting back against an injustice that had been placed upon you."

"Still doesn't make it right, though." Richie shook his head, now disgusted by his actions.

They both sat quietly for a moment.

"I think you're spot on with your theory of good and evil simply being selfish or not, but I feel there is a third category as well."

"How do you figure that?" Richie looked at Lucia in the rear-view mirror.

"I think you can do the wrong thing for the right reasons sometimes. In some situations, I think it has to be done. Take this whole crazy venture, for example." Lucia's face grew red, and she hesitated, as if looking for the right words. "You have forever changed my life."

Richie looked down, not knowing how to respond.

"You have changed my life for the good. I don't know how all this is going to play out, but what if I hadn't met you?"

"If you hadn't met me, you wouldn't be in the mess you're currently in. I managed to get us kidnapped by your own drug kingpin father. That isn't a good thing."

"No, but If I hadn't met you, who knows what could have happened to me? There's no telling where or how I would have ended up. You've inspired me to be a better person, to do something good with my life. That's why I say doing something bad with good intentions is still good, in most cases anyways. Everything isn't black and white. It just isn't."

"Excuse me, sir." A young girl, a worker at the drive-in, had suddenly appeared at Richie's window, startling him.

"Geez, you scared me!" Richie and the young girl laughed for a moment.

"I'm sorry, sir. A man in a Jeep in the very back asked me to bring you this popcorn. He said he owed you a bag."

"Thanks." Richie took the back from her.

"You're welcome. Sorry again for scaring you."

"It's okay." Richie chuckled, as the worker walked off.

"What's up with that?"

"I'm not sure."

At that very moment, a short static-filled white noise immediately followed by a voice came from the bag saying, "Number 44 calling for The Priest. You got your ears on?"

The talking bag of popcorn surprised Richie. He looked back at Lucia for reassurance that he wasn't going crazy. She gave him a look of bewilderment, then looked down at the bag.

The static noise came through again, followed by the voice. "This is Number 44 calling for The Priest, comeback."

Richie looked down into the bag, sifted through the popcorn, and pulled out a long-distance walkie-talkie. *This must be a part of Cotton's plan*, he thought, as he pressed the button on the side. "This is The Priest. Go ahead Number 44."

"Okay, I think I've figured out how to take care of our friends. Over."

"Sounds good, let's hear it. Over."

There was a long pause.

"Are you there, Number 44? This is The Priest. Do you copy?"

"This is Number 44. There's been a change of plans. The police have blocked the exit. I repeat, more police are now on the scene and they have blocked the only way out of here!"

CHAPTER 45

Spills, Chills, and Death-Defying Thrills

"*S*o, *where are we going?*" Mary had sat on the passenger side of the white Monte Carlo Richie was driving.

"*Well, I figured since John let me borrow his aerocoupe, we should do something that will keep us close to the car. He'd have my hide if something happened to this thing. This is one of his favorites. I'd have brought my car, but I don't currently keep any insurance on it since I'm not home much, it just isn't cost-effective. John always lets me drive one of his when I'm in from the road.*"

"*That makes sense. Why waste money if you're not here to use it? That's very nice of your brother to let you drive his cars, but I'm not sure I understand why this is one of his favorites, though. I mean, it is nice and all, but it's just a kinda plain white car.*"

"*It may appear plain, but in 1986 there were only two hundred of these cars made. They were very successful in the stock car racing world.*" Richie had looked over at Mary and she didn't seem to care about the useless facts of John's car, so he changed the course of the conversation and tried to build up excitement for the destination of their current date. "*Anyways, I thought I'd take you to one of the last drive-in theaters on the East Coast. How does that sound? Have you ever been to one?*"

Mary shook her head. "*Sounds like fun! It will definitely be something different.*"

Richie smiled, pleased that Mary seemed to be delighted by his decision to take her there. *"Oh, here we go. We're here already."*

After he had pulled past the entrance sign that read: Lil' Christine's Big Drive-in, Richie proceeded to pay an attendant for their admission. Then, he picked out a perfect spot in front of the giant-sized movie screen. Next, they grabbed some food at the concession stand and made their way back over to John's Monte Carlo.

"Oh, look, it's starting. What are we watching again?"

Richie stopped sipping on his cherry limeade. *"Herbie the Love Bug."*

"Oh no, is it going to be one of those old cheesy sci-fi horror flicks where everything looks so fake?"

"Hey, some of those sci-fi flicks are awesome. But no, Herbie is a lovable Volkswagen Beetle race car that has special powers. He's anthropomorphic. I think that's how you say it. Anyways, I think you will like it. It's a fun little movie."

Mary shrugged. *"Okay."* She settled further down into the seat to make herself more comfortable.

As they took in the sights and sounds of the classic family film, Mary gleefully said, *"I love this movie. He is so cute!"* Then she accidentally knocked over her soda while reaching for the popcorn. Clanking ice followed by a swooshing sound of the drink exiting the cup clamored out. *"Oh no, I'm so sorry, Richie."* She threw napkins on the affected area in a hurried state, hoping to lessen the mess.

Trying to conceal a worried look, Richie unconvincingly attempted to reassure her that it wasn't an issue. *"It's okay. At least it's all on the floorboard. That will be easier to clean than if it had gotten all over the seats."*

"But you said this was one of your brother's favorite cars. Isn't he going to be furious?"

"He won't if he doesn't find out about it. Don't worry, I'll take care of it after I drop you off."

"Well, I hope he doesn't find out about this spill. I was hoping we could take it out again sometime." Mary shyly smiled.

Richie's eyebrows rose. *"Really? So, you do want to go out again sometime? After our last date, I wasn't sure I'd even get you to go out with me tonight. Also, I thought you didn't care for this car?"*

"Well, like you, It's beginning to grow on me." A full-blown flirtatious smile beamed. *"I wasn't feeling so well the last time we went out, but tonight's been wonderful. At this rate, I think I just might be your Love Bug."* She leaned in and the two embraced in a brief but very passionate kiss.

Richie gazed into her beautiful eyes. *"Yeah, I think I'd be okay with that. My own little Love Bug."* Mary smiled and settled against Richie's chest as they continued watching the movie. *"Thanks, Herbie, I owe ya—"*

∞

"One way outta here," Cotton said on the walkie-talkie.

Richie yelled into his handheld radio. "Repeat that, Number 44. Please repeat. Over."

"I said there may be one way out of here. Over."

"Okay, but we've got a problem. The schmuck I was telling you about is in the restroom, and he has the key fob. We're sitting ducks at the moment. The cops will probably nail his ass before he can get back to the car. Is there any way you can pick him up for us?"

"I'm on it, over."

Richie and Lucia both looked toward the building that housed the toilets. A jacked-up blue Jeep pulled up to the door of the men's room.

"That has to be Cotton in that Wrangler. Come on Simms, hurry it up."

"Maybe this is for the best. If he gets arrested here, you most likely will still make it to Oregon in time."

Richie liked the thought of finally getting her father busted, but since Simms had made a contract with The Heat Seeker for him and his family, he couldn't let that happen. He also didn't think it would be wise to let Lucia in on that fact, since she already was having internal struggles with dealing with her criminal father.

Cotton reached over and opened the passenger door to the jacked-up four-wheel drive. Simms was cautious in peeking out the restroom door. He was apparently aware of the growing police presence and was hesitant to make a move.

"Come on! I'm here to help. We got to get you back to Richie!"

"How do I know I can trust you?"

"Look, either you get in the Jeep or I'm going to come in there for the key fob to the Camaro and take it from you! It's your choice."

Simms was visibly anxious and had a hard time deciding what to do. Between the two shouting and the noise of the customized Jeep, it was apparent they had drawn the attention of the police.

"Great job. You took so long deciding what to do that you've now got the cops coming over."

"Damn it!" Simms yelled out in frustration. Then, after a brief pause, he bolted toward Cotton's vehicle, but he didn't go unnoticed by the two officers walking in that direction.

"Halt!"

"Stop right there!"

Both officers ran toward the Jeep.

Simms pulled his pistol and fired several shots toward the two advancing men.

A look of astonishment followed by terror came across Cotton's face. "You're a freaking maniac!"

"Drive, asshole!" Simms slammed the door.

The two officers had returned fire. Cotton immediately put his oversized machine in reverse to escape the incoming bullets. Disturbing thuds reverberated out as the police's projectiles cracked the glass, followed by their ammo peppering the windshield. He went as fast as he could go in reverse, then after reaching the end of the aisle, he spun his Jeep hard to the left and started at a hurried pace toward the front of the drive-in.

Back at the Camaro, after hearing the officers yell into their radios that shots had been fired, Richie spoke out with heavy sarcasm, "Great, here we go."

As Cotton raced toward the screen, other police officers pursued him in their patrol cars, shocking the crowd of moviegoers as they stopped watching the projected car action to view a real car chase unfold right in front of them.

After Cotton got to the front of the drive-in, he turned right and drove by the first row of cars on his way to Richie. One of the police cars pulled in the aisle, blocking his way, causing Cotton to bring the Jeep to a screeching halt. As he put his vehicle in reverse, a second car pulled in behind him with its bright flashing lights and a loud siren blaring out. He was now trapped. So, it seemed.

Cotton wasted no time engaging the four-wheel drive of his off-road capable machine. "Hang on!"

He sped toward the police sedan. The officer exited his car and watched Cotton drive his Jeep over the back of the police cruiser, crushing it. The back glass shattered and the sounds of crunching metal rang out as Cotton's monstrous SUV climbed over its current obstacle.

The officer pulled his weapon out and pointed it at Cotton. "Halt! You could've killed me, asshole!"

As Cotton's rear wheels cleared the car and slammed back down on the ground, he hollered back at the officer, "Calm down. I wasn't going to run over you!" Then he laughed as he looked over at Simms and said, "Just your car!"

Then he made his way over to Richie, but before Simms could get out, another police car was coming toward them.

"Hurry, give Richie the key fob!" Cotton shouted at Simms.

Simms was busy watching the police car come toward them. "I won't make it to the car in time!"

"I know, that's why I said give them the key. The cops will have a harder time catching us both. You can get back in the car with them once we get outta here!"

"Fine, but I'll shoot your ass if you get me caught!"

"I won't, I know what's on the line for Richie." Cotton grabbed the fob from Simms' outreached hand and as he leaned his arm out the window to toss it to Richie, the oncoming police officer was a little more gung ho. He pulled out his weapon and fired at the Jeep while he was still driving. Pulling his arm back in, Cotton dropped the key fob.

Cotton put his blue vehicle in reverse to escape the oncoming cop, but the overzealous officer lost control of his patrol car and slammed into a dark red SUV parked behind Richie.

Richie turned and looked at the crash that had happened just feet behind him. He opened his door to grab the key fob. After picking it up, he glanced at the Charger that had them under surveillance, and the passenger side door was open. He thought that was odd, but he had no time to waste. As he got back in the car, Officer Bullseye, whom Agent Jain ordered to shoot Simms on sight, was aiming his pistol at Lucia's head.

CHAPTER 46

Follow Me

Richie's eyes widened in surprise. "What are you doing?" Officer Bullseye's brows furrowed. He thought he'd be happy to have help show up. "I'm trying to save you from these maniacs."

"She's just as much a hostage as I am."

"It's true." Lucia nodded and flinched away slightly from his gun.

Puzzled, Bullseye looked at Lucia. "I thought Simms was your dad."

"He is, but I've been on the run from that maniac for years."

"I know it sounds crazy, but she's telling the truth."

Bullseye slowly lowered his weapon. Convinced that Richie was telling the truth, he began firmly instructing them, "Well, let's go then. Let's get you two out of here!"

The sound of crunching metal got their attention as Cotton climbed over the same patrol car he had already driven across before as he continued to run from the police cars in an almost comical scene.

Richie pointed to the Jeep. "We can't. That's Cotton McCready in that Jeep. We can't leave him alone with Simms."

"The race car driver?" Bullseye looked perplexed.

"Yes. I can't believe it either, but it's him and we can't get him killed. He's trying to help us, me especially."

"I don't understand. Oh, and by the way, why did you take off like a bat outta hell back at the checkpoint in New Mexico? We coulda ended all this crap back there."

"Listen, man, we ain't got time for this! I'll deliver Simms to you guys on a silver platter." Richie sounded convincing, although he had no idea what he was going to do.

"No, we take him out here! I've got orders!"

Richie buried his face in his hands. He was completely stressed out at this point. Officer Bullseye was going to force his hand. He was going to have to tell him about the Heat Seeker in front of Lucia. "Look, he is going to have my family killed by a supposed notorious hitman called Heat Seeker if I don't help him escape the country."

Both Lucia's and Officer Bullseye's eyebrows rose in concern. Judging from his reaction, he seemed to be familiar with the name: Heat Seeker.

"Nate Rainer, the politician. My family is with him in Oregon. They are there for a wedding in the Mt. Hood area tomorrow at two o'clock. Send guards there, officers, whatever, just protect them!"

"Priest, you got your ears on?" Cotton's voice blasted through the walkie-talkie. "I'm going to have to make us a way out of here."

"Okay, I'm right behind ya. What's the plan? Over?"

"No!" Bullseye shouted. "You two have to come with me."

Richie looked straight into his eyes and pressed the button to start the engine. It roared to life.

Officer Bullseye's face grew intense. "No, shut it down and come with me!"

Richie shook his head. "I can't!"

Officer Bullseye pulled his pistol and pointed it in the car, but not directly at Richie. He was hoping that brandishing his weapon would be enough to get him to cooperate. "Turn it off, Richie! We have to end this here!"

Richie reached for the seatbelt and, as he put it on, Lucia meekly did the same. "You got kids?"

Bullseye continued to hold his pistol out. "No, but my sister does."

"I'd bet she'd go through hell and high water for them and you know that too, right?"

"Damn it, Blackburn! Turn the car off!"

"You know I can't do that."

Cotton was coming back around. Richie got on the walkie-talkie. "I'm falling in behind you 44. Let's do this. Over!"

"Don't do this Richie!"

Richie turned to look at him. "Nate Rainer's wedding tomorrow, Mt. Hood, Oregon. Get security there now!"

Cotton passed the Camaro and Richie immediately pulled out of the parking spot to follow him.

"Damn it, Blackburn!" As the Camaro sped off, Officer Bullseye stood there in disbelief.

Cotton spoke into the walkie-talkie. "Here we go, Priest. Hold on to your cross!"

"Oh, geez!" Richie cried out as the two vehicles rushed straight toward the fence surrounding the antiquated lot.

The old, dried-out wood made an enormous thud followed by cracking sounds as Cotton plowed straight through it with his massive Jeep. He was now kicking up dust with his oversized tires on the arid land surrounding the drive-in while trying to get to the solid pavement of the highway. Richie followed behind him, but he was a little slower than he wanted to be since he was dodging the wood debris from the now torn-up fence. He was having an even harder time seeing through the dust clouds.

"Hurry, boys, block them off!" Cotton yelled into the hand radio.

"What's going on back there?" Richie asked Lucia.

She studied the scene behind them through the rear window. "Best I can tell, Cotton's truck buddies blocked the hole in the fence so the police can't chase us through it. It also looks like they blocked the road."

"Oh, crap. He's going to be in so much trouble because of us."

"It's okay. We'll explain it to them when this is all over."

"If we're around to tell it."

"Speaking of telling things, why didn't you tell me about the contract with the Heat Seeker my father put on your family?"

Before Richie responded, he turned onto the road behind Cotton. "I didn't want to make matters any worse. I hate seeing how bad it hurts you to have a father like that."

"I know what kind of monster he is. You don't have to spare my feelings. Like I said earlier, he's made it clear that he is never going to change. He's made that perfectly clear."

Cotton pulled into a gas station, and Richie pulled up beside him. Simms hopped out immediately and raced over to the Camaro.

Cotton got out as well and went to Richie's window. "Get out of here, man. We'll hold them off as long as possible!"

"I can't thank you enough, Cotton. I'll tell them everything once this is all over. I hope I haven't gotten you in more trouble than you can get out of."

"Don't worry about it. I got good lawyers. Besides, I haven't had that much fun since that time I took home a million bucks for winning a race at Bristol! Now get outta here!" He slammed the top of Richie's door and ran back to his Jeep.

Richie gazed at the famous racer for a moment and gave him a slight head nod before he tore out of the gas station like a maniac and sped down the dark road, hoping to make the best of his longtime hero, Cotton McCready's help.

"Richard, reach under the steering wheel."

"What am I doing? I don't feel anything."

"Further back. I installed two different switches. Flip the one on the right. It will shut off our tail and brake lights. The bastards can't catch what they can't see."

"When did you install them? What does the other one do?" Richie flipped the metal toggle. Then he looked in the rear-view mirror to see if it worked, and it was pitch black behind them.

"The other one kills the headlights. I wired them up while you three went to get gas this morning. You don't elude capture this long without learning all the tricks."

"Do I even want to know why you would have these kinds of switches on you?"

"No, probably not. By the way, this thing looks even more wicked than before with that red halo headlight you picked up. Unfortunately, it makes us stand out, but not as bad as if we didn't have one at all."

"It was the only one that auto parts store had in stock. At least we'll look awesome on our way to the Grim Reaper."

CHAPTER 47

Threatening Security

"Nate. Nate, someone's knocking on the door!" Mary panicked, whispering low, as she nudged his arm, trying to get him to wake up.

After a few groans, and stirring from a deep slumber, he sat up in a panic as he realized what Mary was saying. "Get the police on the phone! I knew I shouldn't have rented a house without a proper security system. The only reason I got this one is because it was so close to the reception hall."

"Mr. Rainer, it's the police. Please open up. We have a potentially threatening matter to talk about."

Mary and Nate gave each other confused looks, then preceded to get dressed enough to answer the door. Mary looked out the window. "It really is them."

He cautiously opened the door to two officers. Judging by their demeanor, he could tell that it wasn't an extremely urgent matter, so he questioned them in a hubristic manner, as he often did with people that he felt were beneath him. "What's the meaning of this? Why are you here disturbing us like this?"

"Mr. Rainer, we have—"

"We are getting married several hours from now. I had my bachelor party last night so that I could spend tonight with my beautiful bride-to-be and here you are ruining it for us!"

Flabbergasted by Nate's rudeness, the officer changed his stance to one of authority. "We have been notified by the FBI that your future wife and her child are potentially in great danger."

"What? That's ridiculous!"

The officer explained the entire situation for the next several minutes.

"This is preposterous! It's obviously a big scheme by Richie to try and postpone the wedding. He's furious that you picked me and now he's got his boss, who we know has a lot of pull, to try and help him out in stopping this wedding."

Mary looked concerned. "I don't know, Nate, this sounds serious. Besides, Richie quit; he had a falling out with Vaughn and stormed out right before he was supposed to go to Europe."

"That's perfect timing, isn't it? Oh, Mary, don't be so gullible. He's an entertainer for a living. He obviously is just doing this so he can have one more last chance to win you back."

"Sir, this isn't a ruse. Richie Blackburn is really being held hostage by Peter Mitchell Simms."

"He says that, but he's probably working for him. He was always one step away from being a criminal."

"That's not true, Nate."

"Yes, it is, Mary! You yourself told me how his brother illegally street raced to pay the bills when Richie was a kid. Like I said, he's always been one step away from being a criminal. How could he not be, considering he was raised by one?"

"Listen, I'm sorry about all this. I know the timing is horrible, but we've got orders to protect you three. More officers will be here soon. This is a credible threat."

"Absolutely not! I will not have our perfect day tarnished by the presence of unwanted and unnecessary police officers.

It will spoil the romantic mood of a beautiful destination wedding and upset our many guests and make them feel uncomfortable."

"That's not true, Nate. They can be here without being seen too much and they won't be in the way. They are here to help. You were just in the bed complaining that the house didn't have a security system and you were ready to call the police until we realized they were already here."

"That was before I knew Richie Blackburn was behind this!" Nate looked at the officers. "You guys can tell me this is a real threat all you want, but I don't believe this for a second. You guys have been duped by a hack wrestler. Now, I must ask you to leave."

"What is the matter with you? It won't hurt anything having them here."

Nate's face grew red, and he became even more agitated. "Yes, it will! This will negatively affect our wedding and the media will most definitely try to cover it and my election campaign will suffer most of all from this. I've worked too hard and come too far to have my career ruined by an elaborate stunt from your ex!"

Suddenly, the cries from a toddler echoed out from the hallway.

"Just great. You've woke Josie up!" Mary started toward her, but stopped and looked over her shoulder. "Do what you want, but it seems you're more worried about your stupid campaign than us!" She continued down the dark hallway, stomping off to Josie's room, furious.

Now consumed with frustration, Nate gave the officers a cold stare. "Get out. Get out now and don't come back!"

"But, sir—"

"Get out now and if I even see the hint of a police officer or even a patrol car here, at my wedding, or at my reception, I will see to it that you are immediately fired and never work in this state again! I'm very good friends with the governor of the state, so I can assure you this isn't an empty threat. I can have your badges for breakfast!"

The officers nodded at Nate's warning and slowly made their way back to their car.

"This is just great!" Nate power walked back to the bedroom and made a call on his cellphone.

Outside, as the two officers got back into their patrol car, the younger one said, "Wow, what an ass! Can you believe that, jerk?"

"Typical politician. You're going to see a lot of that if you stay in this job. You might as well get used to it now."

"I was going to tell him to send his guests up Highway 3 and to stay off of Pine Grove because of that old antique church they are moving."

"Do you mean the old Barton Church?"

"Yeah, they say some of the actual pioneers that came across the country on the Oregon Trail were the ones who built it."

"Is that tomorrow?"

"Yeah. It's going to take up most of the road for quite a while. Everyone around here has known about it for weeks. I thought I'd be nice and warn him about it."

"Oh well, it's his problem, not ours. Piss on that bastard."

∞

Agent Jain was taking a call from Terrance Vaughn. "Mr. Vaughn, It's always a pleasure to hear from you."

"Thank you, Agent Jain. I appreciate your sincerity. I was calling to see if you were able to complete your end of the understanding we have because, from the looks of the news I'm currently watching, that doesn't seem to be the case."

A look of concern came over Jain's face as he tried to keep

his chipper facade. "Uh, Mr. Vaughn, I know this looks bad, but I assure you it's nowhere near as big of a deal as the media is making it. We all know about fake news and all."

"Yes, we do, but here's the thing, though. I'm counting on fake news, and you, to help my problems go away. That's why I made our little agreement in the first place."

"Of course, Mr. Vaughn, and I assure you I will hold up my end of the deal. Richie Blackburn will look like a hero and all of the Infinity Wrestling League's bad press from the flight will disappear. No matter how this all goes down, you will be happy with the result. I assure you of that. Last night was a fluke. We had everything exactly how we wanted it but Cotton McCready's presence messed it all up for us."

"I see. Well, like always, I appreciate your help on this matter and I'll be standing by, waiting for a call from you, stating that all of this is all fixed."

"Of course, sir. We're expecting to finish this up before the weekend is over. Mr. Blackburn has been able to communicate to us that he is still headed to Oregon, so it is just a matter of time at this rate."

"Good, good. I hope to hear from you soon, Agent." Vaughn hung up his phone.

Agent Jain leaned back in his chair. "If we only knew where he was now, damn it!"

∞

Back at the house Nate had rented for the wedding, things seemed to be back in order after he had sweet-talked his way back into Mary's good graces.

"I'm really sorry about everything that happened earlier. I just lost my cool, imagining Richie trying to ruin this for us." They hugged.

"Oh, sweetie, he wouldn't deliberately ruin anything. He

said he just wanted to talk to me before the wedding."

Nate's face turned serious. He broke their warm embrace and looked at her. "What! You've talked to him?"

"Not since Sunday."

"Well, what's changed since then?"

"I talked to Sherrod, his best friend. He didn't say anything about him being held hostage. That was earlier in the week, though. All he said at the time was that Richie might be stopping by before the wedding."

"Hmm, I see. So, this whole thing probably is a giant ruse then. You know this is just like him."

"I don't know, Nate, but this seems really serious."

"It's not outside the realm of possibility that he could pull a stunt like this. You know I'm right on that fact. If he wasn't such a savage, I wouldn't mind him stopping by to properly set you free or even staying for the reception, but after the way he threatened me that one time, I'm still considering taking out a restraining order against him."

"Oh, Nate, he's just very protective of his daughter and he didn't want just anyone being around her. He knows you're okay. He was just rattling your cage." Mary bit her bottom lip to keep from laughing as she visualized Richie threatening Nate. She hugged him. That cheerful thought didn't last long. She was worried about what was really happening with Richie. Nate wasn't amused, though, not at all. He had a scornful look of displeasure plastered on his face.

CHAPTER 48

Flick of the Switch

Richie's music still played from the speakers of the Camaro as it fled down the black highway like a ghost in the dark, thanks to the new switches Simms had installed. Richie kept the tail and brake lights off and turned off the headlights when they weren't an absolute necessity. This allowed him to zig and zag past cars and other minor traffic build-ups with no worry of being spotted. The lonely song currently playing matched Richie's mood. He was thinking about Mary and Josie as he drove fast into the darkness, which was a perfect synonym for his current situation. He had no idea what the immediate future held for him.

"Ah, this damn leg! It won't stop bleeding. I must have injured it further with all the running I did back there at the drive-in. Pull into the next place with a restroom so I can change these bandages."

In just a few minutes, Richie did as he asked and, of course, Simms took the key fob with him.

"Come on," Richie said to Lucia as Simms walked ahead. "We'd better go to the restrooms while we got a chance."

"Wait. Sherrod tried calling earlier. Should you call him back?"

Richie's eyes lit up. "Yeah, give me your phone."

Lucia pressed the send button and extended it up to him. After a few rings, a groggy Sherrod answered.

"Richie, is it you?"

"Hey, Sherrod, sorry to wake you, bro. We saw where you'd called. I wanted to call you a long time ago, but I haven't had the chance. I'm kinda hemmed up here."

Sherrod rolled over onto his back and sat up. "Man, where the hell are you? What is going on? Your face is all over the TV. They're saying you've been kidnapped and held hostage by some big-time drug dude."

"Yeah, that's exactly the case. To top it off, the ass hat put in a contract with the world's greatest hitman for Mary, Josie, and me if I help get him caught."

Sherrod's jaw dropped, and he palmed his forehead. "No way, Rich. What can I do to help? You got any plans on getting out of this?"

"I don't know, bro. It ain't looking good. To beat it all, before this happened, I almost got attacked by some greenhorns for a bounty that damned Vaughn put out on me."

"I'd never take up for Vaughn, but that whole bounty thing was a joke."

"A joke?"

"Yeah. A prank Overkill pulled on his little brother. Apparently, he's always ribbing him and this time it was at your expense, unfortunately."

"That sorry sack. I never did like him."

"Hey, get this, somebody was filming you and your girlfriend at that burger joint that night where it all went down. The part where she punted Benson's nuts over the moon, then dumped that chocolate shake on his head, went viral. There's even a meme of it now. It's freaking hilarious!" Sherrod fell out with laughter, but he cut it short, realizing how bad Richie's situation actually was.

Richie chuckled. "Yeah, it was funny as hell. Benson has had that coming to his ass for years." Then he got very serious.

"Listen, man, if I don't come out of this alive, will you make sure Josie gets everything? The old home place, John's shop, all of his cars, and tools."

Sherrod's face wrinkled up. "Man, don't talk like that, Rich. Everything's gonna be all right."

"I mean it, Sherrod. Don't let the state take my family's history. It belongs to her."

"It belongs to you, and you will be here to take care of it."

"Damn it, Sherrod, I mean it! Listen to me, man! You asked what you could do to help, so this is it. I'm sorry to put this on you, but I don't have anyone else."

Sherrod hung his head. "I hear ya, man, I got it."

"I mean it, Sherrod."

"I will take care of it, I swear, Rich."

Lucia stared at Richie with great intensity. She could tell the conversation with his longtime friend was coming to a close.

"Thanks for always having my back, Sherrod. You're the textbook definition of what a true friend is. It's truly been a blessing to have you in my life."

"Thanks, Rich, I uh, I feel the same way about you, bro." A heavy silence lingered briefly. "Hey, maybe when this is all over, you can work for Hallmark, making greeting cards 'cause that's some deep and mushy sentimental kind of stuff right there."

"You asshole." Richie laughed out.

Sherrod was laughing as well. "Stay safe, Rich."

"You got it, pal." Richie pressed the end-call button and handed the phone back to Lucia without looking at her.

Sherrod looked down at his phone for a few seconds. "Come on, Rich. You got this, brother."

Lucia tapped Richie on the shoulder. "Here he comes. We'd better go to the bathrooms before we get back on the road."

Later on, after passing New Plymouth, Simms said, "Take 26 up here. We need to get off of 84. They will be expecting us to come that way. We will go to Mt. Hood from the south side instead."

Richie looked over at Simms. "Won't that take longer?"

"Not really. We flew through Idaho already, and that's not a small state. We will be just fine and on time."

Richie gazed at Simms. There was something odd. He had a different tone about him, and he was avoiding eye contact even more than usual. There was nothing Richie could really do about it, so he turned left to take Route 26 and then he stomped down on the gas pedal.

The hours, like the miles, ticked by quickly, and it was the same for the songs on Richie's music device. Before they knew it, the sun was rising behind them.

"Don't we turn right soon?"

"No. Just keep going straight."

Puzzled by that answer, Richie frowned. "I can't stay straight. We'll pass by the way to Mt. Hood if I do that."

Simms shrugged. "Oh well. I don't guess we'll be going there then."

Richie suspected as much from Simms. Furious with that arrogant answer, he slammed on the brakes, bringing the speeding Camaro to an immediate halt.

Lucia jolted awake, and Simms dropped his phone from the sudden stop. Surprisingly enough, Simms remained calm, even though anger radiated off him like the heat from a stove.

"Let's go, Richard. We don't have time for this. This isn't some fairy tale where you show up like a knight in shining armor and save the day."

"You lying piece of shit!" Richie smacked the steering wheel. "I knew you would do this. I just knew it!"

"Good, you're a psychic. Now let's get going."

"No! I'm not doing this anymore. This stops now."

Simms squeezed the bridge of his nose and leaned his head back against the headrest. "Do I actually have to remind you what's on the line? We've got to get out of the country."

"You don't have to remind me of anything! It's apparent that you are the one needing reminding. You said yourself you were fleeing the country, and you wanted to find Lucia to tell her goodbye before you left."

Lucia's face projected immense confusion. "What? I thought you had business to deal with in Seattle?"

Simms took a deep breath. "That's not exactly true. I did search for you so that I could tell you goodbye. My fortune is gone and most of everything I own is in these bags I have. Times are changing fast and fleeing the continent was my only chance of survival. But since the Heat Seeker is involved, now we all have to go."

"That's crap and you know it! You're gonna shoot my ass the second I get you to Seattle, and you're going to take your own daughter hostage with you overseas."

Simms cut his eyes at Richie.

"That's the real reason you took out a contract with that hitman so that I would get you all the way there. You never had any intentions of letting me out at Mt. Hood."

Simms chuckled. "What can I say, Richard? You got me!" He continued with his sinister laugh.

Richie looked back at Lucia and she was clearly distressed. "So much for helping your daughter keep her agreement with me and doing something right in her eyes for once."

Simms's face contorted into an almost demonic shape. "What are you going to do about it, tough guy? If you don't drive me there now, I'll shoot you. If you managed to turn me in yourself, your family dies. So, what's it going to be?"

Richie sat quietly, staring at the steering wheel. "You're going to have to kill me now."

Simms laughed. "Don't be ridiculous, Richard, drive."

"Absolutely not! I'm not driving you to Seattle just so you can plug me. You're gonna have to do it here."

"Don't think I won't, jockstrap. It ain't nothing to me!" Simms had become visibly unhinged and lost all control of his temper after continually being put on the spot by Richie. "You don't stay out of the law's grasp this long without being ruthless, and I mean utterly ruthless! I have done unmentionable things, things that would make you unable to sleep for two weeks solid! I've killed kids, old ladies, cripples in wheelchairs. I have sawed up bodies with chainsaws to make them easier to get rid of. Do you know what a mess that makes?" He stopped wailing his arms all about and clenched his fists as he looked straight into Richie's eyes. Without breaking the cold deadly stare, he said, "Have you ever picked pieces of human flesh and bone out of your hair? Have you ever been forced to perform unmentionable sex acts on old women?" Then he got closer to Richie's face. "And men?"

Richie just sat there, looking at Simms, not knowing what to say.

"Don't think for a second I won't pop you right here and now and not think twice about it! Now put the car in gear and drive!"

Richie looked out the windshield for a few seconds, then with a somber look, he turned to Simms. "I'm sorry you've had that type of life. No one deserves that."

"Shut the hell up and drive!" Simms pulled out his pistol and pointed it at Richie. "I don't need your sympathy."

Richie's heart pounded out of control as he gave Simms a blank look. He put his head against the barrel of Simms' pistol in a defiant but humble manner. "I told you I'm not going anywhere, so go ahead and do it." Richie saw flashes of his parents and his brother. He relived moments with Mary and then took a deep breath, closed his eyes tightly, and imagined his beautiful Josie's face as he waited for his life to come to an abrupt end. The very next instant, the loud and disturbing sound of gunfire rang out from inside the Camaro.

CHAPTER 49

Who Saved Who?

Lucia gasped for air as tears streamed down her cheeks like two separate, raging rivers that could have rivaled the mighty Mississippi. It was just days ago, even though in some aspects it felt like months, that Richie and she crossed the Mississippi, and now here she was in their destination state of Oregon. A brief road trip had forever changed everything for her. Her view on life, her actions, and her goals. Nothing was ever going to be the same. Not after this.

A freakish moan-like sound whaled out from Richie. His heart was racing wildly, his skin crawled, and his face was completely absent of color as he grabbed his forehead. After not feeling any wounds there, he franticly reached around to the back of his head and discovered that it was still intact. He looked at the driver's side glass, expecting to see blood splattered all over it, but there was none. The realization was slowly setting in that he hadn't been shot and that he was greatly relieved to still be alive.

"What the—what's going on?" He scanned the car, trying to make sense of what had just transpired. As his senses fully returned from a near-death experience, his eyes locked in on Simms. Blood was trickling out of his mouth and dripping down onto his shirt, running onto his left hand that clutched his chest.

Richie looked back at Lucia, who was in a near-catatonic state. She laid Chico's pistol on the seat next to her, as if deeply repulsed by it. Richie blankly stared at her, not knowing what to say. He was in complete shock by her actions. Grateful but shocked. He looked back at Simms and his lower jaw was slowly and uncontrollably quivering as he gasped for air; his eyes glassed over. Gurgling sounds eerily came from his mouth as he seemed to fade away.

"Get me out of here!" Lucia uncontrollably wept. "Let me out now!"

Getting out, Richie ran around to the passenger side of the Camaro and jerked the door open. Simms had slumped over, revealing a bullet wound to his back. The leather had a small hole in it from where Lucia had shot him through the seat. Now she was panicking and was frantically trying to get out of the back seat. Richie grabbed Simms and hoisted his big, muscular body out of the seat, crashing to the ground with him.

Lucia got out, and she started pacing with her hands deep into her hair, holding her head. Then she clenched her fists and held them out. "Why? Why did you make me do this?" She shouted several more things in Spanish while pointing at Simms. Lucia got down on her knees beside him and put her hands on his torso. The sun had completely risen over the horizon and it shone on Simms' lifeless body.

"I didn't want to do this."

"Of course, you didn't." Richie wanted to comfort her, but he had no idea what to say. She had just killed her own father to save him.

"He just wouldn't stop. It was either this or him killing who knows how many more people before getting killed himself."

"Yeah, he made it clear that he wasn't going to be taken alive, and he was right." Richie paused. "Was that Chico's gun?"

Lucia continued to look down at Simms. Richie bent down beside her and put his arm around her. "Yes. After the crash when Chico was shot, I came to, and it was just lying there beside me, so I grabbed it and stuffed it in my pants. I was really hoping I wouldn't have to use it, but deep down I knew I would."

Richie ripped off the left sleeve of his shirt, revealing more of his muscular, bruised arm. He handed it to Lucia so she could use it to wipe her tear-engulfed face. "I'm so sorry this happened. I can't thank you enough for saving my life, though. And God only knows how many other people you saved."

"I should have done this years ago. I could have saved so many more people."

"You can't worry about the people in the past. This isn't on you, Lucia. No one should have to endure what you have. This is the result of a broken system. Your father slipped through the cracks at a young age and ended up amongst the wrong people. It was a downward spiral from there. I can't say enough how sorry I am that you had to do this, but I do think you managed to finally give him what he couldn't find on this Earth."

"Oh yeah, what's that?" Lucia looked over at Richie while wiping her tear-stained face with his sleeve.

"Peace."

A car pulled up behind the Camaro.

"Oh no! You better get out of here, Richie!" Lucia didn't want him to be tied up for hours in questioning with the authorities before he could get to Mary.

"I can't just leave you here."

"You have to!"

"That seems like a real selfish move. You just shot your father to save my life. I can't run off to deal with my own problems and leave you here holding the bag."

The person who had parked behind their car had gotten out and walked up. "Is everything okay here?"

Lucia and Richie both just looked at him, not knowing what to say.

"Is that man okay?"

Lucia barely spoke above a whisper. "He is now." Then she looked down at him with immeasurable sadness in her eyes, but she had an air about her, as if a tremendous weight had been lifted off her shoulders.

The man came closer and saw the blood around Simms' mouth. "Oh my! That man's in terrible shape! I'll call 911!" He ran back to his car to make the call.

"Go, Richie, go now before the cops show up. I'll explain everything."

"Are you sure you're gonna be okay? It doesn't feel right leaving you here like this."

"I'll be fine now." She looked down at Simms.

Richie stared into her dark, sad, but still amazingly beautiful eyes. "Where do I send my check?"

"Check? What do you mean?"

"The check for payment for your services. We had a deal and you more than held up your end of the bargain. Just as we agreed, you helped get me to Oregon."

Lucia cracked a half-smile and grabbed Richie into a big hug. He picked up a faint whiff of her lovely perfume. He didn't want to let her go, but off in the distance, they could hear sirens coming.

"You better get going." Lucia broke their warm embrace.

He stood still, continuing to stare into her eyes.

"Don't worry; if things don't go as planned, I'll be there for you. Oh, wait, you better take my phone so you can find the wedding venue. I already have it programmed in. It should take you straight to it. Now get going!"

Richie took the phone, and fleetingly walked to The Exorcist. He swiftly opened the driver's door and, before getting in, he gave Lucia one last unfeigned look.

"Oh, I only take cash, by the way!" Lucia half-smiled and waved him off. He smiled back and held his hand up in one last goodbye wave. The sirens were extremely close now, so Richie hopped in the Camaro and took off like a rocket. He watched Lucia in the rear-view mirror until she was out of sight.

CHAPTER 50

Golden Opportunity

Richie had started the last stage of his trek north to Mt. Hood. After driving for a short time since leaving Lucia behind, he had become incredibly tired. So tired that it literally hurt. The continuous cross-country tirade had worn him out physically and emotionally, and driving all night hadn't helped that situation. He had swayed over the yellow line once and almost veered off of the two-lane country road entirely on two different occasions, fighting off sleep. Just up ahead, he saw what appeared to be an old abandoned barn off of the road, so he drove straight to it.

He scanned the immediate area and didn't see anyone around as he pulled into the main opening of the old agriculture structure. He parked where a tractor most likely would have been when not in use on farm fields. He calculated how much time he had to get to the venue, and surprisingly enough, he had plenty to spare before the wedding was scheduled to start, so he set an alarm on Lucia's phone to wake him in an hour. Unfortunately, though, being in the new place had pepped him up a tiny bit despite reclining his seat to make himself more comfortable. Simms' bags on the passenger floorboard caught his eye. He remembered he had more in the trunk as well. With his newfound small boost of energy, he gathered all of Simms' belongings, except for the pistol used to shoot him. He figured the police would need that to verify the story of how Lucia saved him.

With all of Simms' belongings in a pile next to the car, he was about to go through them when he thought of the glove box, so he checked it right away. He laughed out loud after pulling out a bag of circus peanuts Lucia had left for him.

"Thanks, partner." He grinned and left the peanuts in the passenger seat and started going through Simms' bags. "Holy hell, look at all this money!"

After further examining the waterproof bags, he determined that most of it was cash—US hundred-dollar bills to be exact—along with various papers, fake IDs, passports, and credit cards. The rest of it was weapons and ammunition except for a single brown box. With noticeable curiosity, Richie carefully opened the cardboard package and found a ceramic unicorn statue inside.

"Why would he have this? It doesn't make any sense." He looked it over. "I guess I could give it to Josie. She seems to love these things." He placed it in the passenger seat, too.

He took the bags and dumped them in an old well right outside the barn that he saw when he first pulled up to it. He went back to the Camaro and eventually, after settling back down some, he fell asleep, snacking on the surprise gift of his favorite candy from Lucia.

Feeling like mere minutes later, Richie opened his eyes to the sound of Lucia's phone buzzing. He peeled himself from the steering wheel. He had slumped over on it in his rashly planned power nap. He reached for the phone while rubbing his face.

"Hello."

"Where the hell are you, Richie? Are you okay?"

Still trying to wake up, he grimaced. "Who is this?"

"Come on, Rich, how don't you know you're ol' pal? It's your boss, Terrance Vaughn."

In that very instant, as if someone had pressed an on button somewhere on his body, Richie's eyebrows raised and he became fully awake and alive. He uncontrollably blurted out at Vaughn with blatant heavy sarcasm. "Oh, you mean my ol' pal that had me put on the no-flight list? Or is it my ol' pal that screwed me out of my contract money? No wait, I bet it's my ol' pal that crushed my hopes and dreams that I worked over half my life for? Yeah, that's who it is. Sorry, I didn't recognize my ol' pal."

"Come on now, Rich. We're not going to let that little spat we had ruin our partnership, are we?" Vaughn's tone was distinguishably insincere.

"Wow, you are a real piece of work, Vaughn. You just never quit, do you."

"Look, I know you're upset, but now's not the time for this. I just got off the phone with the FBI and they have Simms' body and his daughter, Lacey, but you and the car are still missing."

"Her name is Lucia!"

"Okay, but where are you and my car?"

"On my way to Mt. Hood. I wasn't trying to run from the police. I just need to talk to my ex before she gets married, so please don't report this thing stolen again."

"Well, something doesn't add up then because your friend Lucia said that you were on your way to Mt. Hood as well, but the police couldn't find you. They think you doubled back south or something. They have been scouring the roads for hours trying to find you."

With a look of concern, Richie tilted his head. "Wait, what?"

"After the police couldn't find you anywhere along the way to Mt. Hood, they pulled out of those locations and started combing the surrounding areas instead. What's going on? Where are you?"

Feeling even more concerned and confused, Richie held out the phone to check the current time. An immediate feeling of shock and numbness spread throughout the entirety of his body. "No, damn it, no!"

"What's wrong, Richie?" Vaughn's voice held an actual bit of concern.

"I can't believe this. I can't catch a freaking break!" Richie started The Exorcist and headed toward the road.

"Tell me what's wrong, Rich. I might be able to help."

"I got about an hour and a half to make a three-hour trip, that's what's wrong!"

"Hmm, I see. I might be able to help you with that."

"Really?" Richie was doubtful.

"But before I do, I have a proposition for you."

"Here we go." Shaking his head, Richie gained speed, going up the road.

"Seriously, Richie, hear me out. This is a golden opportunity."

Richie immediately thought of Simms telling Agent Jain that "Golden opportunities were usually for the ones saying it."

"I got a feeling you're going to tell me regardless, so get on with it."

"I'm telling ya, Rich, you're going to love it. We'll talk all about this journey you've been on and really hype it up. You'll be on every morning show, late-night show, midday show; there'll be tons of exposure for the I.W.L!"

"Why should I give a rat's ass about the I.W.L. or you?"

Vaughn slightly raised his voice and spoke a little more seriously. "Look, asshole, I know you stole my car. I don't know how you managed to get kidnapped by the most notorious drug dealer or all of the other details, but Simms' daughter painted a real nice picture that the public as well as the FBI will buy. I'm willing to roll with it and I suggest you do the same!"

Richie's curiosity piqued. "What did she say, exactly?"

"She told the feds that her father originally stole the car from the arena after stealing a mask and ring jacket from the locker room. Apparently, there's video footage that shows that. Then she went on to tell how he raced the hillbillies in Arkansas and the feds were able to verify that story based on what they said after their capture. They said some guy named Peter was the one that showed up in the car. Then she said you all just happened to find my Camaro beside the interstate days later."

"He must have told her that information while I was in the restroom or something because I didn't hear him disclose that." He was pleasantly surprised at Lucia's ability to make such a perfect cover story. "The only part of that information I can verify myself is how we happened to find your Chevrolet beside the road."

"Yeah, well I'm not buying it. I know that it was you that originally stole my car. I'm willing to let that go, though. Bygones can be bygones; I've got a perfect plan. You're going to be the face of the I.W.L., Richie. You might even be the biggest star we've ever had!"

"What about your boy, Badger Timberland? I thought everything was going to revolve around him?"

"Nah, he'll be old news after this story hits the media."

Richie rolled his eyes and shook his head in disgust.

"Everything we had planned for him, we'll do with you instead! We'll put you over on him in record-setting time. Besides, the fans hate him. This will be so huge, Rich. Huge, I'm telling ya!"

"That's all fine and dandy, but I don't think so."

Unhappy with Richie's lack of enthusiasm, Vaughn hesitated in thought. "What if I sweetened the pot a little?

On top of making you the Undisputed World Heavyweight Champion, we'll also make Sherrod and you the Tag Team Champs. I know you two have always wanted to form a team. It will be perfect. How can you say no to that, World Champ, Tag Champ, with your real-life best friend? You'll have it all!"

Still not impressed by Vaughn's bait, Richie switched the topic. "How can you help me get to Mt. Hood on time? You said something earlier about it."

"Oh, yeah, that's easy. I can call the Governor of Oregon and cash in a favor. He begged for ringside seats a while back, so he owes me one. I'll ask him to call off the dogs so you can shoot straight through to Mt. Hood without any worries whatsoever."

"Wow, he can do that?"

"Oh yeah, that's no problem. Everybody's on your side here, Richie. This will be the story of the decade, hell possibly the century! Professional wrestler brings down one of the biggest drug lords of our time. I can see the headlines now. You're going down in history, Rich!"

"That's funny 'cause just a short week ago the whole world was against me."

"Well, the tides have turned in your favor, my boy. I even have an in at the FBI to help make sure this story comes out completely in our favor. So, what do say? Are you in?"

Richie was quiet for a moment as he drove. "Your car will be in Mt. Hood, Oregon. You can have someone pick it up there." He pressed the end call button and nonchalantly tossed the phone over to the passenger seat.

CHAPTER 51

Sacrificial Lamb

Richie downshifted to gain all the speed he possibly could. Confident that Vaughn would still contact the governor, despite turning down his ostentatious offer, and having him call off all the police in the area, he drove as fast as he could without being a complete hazard to surrounding drivers. He was betting on Vaughn's desire to have a great story from all of this, so he would not worry about getting caught, especially after hearing the FBI was going to help this whole situation turn out in Vaughn's favor, so he was going for broke. He was going to do everything he could to get the chance to speak to Mary before the wedding. He had sacrificed too much at this point and too many people had gone out of their way to help him, so he had to see his goal through.

He turned off his music so he could fully concentrate on the road. The mighty engine of the elaborate auto purred in perfection as Richie guided the vessel north to Oregon's highest peak. Fortunately, the traffic was light, most likely due to it being an early Saturday morning.

After a while of driving at such a high rate of speed, the dash's low fuel indicator light came on. Richie had burned through another tank of gas and was now in need of more. Fortunately, a convenience station was up ahead. Moments later, Richie pulled up to the pumps, and as he exited the car, an older gentleman walked up.

"What will it be, premium?"

"Yeah, wait, I thought everybody had to start pumping their own gas here in Oregon back in January?"

"Laws changed that in certain areas. At certain times, customers could pump their own, but it wasn't as big a deal as the Internet made it seem."

"Oh, well, that's good to hear. They made it seem like the entire state was going to burn down." Richie chuckled. "Do you have any Mountain Dews inside?"

"Ice cold."

Minutes later, Richie came out with his drink in hand.

"She's full." The attendant took a long look at the sky. "I hope you don't have outdoor plans today. There's a big storm moving in."

Richie looked up and saw dark clouds off in the distance. "I'm actually on my way to a wedding."

The attendant shook his head in disapproval. "That's a bad sign. They say if it rains on your wedding day, you'll cry the rest of your life."

Richie paid the man. "My granny used to say the same thing."

"Sounds like a smart lady."

"She was a very wise woman indeed." Richie opened the car door. "Thank you, sir."

"Yeah, no problem. You take care now."

In no time, Richie was back on the blacktop, speeding down the highway. He had been making up time at a furious pace and was closing in quickly on his destination, especially considering how far behind he once was.

A short while later, the snow cap-covered protrusion, Richie's destination, Mt. Hood, jutted high into the sky and continued to get larger as he got closer. Becoming confident that he was going to make it on time, he suddenly brought the Camaro to a staggering and screeching halt after cresting a gently rolling hill. The blossoming valley before him was the perfect picture of spring, despite the thunderstorm coming in from the west, and looked like it could have been one of the famous Bob Ross' trademark paintings. Normally such an amazing scene would have invoked feelings of astonishment. However, the green and black Dodge Demon idling at a slight angle in the middle of the road was beyond terrifying and projected an image of supreme horror instead.

In Richie's rush to get to Marry before the wedding, in his totally exhausted state, and after the complete mind-blowing act of Lucia saving his life by shooting her very own father, he had momentarily forgotten about the Heat Seeker. Unfortunately for Richie, though, the Heat Seeker hadn't forgotten him.

Richie's face had grown pale, and he now felt severely sick to his stomach. He sat and stared in astonishment at the killer, not knowing what to do. No other cars were around, and it was just the two men in their respective cars, gazing at each other at about eighty yards apart. Richie just barely could see the haunting hitman behind the wheel. He felt like he was in the final showdown scene of one of the many westerns his late brother, John, and he had watched together countless times over the years.

The Heat Seeker gripped the black steering wheel of his mighty automobile. He occasionally menacingly chewed on a piece of gum with his front teeth that subsequently made his round, wire-framed sunglasses slightly raise and lower on his well-experienced Caucasian face that was adorned by a dark-colored goatee. The black-lensed shades hid his cold and calculating eyes along with a black bandana that hid most of his forehead, which only added to the intimidating air radiating off of him.

In a panicked state, Richie looked out his rear-view mirror, then all about, hoping to find a way out of yet another grave situation. He contemplated turning the car around and simply running to escape the killer, and notifying the authorities in his mad dash to escape the unforgiving villain, but that thought faded fast. He knew deep down he couldn't do that. He had come too far and was way too close to his destination to just give up and run. "That's what a coward would do," he mumbled as a sudden flash of lightning pierced through the gray clouds off in the distance. He thought about what he said after his last match, about how all his opponents were mere speed bumps on his glorious highway to heaven. With aggression and adrenaline growing inside him at an alarming rate, he yelled, "Yeah, that's right. You're just another speed bump in my way." He looked at his cross, still hanging from the rear-view mirror. He made the sign of the cross on himself in a speedy and almost whimsical manner. Then he turned his music back on just before stomping hard onto the gas pedal and dumping the clutch.

The engine let out an almost ear-shattering roar and tire smoke engulfed the immediate area around The Exorcist as the car moved increasingly fast. The Heat Seeker didn't even bat an eye as he spat his gum out the rolled-down window, putting his ferocious Demon into gear.

Both of the mighty cars raced toward each other at an astounding pace on the yellow line of the narrow two-lane road. In mere seconds, they were twenty feet from each other. The Heat Seeker threw his Dodge sideways, hoping to make Richie run off the road, causing him to crash. His plan almost worked as Richie narrowly missed the menacing green machine as he swerved onto the grass right beside the road. The Camaro slid at a slight angle, throwing sod high into the air while leaving a set of tire tracks in the earth behind him. Richie had turned into the slide, barely keeping control of the car, but he kept the gas pedal pressed to the floor and eventually got back onto the road, gaining some serious speed. The Heat Seeker still had an emotionless face as he calmly but quickly got his car turned around and relentlessly pursued Richie.

Richie tightly gripped the steering wheel as he maneuvered his mighty chariot up the highway. He had gotten a decent lead on his foe and was hoping to keep it. Fortunately for him, traffic was still light, and he just blew right by any vehicles that he came upon. Unfortunately, though, the Heat Seeker was making up ground quick in the straights.

"Come on, pal, don't fail me now," Richie said to the Camaro in a hopeful tone. "We don't have too much further to go." He was counting on there being some sort of police presence at the wedding. Especially since he had told Officer Bullseye about the dire situation. He was now offering himself as the bait for the Heat Seeker, hoping the authorities could take him into custody once he arrived. If this plan didn't work out, at least he would save his family by sacrificing himself for them.

It had just been minutes since the astounding chase had begun, but to Richie, it felt like months. The Exorcist was now covered with road grime, dust, and sported a bug-covered windshield. Despite all that, though, its less-than-perfect appearance still looked as ferocious as ever, and the red halo headlight definitely added to that perception. The Demon was just as fearsome, if not more so, especially because of the imposing driver. The remains of the right-side rearview mirror dangled all about in the wind as the Dodge closed in on the Chevrolet.

Richie was still gaining speed as he drove, as he had never driven before. The radio still blasted out his favorite tunes as his eyes now lay upon a damning sight ahead.

"No, no, no, not now!" He downshifted through the gears, bringing The Exorcist to a stop.

∞

"Hold up. That looks like an injured dog over there," Richie had said to his brother, John, from the passenger seat of his shop truck, as they sat idle at a stop sign.

"Looks like a golden retriever. It probably got clipped by a car. That'd be my guess, judging by the way it's limping."

"Should we take it to a vet?"

"We don't really have time. Didn't you say we had to get you to the airport before five p.m.?"

"Yeah, but I'd really hate to leave that poor thing out here suffering. It doesn't look like a stray. It's got a collar, plus it's too clean."

"Yeah, there are probably a couple of kids somewhere crying their eyes out 'cause Fido is missing. We can drop it by Old Man Sheppard's right quick. Plus, Vern was telling me in the shop one day that he's got some hot chick intern working there now. Maybe you can finally get a date for once." John chuckled as he pulled up next to the injured animal.

"Well, first off, Vern thinks any woman with a pulse is hot, and second, I can get a date just fine. I don't have time to be dating right now. I'm always gone."

"I know, dumbass, I'm just busting balls. Now grab that pooch and let's skedaddle."

Richie hopped out of the truck and slowly approached the whimpering dog.

"Hey, be careful! Injured animals can be dangerous."

The canine came up to Richie and lay down at his feet. He bent down to pet it and it allowed him to do so with no problems.

"Seems friendly enough." Richie carefully placed it in the back of John's truck.

A short while later, Richie was carrying the Scottish gundog into the veterinary clinic. A beautiful young lady ran over to assist him.

"What happened to your dog?" She immediately instructed Richie to bring it into one of the examination rooms before he could answer.

The intern's beauty caught Richie off guard. *Wow, Vern was right for once, he thought. "It's, uh, it's not my dog. My brother and I found it beside the road. Best we could figure it got clipped by a car."*

"I figured it was something like that since you were carrying it in." She checked the tag. Then she grabbed the dog under the ears. *"What happened to you, Josie?"*

"Josie?"

"That's what her tag says her name is."

"That's what my grandmother's name was." Richie half-smiled.

"That's such a lovely name."

"She was a lovely lady."

"What about you?"

"What about me?" Richie gave her a confused look.

"What's your name?"

"Oh, I'm Richie. And you are?"

"Mary."

"It's nice to meet you. It looks like you are really good with animals." He watched her work on the new patient. *"I really like animals, too, but I don't have much experience with them. I used to watch the Croc Hunter all the time back in the day."*

"He was a legend, that's for sure."

"Well, it was really nice meeting you. I have to get going."

"Hear, wait a second." She pulled out a pen and quickly jotted something down on a pad of paper. *"This is my number. If you ever want to learn more about animals, you can give me a call."*

Richie smiled as he took the piece of paper from Mary. *"Thank—"*

∞

"You've got to be kidding!" Richie pulled up behind another car. Several men on horses were herding sheep across the road. "This is it. I'm dead."

CHAPTER 52

Comin' in Hot

In an imposing and eerie fashion, the green Demon slowly rolled up beside Richie. The demonic sounding engine pounded its sound into the pavement, which caused it to bounce off the hardtop and echo out. Richie just kept looking straight ahead as he seriously dreaded looking over. He just knew there would be a pistol pointing straight at his head, and he really didn't want to see that. Both engines were so loud idling that it slowed the sheep down as they crossed the road, and there seemed to be hundreds. There was nowhere for Richie to go, and after noticing that two sheepherders were giving him dirty looks, he turned off the Camaro. The Heat Seeker followed suit, doing the same to his elaborate automobile.

Finally, after a few seconds, Richie took a deep breath and turned his head to the left. He saw the Heat Seeker just sitting there, looking straight ahead. His calmness seemed eerie to Richie, so he looked straight ahead.

A rider helping to contain the sheep dismounted his horse and walked over to the cars that were accumulating. "I'm real sorry, folks. If you can just bear with us for a few more minutes, we'll be out of everybody's way real soon." The young man's tone was genuine, yet nervous.

The Heat Seeker leaned his head out the window. "It's all right, brother, take your time. Some of us ain't got no place special to be." With definite deliberation, he unwrapped another stick of gum and began chewing it with his front teeth in an inauspicious manner, the same as he did before.

Richie sat motionless while he gazed through the windshield, watching the storm still slowly rolling in. He wanted to say something to the man who accepted orders to kill him, but he didn't know how to go about starting a conversation with a person like that. *How do you converse with a calculating murderer that's trying to kill you?* he thought. He sat there in silence and listened to the sheep's feet pounding the pavement with an occasional bah here and there and his engine, as well as the Heat Seeker's making popping and cracking sounds as they cooled down after being turned off.

Richie finally just blurted something out. "You don't have to do this, you know." Richie slightly leaned his head out of his window, but he wasn't directly looking at the professional killer.

The Heat Seeker continued to chew his gum, but now in a more malevolent manner as he looked straight ahead. "Yeah, I do." A small clap of thunder bellowed out far off in the distance.

"I didn't kill Simms. His own daughter did."

"Wow, that's harsh. She must be just like him. Ousting her own dad to take over his empire."

"No, she's nothing like him. She's a hero. She did it to save me as well as herself. Besides, Simms' empire is gone. That's why he was fleeing the country in the first place."

The Heat Seeker noted with a head nod. "That explains the deal he made with me, then."

"A deal you don't have to keep. My family had nothing to do with this!"

The Heat Seeker stopped chewing his gum and looked straight over at Richie. "What are you talking about?"

"The hit Simms put on my family and me with you if he didn't manage to escape the country. That's why you're here now, isn't it?"

The Heat Seeker shook his head. "The deal we made never mentioned your family, just you."

Richie looked dead at the Heat Seeker, then through the windshield before chuckling. "That bastard."

The last of the sheep were getting ready to cross the road.

"You still don't have to do this. What if I gave you this car? You're obviously a guy that has good taste in vehicles. I know you could really appreciate a ride like this."

"Well, even if that was your car to give away, I still have a deal to fulfill."

"A deal with a dead man. I get that you are a man of principle and that's very admirable, but I've got a daughter that needs raising."

"That's very touching, but it doesn't change anything. When those heat-packing cowboys clear out, I'm going to shoot you. I'm sorry. It's nothing personal, but when I'm hired, I always complete the job."

Richie looked down in defeat. During this entire road trip from hell, he'd gotten out of every grim situation he faced, but this was it. It was truly over. While he was looking down, something caught his eye. It appeared to be a rattlesnake that had crawled out from under the passenger seatbelt buckle. Every muscle in Richie's body clenched, completely paralyzing him with fear. The snake continued to slither out from the hole, moving toward the gear shifter. Its head circled the shifter's leather boot effortlessly before returning to the passenger seat. Richie could see, without a doubt, that it was a rattlesnake. It had looked exactly like the one Skeeter threw on the hood back at the junkyard, but only this one was smaller and didn't have a rattle. Then it occurred to him.

It most likely got into the car when he left the door open to save Lucia from the Tramp Clan.

Richie sat as still as a statue, without taking his eyes off the stowaway serpent. He could hear the cars in front of him driving away and the noise from the sheep getting fainter as they traveled further from the road.

This is it, Richie thought. *I'm probably going to die anyway, so here goes nothing!*

In one fell swoop, Richie grabbed the rattleless rattlesnake and hurled it straight into the Dodge. The Heat Seeker had his pistol drawn and pointed right at him, just as Richie suspected, and the snake landed right on the hitman's shoulder. Almost instantly, the venomous viper latched onto his right cheek and he let out a spine-chilling scream, causing his gum to spill from his mouth. He dropped the gun, as he pulled the snake off of his face.

While The Heat Seeker was busy getting rid of the fang-ridden reptile, Richie started up The Exorcist and took off in a flash.

The Heat Seeker finally threw the snake out of his window and got the Demon started up. He wasn't cool or collected anymore. Instead, he was absolutely furious, and every jerky and agitated movement he made showcased that.

"You're dead, shit bag! You are so dead!" As his mean green machine got up to speed, he looked at his snake-bitten face in the rear-view mirror. His sunglasses had come off in the scramble to expel the snake from the car, exposing his dark, sinister eyes.

Richie's heart was pounding almost as fast as the pistons in the engine. He was in total disbelief of what had just happened but was trying to shake it off and take full advantage of his head start on The Heat Seeker. Doubts of it lasting long, though, were arising as the road opened up into four lanes, and it was now a straight shot for as far as Richie could see. Both cars were pretty well equal in most ways, but the Demon had a slight advantage in going straight where The Exorcist could handle corners better.

"I've got you now!" The Heat Seeker clamped down like a vise on his cheek as he gripped the steering wheel with the other hand.

Richie watched the rear-view mirror with great intensity, similar to a hawk eyeing up its prey. He was beyond disheartened to watch it fill up with the black and green car. "What is wrong with this guy? If the idiot had any sense, he'd be on his way to a hospital!"

The two cars were an absolutely astounding sight as they thundered down the road, nose to tail, with actual thunder clapping above them. Occasional streaks of lightning stretched across the mostly gray sky, adding to the stunning spectacle. The few motorists they passed, they left speechless and wondering if they really saw two cars rocketing past or was it just their imaginations.

Richie had kept his foe behind him thus far. He felt like his longtime hero and now friend, Cotton McCready, holding off his competitors at the high banks of Daytona. He blocked every move The Heat Seeker had tried. After a few minutes of being stuck behind Richie, The Heat Seeker was really losing what was left of his cool. He was in agonizing pain and wanted to hurry and end this prodigious duel.

Up ahead, the road merging into two lanes distracted Richie just enough for the Heat Seeker to get to the front of his car beside Richie's left quarter panel. The hitman was finally in the position to make the move he'd been working for. Both engines revved out loud as they raced up the road. The Heat Seeker was on the wrong side of the road as he pulled up beside Richie with his pistol in hand, pointed in his direction.

As Richie was about to turn his head in the hitman's direction, he saw a very faint orange and yellow flash just over the current crest they were rapidly approaching. He was going way too fast to even know for sure, so right at the top of a slight incline on the highway, he slammed on the brakes, creating the first of two three-sixty-degree spins.

Richie was holding onto the steering wheel for dear life as The Exorcist spun out of control. Meanwhile, the uneaten circus peanuts came out of the bag and were strewn all over the interior of the car. The Heat Seeker zoomed right past a caution light-equipped construction truck and drove straight toward a rather large antique church that was being moved. It was the very same one the officers were talking about the night before at Nate and Mary's place. The Exorcist Camaro came to a stop right in time for Richie to witness the ferocious Dodge Demon plow up under the old structure as it just barely hung off of the enormous trailer that was hauling it. As fast as a heartbeat, the blisteringly quick vehicle came to an immediate stop and collapsed like an accordion, as it rammed into the thick, heavy steel of the flatbed hauler, causing a massive, ear-shattering explosion with insanely intense flames. The eruption seemed to come from another world, instantaneously catching the old church on fire. The entire area looked like it could have been a direct window to hell.

Richie watched in complete awe as he drove on the shoulder of the road to get by Dante's Inferno-like scene. He wanted to help the movers, but there was nothing he could really do as they all were frantically fleeing the fire, so he picked his speed back up and drove onward to the wedding. Glancing at the immense flames and billowing black smoke in his rear-view mirror, he looked down at his silver cross. It was reflecting an uncanny orange glow from the fire as the rain fell.

A short while later, Richie was within minutes of the venue. He had been listening to his radio and reflecting on his quizzical, outlandish, and downright unbelievable road trip as he drove up the winding road leading to the event. The rain had continued to pour down since leaving the Heat Seeker in a burning pile of twisted metal, but now it was slacking off and the sky was quickly clearing up. He was late. The ceremony should have already been underway, but he hoped that the rain had postponed it.

"You have arrived at your destination," Lucia's phone said from the passenger seat.

Richie was thorough in scanning the area, looking for Mary as he drove through the large piece of property, praying he wasn't too late. After rounding the corner of a very nice log building, he laid his eyes on the beloved mother of his child. She was a stunning sight in her beautiful bright white wedding dress, and the majestic Mt. Hood behind her made for a breathtaking backdrop.

Richie drove straight up to the aisle and, in his exhausted state, accidentally knocked over a few empty chairs in the back row of the sophisticated setup. He used up his second wind, escaping the Heat Seeker. Now all of his adrenaline was gone. Pain encompassed his entire body, and he'd never been so tired in his life, but he forced himself to suck it up, as his brother, John, would have instructed him to do.

The audience had taken notice of him because of The Exorcist's loud engine, but after hearing the chairs crash over, they all looked back at him as well as the bride and groom. Richie flung the Camaro door open, and pulled himself out of the cab. Nate's eyes widened, and his face turned red as he demanded to know, "What's he doing here?"

Mary was completely astounded as she gazed at the father of her daughter. *Those police officers were right last night*, she realized. She looked over at Nate and thought, *What an ass. He couldn't even let the police do their job for fear of it causing him some embarrassment in his precious career. On the other hand, Richie not only quit his dream job but he risked his life, and it looks like he has gone through absolute hell for just a chance to talk.* It was now obvious to her that this wedding was a mistake. The only man for her was at the back of the aisle. That was who she truly loved, and it was beyond obvious he loved her, but she couldn't help but wonder if this was the best decision for Josie.

Holding on to the car's door, Richie took a few steps and collapsed to one knee as he stared up the flower-ridden walkway. He looked worse for wear with his torn shirt that was sporting his wrestling character's face, along with the blood from Simms. His face was still riddled with bruises and abrasions from the battles along the way there.

Richie's eyes locked on to his precious baby, Josie, his little daughter, adorned in a ridiculously cute and tiny dress, who now looked up at Mary as she held onto her flower basket. She gently tugged at her mother's veil to get her attention. It was in that moment that Mary could see that Josie was just as surprised and Mary felt relief with her new decision to give him another chance. Josie was noticeably full of excitement at the sight of her father as she pointed straight to Richie and called out, "Daddy!"

EPILOGUE

“That should be good there. You can turn it off now,” a man in a gray and blue striped shirt said to another man dressed the same way.

“Are you sure?” The other man rolled down the window of the car he was backing up. “You know how picky he can be. I mean, we are talking about Terrence Vaughn here.”

“Yeah, I know. If he ain’t happy with that, he can kiss our ass and park it himself. We just got paid to fix that hole in the seat. He’s lucky we didn’t make him come and pick it up himself.”

The other man turned the black beast off and exited the rarity very carefully. “It’s hard to believe the story behind this car.”

“I know. I heard they wanted to do a movie about it but The Priest wouldn’t sell his part of the rights to do it or something along those lines. I can’t exactly remember.”

“That’s crazy.”

The two men turned off the lights as they exited the building.

The entire shop, which was filled with rare and expensive cars, was now almost black and silent, except for The Exorcist Camaro’s red halo replacement light on the right side. In the enveloping darkness, it and it alone came on and shone red.